Queneau's
Alphabet

A Story Cycle

STEVE RASNIC TEM

There is beauty in fundamental things, and nothing is more fundamental than destruction. I could watch a forest burn, or a field, or a house, for hours.

I can still smell the smoke. It's taken residence in my nasal passages, and I can't get it out. I liked setting fires when I was little, and then I stopped. But I would have these gaps where I couldn't remember what I did. I hope I didn't hurt anybody.

Your ABC's. It's one of the first things you learn. I learned mine walking this street with my mother and looking at the large wooden letters mounted on the houses. The houses on Alphabet Row have letters instead of numbers, twenty-six houses, one for each letter, thanks to John D. Queneau, the rich fellow who owned the land and built all these houses. At the end of the street, he constructed the library bearing his name, QUENEAU in huge stone letters beneath the spired roof. It's a grand Gothic building full of surprises. The descender at the end of the Q hangs like a dragon's tail over the front entrance.

My mom is the head librarian. Our house was on the corner across the street. Grandad willed this ruin to Mom, and she tried to fix it up, but she never had much money. Grandad was obsessed with all things Egyptian and remade his house using chicken wire, plaster, and paint to resemble an ancient tomb. The result was like a decaying movie set. Over the front door hung a painting of the sun with wings. Just under the roof were depictions of beetles. Hieroglyphs were crudely scratched into the exterior walls and much of the interior. Everything was crumbling. Mom worried somebody would report us and the house would be condemned. They would have done us a favor.

Contents

A is for Alphabet..1

B is for Baby...16

C is for Clown...23

D is for Dog..30

E is for Eye...35

F is for the Farm..45

G is for Ghost...62

H is for the Hunt..69

I is for Infestation 81

J is for Jolly..92

K is for Killer...104

L is for Love...116

M is for Mother...120

N is for Night..132

O is for Occult..144

P is for Phantasies...158

Q is for Queneau...169

R is for Remains 179

S is for Subsidence..189

T is for Tutti i Morti..203

U is for Underground...212

V is for Vermin 221

W is for Whispers.. 238

X is for Xenophobe... 247

Y is for Yesterday.. 257

Z is for Zombie 266

& 275

A is for Alphabet

There is beauty in fundamental things, and nothing is more fundamental than destruction. I could watch a forest burn, or a field, or a house, for hours.

I can still smell the smoke. It's taken residence in my nasal passages, and I can't get it out. I liked setting fires when I was little, and then I stopped. But I would have these gaps where I couldn't remember what I did. I hope I didn't hurt anybody.

Your ABC's. It's one of the first things you learn. I learned mine walking this street with my mother and looking at the large wooden letters mounted on the houses. The houses on Alphabet Row have letters instead of numbers, twenty-six houses, one for each letter, thanks to John D. Queneau, the rich fellow who owned the land and built all these houses. At the end of the street, he constructed the library bearing his name, QUENEAU in huge stone letters beneath the spired roof. It's a grand Gothic building full of surprises. The descender at the end of the Q hangs like a dragon's tail over the front entrance.

My mom is the head librarian. Our house was on the corner across the street. Grandad willed this ruin to Mom, and she tried to fix it up, but she never had much money. Grandad was obsessed with all things Egyptian and remade his house using chicken wire, plaster, and paint to resemble an ancient tomb. The result was like a decaying movie set. Over the front door hung a painting of the sun with wings. Just under the roof were depictions of beetles. Hieroglyphs were crudely scratched into the exterior walls and much of the interior. Everything was crumbling. Mom worried somebody would report us and the house would be condemned. They would have done us a favor.

Every day when I was little my mom would walk me down the street and we would say the letters together and she'd ask me for words starting with those letters. A is for Apple, but also Arnold, which is my name, although everybody calls me Arnie. B is for Ball, or Bat, C is for Cat, or Can, or Crash, and on and on through Z (Zebra, Zoo, Zoom). She said sometimes if you find the right word you can learn something important about yourself. A lot of those letters are gone now, due to vandalism or the owners taking them down, which is a real shame.

I got to know those houses, but Mom never let me get too close. I wasn't allowed to trick or treat on our street, or to fundraise for scouts, or even step onto anyone's lawn. When I asked her why, all she would say was "Because I said so." I discovered she wasn't the only parent with that rule.

I have, or had, three close friends. Carl, Doug, and Roger, each outcasts in our own way, so maybe our friendship was destined. But destiny is something I hate to think about.

We had our own dark versions of the alphabet, producing new variations as we tried to top each other. A is for Asshole, B is for Butchered, C is for Clown. Maybe "clown" doesn't seem all that dark, but you never met the lady who lived at #C Alphabet Row. D is for Dracula. G is for Ghoul. E is for Eviscerate. Carl taught us that word.

We filled our time playing with Roger's Atari, reading comic books and other cool stuff at Queneau's Library, and riding our bikes around the neighborhood looking for clues. We considered ourselves sage detectives. But we were just being snoops. Terrible things happened in the neighborhood, most without our knowledge.

"Hey you guys!" Roger rolled into the library reading room like somebody shot him. At fourteen he was a stumbling disaster, always in a stained T-shirt, constantly screwing up. I wonder if he might have grown out of that if he'd had enough time. His hip caught a library cart and an avalanche of books spread across the floor. Roger had little impulse control. I could relate.

"Oh my God!" he shouted dramatically and fell to his knees on the books, crushing and tearing pages. An elderly librarian peeked in, sighed, and went away, probably to tell my mom. I pulled him off the damaged books, and Carl and Doug did what they could to fix things. I felt bad for Roger, who sat like a pile of dirty laundry, tears in his eyes.

Doug fiddled with one of the cart's wheels, trying to straighten a bent piece. He was our mechanic. A little cranky, but there were reasons. He didn't talk much about his home life, but everybody saw the bruises.

"Your mom's going to kick us out again," Carl said. "Could you get us into the basement? There are some books I'd like to look at."

Carl was some kind of genius. Everybody thought so. He wanted to be an astrophysicist someday. He could have been anything, really. He was that smart. I was never sure what I wanted to be. Maybe a reporter, an author, something to do with words. Now I know that's never going to happen.

We accessed the lower levels via an ancient, rickety elevator. I knew the security code from past visits with my mom. I'd seen the first basement, but Mom said there were at least three more below. *At least.* She worked there—didn't she know exactly?

The first basement was a mix of rare books, battered editions, odd items such as phone books going back to the Forties, old maps, newspapers and magazines, and a lot of what Mom called ephemera. They let researchers study the collection, but much wasn't even catalogued. Mom said most of the staff wouldn't even go down there.

Sudden movement disturbed one of the distant stacks. Some books shifted and stuff fell. I hoped it wasn't rats. I hate rats. And one thing I've discovered—wherever, or whenever you go, there's going to be rats.

Carl gave us each a small but powerful flashlight from the backpack he always carried. We split up to explore. Roger had the notion he'd find some valuable old comic books. I knew there was nothing that exciting but didn't want to discourage him. Doug was interested in anything mechanical, so he went right for the collection of *Popular Mechanics*. I liked going where others rarely went, so I just browsed.

The center of the vast room was filled with tightly spaced metal shelving, labeled Fiction, Physics, Mechanics, Crime, etc., although the jumbled contents weren't easily classified. It was a sore point for Mom, but they didn't have the staff to organize it. I kept thinking how fast it might all go up with a well-placed match.

Carl waded into the shelves labeled Metaphysics. He had a notebook and a tape recorder. I wasn't even sure what Metaphysics was.

It was hot and stuffy, with little ventilation. My burn scar started bothering me, as if it wanted me to know it was still there. It's why I wear turtlenecks all the time. I tried not to scratch it. The warped skin is sensitive, and sometimes it bleeds. It looks like a giant bite mark across my chest with a narrow tongue running up my neck and licking my jaw, the part the turtleneck can't hide.

I heard footsteps and watched a short figure in a heavy overcoat and stocking cap cross between the stacks at the end of the row. Whoever it was, he must have been boiling inside that getup. Something seemed so familiar about his size, his posture, and the way he walked.

I took off after him, but by the time I reached the end of the row he was gone. I listened but heard nothing. I heard footsteps again and saw motion through the next row. I ran around the end and straight into Carl, who yelped. I laughed. I'd never heard him yelp before.

"Jesus, Arnie, you scared me. I need to get home. Let's grab Doug and Roger and go."

"Sure. But ... could you come over to my house after dinner? There's something from Grandad's old collection I want to show you."

I always wanted to impress Carl, and I thought at last I had something to amaze even him.

An hour after dinner and Carl still hadn't shown up. It made me angrier than it deserved, but that's me. I have a problem with anger. If I did half the things I imagined, or dreamed, I'd be in jail. I've never hit anyone, ever, but I've done other things. I take meds for it. Some days they work better than others. Sometimes the only way I can release the tension is to do something bad. But mostly I do bad things to my own stuff.

I could hear Mom and her latest boyfriend arguing downstairs, so I was thinking it was a good thing Carl didn't come. There was a knock on my door. Carl was standing there red-faced with embarrassment. I pulled him inside.

"Sorry for the drama."

"S'okay. You have something to show me?"

I revealed the four large metal disks I discovered among my grandfather's stuff in the attic. He examined them.

"More or less identical. Looks like a mix of copper and some gold maybe, a little silver. Each side bears a large central figure, with writing and designs covering the background. Egyptian. Thoth and Khonsu, I believe, both moon gods. You've heard of the Game of the Moon?"

I shook my head, embarrassed. Given my grandad's Egyptian interests, I should have known.

"Khonsu, the measurer of time, wanted to know the secrets in the shadows where his light didn't touch. He envied Thoth, who knew your thoughts before they reached your lips. They played a game, each wagering a part of his power. Thoth won a piece of Khonsu's light and placed it in his crown and Khonsu could no longer show his full light. That's why the moon grows brighter and larger, and then it dims until it finally goes dark." He put the disks back on my desk. "They're in excellent condition. You should donate them to a museum. They might credit you on the exhibit. Wouldn't that be great?"

"There's more to it than that. I was trying to make one spin on its edge, like a top, you know? When suddenly it wasn't there. I thought it fell off my desk. I couldn't find it anywhere. Here, watch this."

I was nervous. What if I couldn't repeat the effect? The first two times the disk wobbled and fell over, but I got it spinning again. The disk disappeared. I was so pleased when Carl gasped. Two minutes later the disk reappeared.

Carl picked it up and examined it thoughtfully. "Try spinning it harder." I did, and the disk spun for a longer time, disappeared, and didn't reappear for another ten minutes. Carl smiled. "You know what they sometimes call Khonsu? The *traveler.* As in *time traveler.* I think this disk is traveling through time. Let's try something."

Carl took a large glass jar off my shelves. It used to contain popcorn. This time when I spun the disk he put the jar over it and after a few seconds both disk and jar disappeared and reappeared minutes later. "Do you still have frogs in your backyard?"

"You're not going to hurt them are you?"

He grinned. "Of course not. Bring me one."

This time after covering the spinning disk Carl plopped a frog down on top of the jar. The frog sat impassively, then the frog, jar, and disk all disappeared. When they reappeared, the frog looked pissed.

"No effect on the frog it seems," Carl announced, "although we can't say what's going on psychologically with this guy. You know, the weird thing is, I don't think the earth's rotation is affecting this."

"*That's* the weird thing?"

"Do you mind if I borrow this disk, medallion, or whatever it is, and play with it at home? And don't tell the other guys yet. We don't want to jump the gun here."

"Do whatever you like. But don't lose it."

I woke up in the middle of the night with a light shining in my face. It was Carl holding one of his little flashlights, grinning. He had a weird contraption hanging around his waist: an old outdoor light fixture with the disk inside and some electronics and batteries mounted on top. "Greetings from the future!" he said.

I sat up. "That didn't take long."

"It's been three weeks. If you spin the disk clockwise, you go forward in time, but counterclockwise takes you back. Now that I've got the kinks worked out I can build a more compact version for all four bikes. Think about what you want to do with our new toy, and I'll see you in, oh, about three weeks." Carl pressed a button, the disk started spinning, and he disappeared.

Three weeks later Carl came to my house with the same contraption. "If it worked, you've already seen this, right?"

"Um … right."

"The top and bottom clamps make it spin and introduce a slight wobble if we want to offset the destination location. There are dials on top for offset and the plus/minus switch indicates time forwards or backwards. You ready?" Before I could answer Carl disappeared and came back within an eyeblink. "I just visited you in the middle of the night, three weeks ago. Boy, did you look surprised!"

———

Carl couldn't assure us it would be safe. But we all understood that, didn't we?

Doug and Carl had the devices mounted on all four bikes in no time. Doug wasn't satisfied. "I wish we could make them a little more aerodynamic."

Carl shook his head. "Aerodynamics are irrelevant to time travel. You're in one time and place, then you're in another. The lanterns give them a Victorian look, like in the movie *The Time Machine*?"

"Never saw it," Doug said distractedly, busy with some last-minute bolt tightening. "I hope none come apart in transit."

Roger jumped around like he had to pee. "Does it use antimatter?"

Carl gazed at him a moment, sighed, and said "No."

I felt increasingly anxious. I trusted Carl knew what he was doing. He was a genius, right? But still, he was just a kid. "Carl, how do we evaluate these?"

"We can leave anytime. It's up to you guys."

Doug frowned. "Anytime is better than now."

Carl gathered us around his bike. "If you look through the aperture you can see how much time it's set for in years, days, hours, and minutes. The three little dials underneath control that, plus the distance offset. The plus/minus switch toggles between future and past. The green switch triggers the device. Then there's the red switch which returns you to wherever you started from. I think we should all have the same settings, so no one goes to a time alone. That should be a rule."

Roger was the only one who seemed super excited by the possibilities. "If we set it for eight years from now we can drink alcohol!" Doug snickered.

"Well, that's ambiguous," Carl said.

"What does that mean?"

"The world will have moved on, but I think we'll still look fourteen years old. Maybe we'll be twenty-two psychologically, but I don't know for sure. It's a conundrum. Roger, that means it's a difficult problem to solve. Let's set it for twenty-one days ahead this first time."

Anxiety was making me fluttery, but I made the setting anyway, and helped Roger, whose sausage fingers fumbled with the small dials. The four of us pointed our bikes toward a clump of trees at the far edge of the park. When Carl gave the word we started peddling hard toward those trees. When he shouted "Now!" we all flipped the bright green switch.

I expected an instantaneous transition, but instead I was overwhelmed by this unpleasant vertigo, and a premonition the world was about to explode. I was so angry I started shouting. Then I was hanging upside-down, and something had me by the foot shaking me so hard I thought my internal organs were going to fall out of my mouth. When my head cleared we were under those trees, our bike tires inches deep in a carpet of yellow and red leaves. It had been almost fall when we started. Now we were well into the season. Dark clouds crowded the sky, and I could see distant lightning flashes. The other guys were laughing, gone goofy from the thrill. I, on the other hand, struggled not to throw up.

"Let's do it again!" Roger shouted. "But for years ahead this time! Make it a hundred!"

Thankfully, Carl nixed the idea. "It's late. I don't think we're ready to time travel in the dark. And a century? Do you realize how much things change over a century? Use some sense."

Carl restricted us to short trips at first: a month ahead, two months, then a year, a few years. He had stringent rules for our journeys: we couldn't touch anything, or interact with anyone, and we had to remain as inconspicuous as possible, which Roger violated all the time. He was too excitable. "Hey, you guys, look at that!" Heads would turn, and Carl would try to get us back to our own time while minimizing disruptions. Carl was concerned about disturbing the timeline, and creating "multiverses," which the rest of us couldn't fully appreciate. I mean, how do you worry about something you can't see or imagine?

But Carl still planned the trips and carried them out, lead us forward and even backwards in time. Most of these voyages made me ill, sometimes violently so. I asked the others how they felt. Doug said he did get a little queasy once or twice. Roger didn't seem to understand what I was talking about. Carl, on the other hand, became quite concerned, and asked me detailed questions, even suggesting I might stay at home and rest while they adventured whenever. That's when I shut up about it. I didn't want to be left behind. I was also worried about my friends. I wanted to be there for them if they got into trouble.

Despite the illness, I enjoyed our "backwards" trips the most. We all did. Returning to a particularly fine summer's day.

Or re-seeing a movie in the same theater we first experienced it. We just had to be careful not to run into our former selves. Carl had a sixth sense for that sort of thing.

I always arrived later than the others. Sometimes by as much as a half hour. I know I went somewhere during that time, did some things, saw some things, but I couldn't remember the details. Carl wasn't too concerned. He called it an "anomalous result."

The most interesting part of our trips was watching my neighborhood of Alphabet Row, and how much it transformed over the years, observing the evolving architecture, seeing patterns repeat themselves, witnessing people move in and out of these houses, some going to better, spiffier neighborhoods, and others leaving in an ambulance or hearse.

We weren't allowed to alter anything, at least not according to the rules Carl laid down for us. We were sworn to follow his directions precisely so we would have similar, safe, and repeatable experiences. But anomalous results did occur.

On an early trip I heard a baby crying. Not a hungry cry, or a wet diaper cry (I knew about these things from visits with my cousins), but a full-throated howl of pain and desolation. A cry no one else heard. "How can you not hear?" I asked. "It's a suffering baby, a baby that needs our help."

"Sorry, Arnie. I don't hear a thing," Doug said, and the others agreed.

Yet no matter how far forward or how far back we traveled, I heard the screaming baby at every stop.

Then there were the ones who chased after our bikes, like the lady with all the makeup, the "clown" lady. It looked as if she'd been waiting for us, but how could she know we were coming?

Once we ran into an old hound, too old and feeble to keep up, but somehow it still managed, and took a bite from one of Roger's sneakers.

Other times it was ghosts in various stages of decay. Or maybe their not-quite-thereness was an artifact due to time travel. And once a vine wriggled out from under a house's foundation and tried to bring Doug's bike down. A last-minute maneuver prevented a crash. Another time we had to avoid a flood of rats covering the entire street.

For Carl, it was an "insect" swarm pouring off a lawn and sending out insect soldiers to attack his back wheel. I was riding behind him, and I saw them eating the asphalt right from under him.

But for me it was always the people who triggered the worst terror. The drunk Santa Claus who tried to grab my handlebars. The naked human who ran on all fours like an animal—it got so close to me, and I swear it had these long teeth hanging down in front like a rat's.

We, and our bikes, were a dream, or a nightmare, the entire neighborhood was having.

Traveling back and forth through time we were able to identify the problem houses, the ones which were shrinking, or growing, or changing more frequently than the normal passage of time should allow. The bad houses and the ones even worse.

Doug had never been good about following rules. Sometimes he brought things back from our trips: a weathervane, an antique tricycle, and once a flashlight emitting a thick, gray light. More than once he took trips on his own.

He couldn't accept that he wasn't supposed to do anything even if he saw a threat. He got some spray paint and tagged the doors of a few of those bad houses, an X, a V, or a K, signs which he hoped might warn folks there was a problem inside. We tried to stop him. But Doug managed to mark these houses anyway.

Carl was livid. He said Doug had no idea what kind of mischief he may have caused. But Carl himself wasn't averse to pushing limits. He decided our next trip would be twelve years ahead. He said he wanted to see how the neighborhood evolved. I think he hoped to get a glimpse of us—especially himself—as adults.

He made us start near my house. He said it would be safe—my mom wasn't home. I didn't want to see my house twelve years into the future. I suppose I could have refused, but would it have made any difference in the end?

The side effects were worse than before, with shifting visions of fire and destruction, perspectives turned sideways and inside out, library walls crumbling, and my mother's upset—I heard her wailing. I arrived in the front yard much later than the others, fell off my bike, and had to struggle to my feet.

The others didn't even notice me. They were staring at my house. It was dark with no moon, and difficult to see. No one was at home. All the lights were out.

I realized parts of the house were missing, pieces scattered around the lawn. Black streaks reached from the first floor to the roofline. Gaping mouths full of sooty debris and broken timbers had eaten the downstairs where the living room used to be, and most of the second story, including my room, were gone. Police tape stretched across the emptiness. A "Keep Out" sign was propped up by the front steps.

Doug turned his head and looked at me. "Dude, your house. You…" He stopped. I didn't understand the expression on his face.

Carl and Roger turned around and let their bikes go, letting them crash together. What were they thinking? If they damaged the equipment they might be stuck in this time.

"Arnie, your abdomen. And your legs!" Carl sounded genuinely concerned. I looked down. Most of my belly was gone. I could see right through it into dangling intestines and a few gleaming ribs. I had no legs at all.

What we are and what we'll be. Carl was always saying that, like it was all that mattered. I never understood what my friend meant, but as time moves on—racing ahead, doubling back—I can feel myself getting closer.

Carl tried to fix things, because that's what Carl does. First he tried to determine what actually occurred. Twelve years on from my fourteenth year my house burned/will burn, severely scarring my mother and killing me. The cause will remain officially undetermined, but I will always wonder if it's because of something I did. Maybe I got angry and did something foolish.

I'm destined never to know. I've waited over twenty years, physically here and not-here, and the event still hasn't been part of my lived experience—I'm never there as the flames consume my world—but it *did* happen. I *did* die. My mother is *still* disfigured. Sometimes at night I wander through Queneau's Library in my current, undefinable shape, and I see her inside her office, a 3D-printed plastic compression mask strapped to her head to cover her severe facial burns, so she can still work more or less in peace without people's stares and pity.

When you journey forward past the point of your own death the universe runs out of rules. You're not exactly a ghost, but you're not completely real either. Oh, you think like you're real. You certainly suffer like it.

Carl felt responsible. I love him for that, but it's not untrue. He took Roger and Doug on trip after trip, forward and back, trying to find a solution, until Doug quit, or at least disappeared, went somewhere and somewhen on his own. No one has heard from him since.

Roger, on the other hand—I still hope he's okay somehow. On his final trip his bike came through, but he wasn't on it. There was blood on the seat, and smeared across the handlebars, and bits of flesh snagged on some sharp edges. The time apparatus was shattered, the disk gone, with one of Roger's fingers stuck inside.

It's just me and Carl now, and I'm not much company. He travels up and down the timestream trying to find our lost friends and some way to reverse my condition. He stopped talking about becoming an astrophysicist a long time ago.

That was him in the Queneau basement, the figure in the wool cap and heavy coat. He spends a lot of time researching. His body isn't good at regulating temperature anymore. Another anomalous result, I suppose, of too much time travel.

I feel I got everything I deserved. I too travel the timeline, sticking to this neighborhood where I have lived all my life. Like a tide, time spreads across the neighborhood, and every time it recedes it takes some things away, and leaves others behind, but the overall effect is a diminishment, a slow devour of everything I've ever known.

I still say the letters almost every day. A is for the Anomalies. E is for Endless. D is for Destiny, but also Despair. C is for Consequences, and Cruel, and the terrible Cost. And P, I think P is for Pyromania.

B is for Baby

Wendy didn't like the new baby. Not at all.

She didn't understand why. It didn't make any sense. She'd always loved babies. She'd always loved everybody's babies. They were small and cute and soft and wore pretty things—even the boy babies—and they laughed sometimes when you picked them up, or sometimes they cried but that was okay too. They were kind of like dolls only better. She could hardly wait to have one of her own, even though she was only twelve, and she'd begged her mother for a very long time to have one.

So her mother finally had one. And Wendy couldn't stand to be near it. She never expected it to be so floppy and breakable. The babies she'd held before didn't seem so fragile, but they had been a little older. Maybe her mother should have waited until the baby had grown a little before letting it outside her womb. This baby couldn't hold up its own head. At least Wendy's dolls could hold up their own heads.

Wendy wasn't all the way sure, but she thought her momma had the baby because her dad wanted her to. They argued a lot. The last time Wendy could remember them being nice to each other was back when she was ten. They went out to dinner and dancing almost every weekend. They hadn't gone dancing in a very long time. They sat at home and watched TV. Sometimes her dad went out with his friends. Sometimes Mom smoked a lot of cigarettes by herself, just sitting at the kitchen table, not doing anything else.

They argued about a lot of things, mostly money and stuff like that. And they argued about babies. Dad wanted another one and Mom didn't. They argued a lot and they drank a lot and her mom was sad a lot and one day when she was especially sad she told Wendy she was going to have another baby. Wendy could hardly stand it, she was so excited. She helped her dad paint the big letter B by their front door a bright baby blue. Once the baby saw that he would know this was exactly where he belonged.

"Can I babysit it? Can I take it to school? Can we play dress-up sometimes and it could pretend it was my kid and we just got back from the Bahamas?"

Her mother told her to settle down and leave her alone for a while.

They never let Wendy see the baby when it was still in the hospital. Dad said the baby was sick and wasn't ready to come home. Dad was there a lot, or he was out with his friends and Wendy had to stay with Mrs. Zamora on the next block where the houses were numbered rather than lettered. "You'll see him soon enough when your mom brings him home," her dad kept saying. "Just remember he's very small and very fragile. You have to be careful with him. He isn't your doll."

That turned out to be so true. This new baby made a lousy doll.

Finally, they did bring him home to Alphabet Row and Wendy didn't feel anything like she thought she was going to feel. She'd seen a lot of babies and she'd learned all about babies in Health class but she'd never felt like this. This baby was almost too soft, too wrinkled, too little. It had eyes like little black beads—eyes so little and so black you couldn't tell if it was looking at you or not. She couldn't stand the thought of it in her mother's belly. It made her think of centipedes, worms, and snakes. A baby like this belonged outside in the garden churning up the dirt so the flowers would grow better, not inside their house around all their nice things.

She knew it wasn't an *it* anymore. It was a *he*. The baby's name was Michael, just like her dad's. Michael Lewis Rasmussen Junior. It sounded strange, such a big name for a little wrinkled thing. Once she said to it over and over, "Michael Lewis Rasmussen Junior Michael Lewis Rasmussen Junior Michael Lewis Rasmussen Junior," until her mouth was so full of spit she couldn't talk anymore.

But it didn't move. It didn't act like it heard her. Lying on its back it looked like a bug, legs wiggling in the air like it was trying to turn over. Wendy imagined some bad person, some robber or kidnapper, taking it and cutting off all its arms and legs. Then it would look like one of those little white worms she'd seen come out of the dead cat behind the alley. "Grubs," her mother called them. It was a good name for it. A good name for something that squeezed out of you.

Its mouth was round, so round Wendy thought it might be the only thing perfect about the baby. But there were almost no lips—this almost perfect round hole and no lips, and all red inside.

Even though it had no teeth she couldn't stand to watch her mom nurse it, putting that round hole up over her nipple. She'd always loved to watch mommas nurse before. Mrs. Taylor used to let her watch her nurse her baby all the time.

It looked like they almost forgot its nose, just a couple of holes for the snot to get out.

When they first brought the baby home Wendy had been so excited she ran a little too fast and almost ran over her mother. She stumbled right up against the baby, and although her dad was yelling at her to be more careful, she was so thrilled to see the little thing she just had to reach out and touch it.

It was like touching dough. She snatched her hand back. For a second she wondered if her parents were playing an awful trick on her, and that wasn't a baby her mother was holding at all, but some kind of underground thing they dug out of the yard.

But then its cold black button eyes peered over the blue blanket. Staring right at her, as if it was just as surprised, and scared, to be seeing her.

"Kiss your new little brother," her father commanded in a tired voice.

Wendy shook her head and backed away.

"Come on, Wendy," her mom said. "You've been more excited than anybody about the baby coming."

Wendy walked slowly up to the blue bundle and nervously puckered her lips. Her mom pushed the blue bundle toward her face.

The baby had turned blue. The baby had stopped breathing.

Wendy screamed. And then the baby looked pink again. It smiled at her as her parents started shouting, like it tried to fool her on purpose. It wanted their parents to kick her out of the house so it could take her place.

After that Wendy watched the baby as closely as she could. She made sure she never turned her back on it. When it cried it sucked all the air out of the room. Mom and Dad were always so tired because they couldn't breathe. After a while her dad started going out with his friends again. And her mom started going out to the neighbors more and more often. And almost every time she was left alone with the baby. They said she was old enough now and the baby was big enough.

She took care of the baby. She didn't let anything happen to it or anything—she just watched it. It wasn't cute like a doll. She didn't know why she ever thought babies were cute. It was always hungry, and she got good at feeding it with the bottle, because she knew if she didn't feed it, it would probably try to eat her. Sometimes it latched its mouth onto her arm and sucked so hard her skin turned pale, like it was practicing for when they ran out of formula and the only food available was Wendy's arm.

She brought these baby picture books home from the library at the end of the street, and sometimes she'd look at the pictures of other babies and compare them to this baby. She knew something was very different. She just couldn't tell what.

"Baba," she'd say. "Baba look up at me." And the baby would look up at her and then she'd look at some other baby's face in the book. "Baba" was what Mom and Dad called it now. She guessed Michael Lewis Rasmussen Junior was too much for them, too.

"Baba make boo boo," or "Baba gots 'um booby," they'd say, tickling him, trying to make him laugh. He almost never laughed, but her mom and dad didn't seem to notice. They embarrassed her. She had to go to her room when they started that stuff.

Sometimes when she was alone with the baby it would squirm and wiggle on the floor like a giant pale worm. A wrinkled, smelly grub like something in the garden. She started calling it "Grub," but not in front of Mom and Dad. Maybe it did belong in the garden, and they were wrong for keeping it inside.

She dug out the library book about how babies are born. It had lots of pictures of babies while they were still in their mommas' stomachs. Sometimes the early pictures bothered her, especially the ones that showed how early babies, e-m-b-r-y-o-s, of people, horses, pigs, whales, how they all looked alike. Almost exactly alike. Maybe Mom and Dad brought the wrong thing home from the hospital.

"Hey, Grub!" she called. It looked up at her with its huge round head, its tiny beady eyes. "E-m-b-r-y-o," she spelled. It twisted and squirmed like a tadpole out of water, flopping on the living room rug. "Grub, Grub, Grub," she said, then made a big sigh, as if it had been very bad. It smiled a little doughy smile and made a sound like a baboon. For sure someone had made a bad mistake, and her real baby brother was in a barn somewhere, or maybe swimming in the ocean.

One night she fell asleep waiting for her mom and dad to come home. She dreamed about waking up, going into Grub's room, and looking into his bassinet. And seeing a mound of rotting hamburger on his blue blanket, and that awful hamburger had one dark little eye and a round mouth with no lips. The bright red inside his mouth wanted her to put her finger in there so he could eat.

When she really did wake up she discovered that her mom and dad still weren't home yet. They were terrible parents and always had been, leaving her alone with something that wasn't even human. She went over to Grub and watched him while he slept. She picked him up and held him tight and kissed him on his little round mouth. Then she put him back down again. He still wasn't awake. She stroked the skin on his belly and listened to him snore. Then she reached under her shirt and stroked the soft skin of her own belly, and the even softer, more tender skin of her new breasts.

She reached down with her other hand and touched his belly again. She could feel the edges of scales, hard, and a little sharp. And he smelled bad. She pulled her hand away, but after a few minutes she put it back again. He was a strange little thing, and unlike any creature she'd seen before.

But she still kept touching him, stroking him, watching him sleep. Touching him didn't feel bad at all. She knew she couldn't tell anyone what he was really like. But he was her little brother now, and soon it would be the two of them against the rest of the world.

C is for Clown

Iris thought it was the women who *didn't* wear makeup who had something to hide. She distrusted these pale-skinned beauties, perceiving their plain faces as careful attempts to maintain a blank slate, devoid of revelation. Scarce eyebrows and receding mouth lines and colorless skin, hair pulled back, and clothing subdued: they gave Iris the creeps. She had no idea what they might be trying to hide, but because she knew her own few secrets, the thought of their hidden agendas chilled her.

She spent years observing the other women of Alphabet Row and noticed that the scarcity of makeup was currently at its peak of popularity. The climate of the country, she supposed—which seemed to her to be one of a new reticence, a conservative cautiousness of expression, but that brought little comfort.

Most women had faces like barn doors anyway, only as pretty as their paint jobs. Her father used to say that, and even though he was a complete son-of-a-bitch she thought he'd been right about that one thing. Women's naked faces weren't all that expressive. Probably something to do with evolution. Once the need to communicate fear, pain, hunger, and all those other survival-intensive messages had been somewhat ameliorated, thanks to developments in the medical and communications fields, there wasn't so much need to use the face. In fact, use your face too much and people might think you were a chimpanzee.

Take that librarian, for instance. Never used makeup at all. Iris could tell she was shy to begin with, but the lack of makeup had damn-near receded the poor girl into the dusty background of that library. Her face appeared to be more gray every time Iris went in there. Like book pages that had been turned so much the type was rubbing across the page, so that the words got dimmer and dimmer until someday they were bound to disappear.

Iris thought of the woman's nose wearing away into the planes of her cheeks, her eyes fading to pewter, her lips shrinking into the line of her mouth, and then even the line disappearing. She couldn't imagine the librarian missing that mouth, she so seldom used it.

Such women had no character.

No wonder the woman lost her face in that terrible fire. She didn't deserve a pretty face.

She reconsidered that thought as she applied the morning's makeup. Character was something you held inside yourself. That was true enough. But character didn't do you much good if no one knew it was there. And a person might have several, even dozens of characters inside herself. Particularly if you were a complex sort of person. And the only way to show each of those characters was to do something to your face.

This morning she was going to be "Morning Glory Iris." That seemed the absolute best way to put some cheer into the day. Morning Glory Iris with bright red cheeks and bright blue eyes and lips that were sunny and full. She spent an hour with her powders, paints, and liners, taking out old lines and putting the new ones in, slowly bringing out and accentuating the sunnier side of her nature.

By noon, before the makeup began to melt in the summer heat, she would decide to be someone else. Perhaps someone cooler. Blue Iris. Or maybe After Dark Iris.

The doorbell went off, straining for higher and higher tones. Iris dropped a bright scarf—yellow, to bring out her lips—over her shoulders. Then she went to the door and peered through the peephole.

Cop. Officer Bob, she called him. With his fat little tummy and his round, idiot's face. A sloppy grin—too active for that pasty face. Like a cheap animation. A low-budget cartoon.

She dropped her bright scarf into the corner and pulled out a dark shawl from the closet. She took some of her eye shadow on her fingertip and rubbed it haphazardly into her cheeks, then blended it with her other makeup. She glanced at her shadowy image in the mirror by the door. "Old Maid Iris," she whispered to the glass. Then she opened the door.

Officer Bob squinted as he peered into the dim entranceway. "That you, Miss Iris?" he drawled in a voice almost southern in its lilt. She almost expected him to pull out a corncob pipe and dance a little jig. "Sorry to be bothering you again."

Again. He'd been by three, four times in the past six months.

"May I help you?" Iris croaked.

Officer Bob appeared to be looking past her, at the bright red-striped wallpaper, the huge blue dots floating among the stripes like balloons. "Well, ma'am. Got a few people missing again. Don't like to bother you, but I've been talking to everybody in the neighborhood."

"People are missing from this neighborhood?" she asked quietly.

"Well, just one from Alphabet Row. Little Missy Reynolds, four years old, from just down the street? Her family moved in less than a month ago?"

"A *sweet* thing," she said.

"Yes, ma'am. Well, there's her, missing two days now, then I've got one of those subscription salesmen, some college kid from out of town, and a newspaper boy from three blocks over."

"How tragic."

"Yes, ma'am. You wouldn't have seen anyone like that, now would you?"

"No. No one *ever* comes by here. My family doesn't even visit."

"Yes, ma'am." Officer Bob scratched his head. His eyes rolled a bit, somewhat comically. "But do you mind if I leave some pictures with you? In case you see somebody?"

"Oh, well ..." Before she could stop him, Officer Bob had forced his way inside the entrance way.

"*My goodness!*" he said, laughing nervously. "Looks kind of like a carnival in here."

Iris tried to keep most of her face behind the shawl. She peered around, attempting to see her house the way Officer Bob must be seeing it. Red-striped and blue-dotted wallpaper, Tiffany lights, bright-green wood furniture, shiny red- and yellow-colored plastic glasses, plates, radio. She saw nothing to remark on.

He looked a little worried. "Nice," he said.

She was Blue Iris that afternoon when she heard the scratching at the door. But nothing much bothered her when she was Blue Iris, so she ignored the scratching for a long time. Eventually, however, she began thinking of the damage that scratching must be doing to her candy-apple door. So she finally got up and walked slowly toward the door, touching the pale-blue shadows on her face here and there, seeking any signs of nasty perspiration, willing coolness into her skin.

The scratching increased as she approached the door. She could feel irritation beginning to burn just under the surface of her skin, but she was Blue Iris now, not Tiger Iris or Bear Iris and certainly not Clown Iris, so now was not the time to be irritated. It would be quite out of character.

When she opened the door she didn't see anything at first. Then the darkest of the shadows at her feet suddenly slipped through the doorway.

She spun around and followed the black cut-out of cat as it padded up her stairs. It twisted its neck suddenly—she was sure the neck had no more thickness than construction paper—and opened two burning yellow eyes. It sprung open a mouth full of sharp and hissed. Its crooked tail had a hook. It wrapped its hook around a stair rail to catapult itself faster up the stairs. Iris's mouth fell open into a scream, breaking her blue face wide open.

Taking the steps two at a time, Iris lurched clumsily after the cat. She could feel the sweat oozing out of her hairline, turning the makeup on her forehead to mud. The cat leapt and somersaulted just ahead of her, then jumped up on the Creeping Charlie that grew up the stair banister leading to the house's tiny attic. The ends of the plant stirred, and Iris imagined them reaching up and curling around the cat's neck, throttling it so hard it would fall into a dozen clean slices of black-cat meatloaf.

But the cat was too quick for the plant and was soon upstairs tearing around her attic room, the one space where no one else was allowed, unless Iris herself carried them up there. She could feel her anger building, washing away all the soothing, placating voices inside. She imagined the veins in her face swelling, burrowing larvae-like throughout her skin, creeping eruptions burning bright patterns into her face.

When she reached the attic door she locked it, trapping the black cat inside with the others. As she started back down the stairs to her makeup room, she considered her options. A boulder dropped from a cliff to flatten the thing. A shotgun to blast it into hundreds of miniature black cats. An Acme rocket to tie it to, launch it into the moon where it would put out the eye of a face which this evening looked every bit like W.C. Fields.

All things were possible if you were in the right character.

Blue Iris, Pretty Iris, Determined Iris was on her way downstairs when she again heard a light tap-tapping at her candy apple door. She thought she should ignore it. She wasn't in character, she wasn't in any character at the moment. But it might be another cat, or better yet, it might be some Sad Sack of a stray dog who'd just be hungry enough.

She looked through the peephole and didn't see a thing. That got her hopes up that indeed it might be a dog.

She opened the door slowly so as not to scare the poor little hungry thing and found a child on her doorstep. A little girl. She looked familiar. Iris thought she might live in the neighborhood.

The little girl looked startled, and Iris thought about her own face, and not having looked in the mirror since all her exertions she had no idea who or what she looked like. She thought she might look very much like a scary crone.

But the girl firmed her quivering lips. She took a step forward and said, "Have you seen my kitty? My kitty's name is Blackie. My baby brother and I were playing with him and now I can't find him. Blackie, I mean. My baby brother's still at home, waiting for Mom and Dad to come home."

Helpful Iris looked into the little girl's eyes, and they were *ludicrous*. They were these huge, shiny, glassy dark eyes like you saw on dolls or in those syrupy pictures of puppies, kittens, and waifs. These could *not* be real. It was just all too good to be true. Huge, gigantic eyes like black saucers.

"Would you like a cookie, little girl, while we talk about where to look for your poor missing cat?" asked Grandma Iris.

And, of course, the girl with the huge eyes nodded yes. Vigorously.

Iris went up to her makeup room to make herself more presentable while the child consumed her cookies and milk. She promised she would not be long. Iris made her face as white as she could. Then she made her eyes as red as she could. Then she took her brightest, bloodiest red lipstick and drew on the huge candy apple teeth. And just like that Clown Iris had arrived.

D is for Dog

As far as she knew Anna Lee was the oldest person living on Alphabet Row. She had no illusions about herself. She thought mostly about herself these days, but then, wasn't that an elderly person's right? Life didn't bring her much fun anymore, but who needed fun at her age? She was lucky just to be alive. She'd outlived her husband a good twenty years and might outlive him twenty more. Old and dour: that described her to a T. She wasn't ashamed of it.

Nothing bothered her. Not the kids playing ball and running across her yard. Not the dwindling number of visitors to her home. And surely not the adults with their parties and other goings on she never was invited to. She didn't care. She hardly noticed there were other people in the neighborhood. Nothing ever bothered her. Then one day the dog was there.

Like most days this time of year she had been in the garden. She'd been bending over pulling up onions, dropping them into the old red handbag she used as a garden sack. And suddenly there he was, his cold breath on her neck. When she looked up she was staring right into his mouth.

He gave her quite a fright. For a brief moment she imagined she was staring into her own mouth: an old, pale, fleshy cavern, several broken and yellowed teeth, the stumps beginning to rot from lack of care and insurance. A diseased mouth. She imagined she could see the sickness spreading into the gums, the soft pale flesh that covered the roof.

The dog's breath was hideous. Everything he'd eaten for a week or more had left its taint: rotted food, small dead animals, sewer material. An old stray's diet. A dying thing's diet.

The dog lowered its muzzle and stared at her with rheumy, dreary eyes. A hard dullness at their core.

She threw a cabbage head at him and he loped away. The long scars down his side wriggled like worms. He turned his head once and stared at her again. His foul breath was still alive in her nostrils, probably breeding disease.

The brief encounter virtually exhausted Anna Lee, and she spent the rest of the day dozing in the overstuffed chair by the parlor window. Every now and then she was alert enough to note the dwindling daylight, which served only to spark a renewed round of dreams.

The dog might have been one of her late husband's runaways, she thought. But that was impossible, wasn't it? He'd been gone twenty years now. But for some reason she just couldn't let go of the idea. The man had dearly loved dogs, the uglier the better, and always kept on hand a hound or too. Hellhounds, she'd called them, the way the old dogs messed themselves and everything they touched. Like her husband his last year, slobbering and incontinent. Dizzy with an exhaustion which would not go away, an exhaustion which flowed so heavily the man grew dumb with it. That's what it was like to die, she'd concluded, watching him—your will, your mind diminishing until it was the first thing gone to dust, a foretelling of what was to come.

When she awakened the parlor was brimful with darkness. Not even streetlights could penetrate the enormous hedge that bordered that side of the house. Once again she wished she'd never planted it. She hated the dark. Most of all she hated not being able to find the ceiling. It was as if the sky had blown away, and she was floating up into all that emptiness. Destiny. The end of time.

And though she couldn't see him, she could smell that dog's horrible breath. He was in the room with her, waiting, biding his time, the stinking remains of a dead mouse coating his dull and rotting teeth.

She didn't know why she thought of the dog as a "he." Maybe it was the way the thing reminded her of her husband. The old fool had loved his smelly old dogs, his hellhounds. D is for Dog. H is for Hubby. F is for Fool. And D is also for Dirty, Deceased, and Dead.

She tried to get up, force herself over to the light switch. But something kept her pressed against the chair. The weight increased. Something heavy had flopped into her lap. And that horrible smell was even worse. She was dizzy with exhaustion and disgust.

Now there was a droning sound, like a lawnmower, a hive full of bees. Somewhere in the distance. Then right in her ear. The dog's foul breath whispered to her about all the horrible places it had been.

Anna Lee screamed and pushed away with her hands and knees. The thing was terrible to touch, a hide so oily it didn't feel like fur. She heard him grunt and crash against the wall.

The parlor light came on with a dim yellow burn. The dog lay still against the pale wainscoting. A greasy smudge marked where it hit the wall and slid to the floor. She could not believe she had the strength to do that. She got a broom and poked the thing. It didn't move.

She had a funny thought. She was angry at the dog, angry because of the suddenness of its death. *Why should a dog be allowed a sudden death when my husband had to linger?*

Dragging the dog out to the alley left her dizzy, and she thought several times she should call someone—the sanitation people, the police, maybe that quiet man with the glasses who lived next door—but she didn't want anyone to see the dead animal in her house, or the greasy spot it left on her wall. She didn't know why, it just didn't seem proper. People might talk.

She couldn't just leave its body lying there—that wouldn't be right. She moved one of her trash cans over to the dog, and then realized she couldn't stand the thought of the sanitation men finding the dog in her trashcan. So she took a deep breath and dragged the carcass a little farther down the alley. Each time its bloated belly caught on a stone the whole body shook a little and she had to take another shuddery breath. She stopped in front of one of her neighbor's cans.

She stared at the dog's body and the trashcan in dismay. She'd never be able to lift that much weight. She looked around. The darkness was a powdery soot color. Her eyes were the first thing going, the first thing turning to dust. She could see the dust in the dark air, and she knew it was the dust of her own eyeballs disintegrating that she was seeing. She was fading one piece at a time.

She looked back down at the dog. Then she tipped the can over, spilling a little garbage on top of the dog. She turned the can all the way over and tried to put it upside-down to cover him. But he wouldn't quite fit. Greasy parts of the dog stuck out here and there. She went round and round the can until she was dizzy again, kicking at those exposed dog parts until the last one slipped under the metal rim and the can slid completely over the body with a satisfying clunk.

Then Anna Lee dragged herself upstairs and fell exhausted into bed.

Dawn came slowly. Dawn was arriving later and later in the day. Sometimes she thought about calling the TV weather people about that. They knew about climate, certainly. The only reason she hadn't called yet was she wasn't quite sure if dawn fell under the category of climate.

She rolled over slowly to give her husband one last hug before getting up.

And felt the greasy hair, the too-loose skin.

Her eyes fell open. She was surprised by her own calm. The dog's stench was a powerful presence in the room, but for some reason she did not find it terribly offensive now. It was like some exotic incense, a perfumed vapor that drifted through the room and penetrated her skin directly, making her head buzz.

The dog's dumb expression held no clues. His eyes were dull. His eyelids drooped. Once again when he opened his mouth she imagined she was looking inside her own body.

She tried to say her husband's name, but she could no longer remember it. She could feel remote parts of her turning into dust. She could feel herself diminish.

She'd said it to her husband many times. She remembered the complaint clearly. "We're going to the dogs," she'd said. She'd said that very thing.

E is for Eye

Sean had always had a weak left eye. He'd seen numerous doctors over the years, but an adequate diagnosis failed to emerge. "It's like amblyopia but not exactly," was an analysis he'd heard more than once. The condition was also known as "lazy eye," which he took as an insult, as if somehow, he wasn't trying hard enough. "A possibility of strabismus" was another threatening prognosis pronounced by an adult far above his head. In fact, a great many things were said by the doctors, most of which frightened him, as he sat in a chair he could not escape, his vision blurred by the drops they used. "Atrophy" was a word he particularly recalled, as some fuzzy expert hung over him, prodding with meaty fingers.

"At least you're not crying tears of blood." Had someone said that, or had he imagined it? Sources became elusive when you couldn't see them.

His brain chose to accept the images from his stronger eye and ignore the images from the weaker. The lack of certainty seemed to make little difference in treatment. When he was a kid, they put a patch over his strong eye. His "mighty right," he called it. The patch annoyed him, especially at night. It would itch but he couldn't scratch or rub it, and sometimes it would throb painfully as if attempting to eject the patch all by itself.

Over time his weak eye began to correct itself, although not entirely. He once overheard his father tell his mother, "Well, he'll never be a pilot." That was okay with him. Sean was terrified of heights. He liked wearing glasses. He enjoyed reading, and the special lenses and thick frames his mother picked out made it easier to cancel the rest of the world and focus on the imaginary universe of the book. He also had a better view of what exactly was on his dinner plate and became a picky eater.

Sean had that first pair of glasses tucked into a drawer. He'd had many pairs since then because his vision was so unstable. As a teenager he'd been foolish enough to tape his right eye shut again and deliberately strain his left eye so he might experience numerous confusing but oddly entertaining spatial effects. His father caught him and called him a fool.

Over time he discovered he required several different pairs of glasses just to navigate through an average day, glasses for reading and glasses for driving, another pair for walks and another for watching TV, with different prescriptions, tinting, size and shape of lens, and of course a different lens for the left and right eye. All had to be changed as he grew into adulthood.

Periodically confidence in his doctors eroded and he changed ophthalmologists. They were all enthusiastic at first, fascinated by his unusual condition. Their excitement tended to wane as his eyes thwarted their best efforts. He developed pressure issues and endured tests for glaucoma, cataracts, and central serous chorioretinopathy. None of these examinations were encouraging, serving only to agitate the fragile acceptance he'd built over time.

He moved into the empty bungalow on Alphabet Row when he retired from teaching. It was a small, drab house obscured by evergreens, much like all the other dreary homes on the street, whatever character it once had erased by a series of ill-considered renovations. This was typical, he knew. Every few decades homeowners craved simplicity, and once stripped away, interesting architectural details were seldom restored. Although he respected the idea of ornateness, he couldn't see well enough to properly appreciate it. For him, a plain house like every other house was fine.

The house wasn't enormous, but appeared sufficiently large when he bought it, but the rooms proved a poor fit for his furniture, his four-poster too long for the oddly shaped bedroom, his dining table and chairs too wide for easy passage, and his beautiful antique sideboard wouldn't pass through the entrance. He had either to replace cherished pieces with something smaller or give them away, and even then, he was left with little elbowroom.

Sean was embarrassed to have made such a basic error. He'd made measurements, and he had a copy of the floor plan. Houses shrank once the furniture was moved in—that's what his mother used to say. He knew he was bad with spatial issues. He just hadn't expected such an extreme consequence.

Almost immediately he fell into a regimented schedule, his "old man's routine." On Monday mornings he walked several blocks to a small bodega for a week's groceries. Not having a car, it was the most he could carry in his little cart. Every afternoon after lunch he read in his one comfortable chair under his one good floor lamp and worked on his diary. Books in progress were stacked on the floor on the right. Books to take back to the library or re-shelve in his own collection were stacked on the left. Whenever he confused the two, he became upset. A small side table slightly in front of him bore his diary and held his various pairs of glasses in a lined drawer.

Sean had come to appreciate the predictable moments of fiction: the call to action, the argument against, the dark night of the soul, the reversal, the eventual triumph, or defeat. In his own story he feared the author was frequently on the verge of losing the plot, seduced by a variety of irrelevancies sure to engulf him if he were to lose focus. He'd never found a pair of glasses able to remedy that.

On Fridays he read until early afternoon before eating a sandwich and heading out to the old library at the other end of the Row. When the library closed at five, he crossed at the corner and walked three more blocks to a movie theater to see one of the new releases. He loved movies, but the dark scenes were sometimes difficult for him to make sense of. So he imagined what he could not see clearly.

On this Friday Sean arrived at the library later than usual. A struggle with an elegiac scene in a newly translated foreign novel delayed him. He had no idea what was actually going on but felt compelled to read to the end of the chapter. He scribbled his reaction in his diary noting the author's eccentric dreamlike style, which sparked a recollection of the eerie dream he'd had the night before—finally having gone completely blind he'd been lost in a strange city where people mistook him for someone else. Now he worried whether he'd locked the door behind him. He'd forgotten to eat his sandwich and would have to buy a too-salty or too-sugary snack at the movie, which would doubtless keep him up past his regular bedtime, increasing the chances of another disturbing dream and an exhausting day after.

He slipped on his reading glasses to examine the local newspaper and knew something was wrong. The large headlines leaned off the page and the smaller print blurred into a greasy smear. He'd been reading for quite a while that day, and sometimes it took a while for his eyes to adjust. He massaged them gently. They stung, felt oddly gritty. He took his hands away and tried the glasses again. He recognized many words, but they appeared strung together in an elliptical fashion. He got out a tissue to clean them, slipped them back on, and experienced no improvement. He searched his coat for another pair, but these were even worse, creating painful haloes wherever he looked. A third pair retrieved from an inside pocket were emphatically blurry and he took them off.

Sean didn't understand how he could have made such a mistake. Three wrong pairs? Which had he worn walking to the library? He searched his chair, nearby tables, and the floor, but didn't find another set.

He supposed he should go home and call it a night, find the proper pairs in the morning. But he was nagged by the notion he'd brought the correct glasses after all, and his vision had suddenly suffered a cataclysmic failure.

If he returned home, he would miss the movie. Friday had always been movie night. Sean hated violating his schedule, and hated disappointment even more. He was aging rapidly. How many more movie nights did he have?

He'd always had to make adjustments to accommodate his odd way of seeing. His eyes would be sore afterwards, but he thought he could follow the storyline—he'd become adept at filling in the blanks when the world left out random pieces. At least he was eager to try.

Sean set out for the theater early, letting his feet find each edge before committing, counting off the eight steps down from the library entrance and easing onto the sidewalk. He knew the street corner where he had to begin and understood the general direction he needed to travel. There were traffic lights and pedestrian lights the entire way, so a safe trip seemed possible.

He discovered those lights were not as reliable or as distinctive as he'd hoped. They blurred together, the electric colors shifting and melting into a psychedelic effect. At some points he didn't know if he was looking at traffic lights or the neon sign of a business. Several colors were more vivid than others, as if those were the ones he should pay attention to. His eyes teared up and his depth perception failed him. It became difficult to track moving objects. He couldn't tell if traffic had veered dangerously close. The painful headlights sometimes made it necessary to look down at his feet: two furry animals lurching across the glossy pavement ahead of him.

Thankfully, a growing crowd pushed down the sidewalk in the same direction, so he made himself part of their multilegged army. They were unexpectedly loud and excited, and he was carried along in their ecstatic dance. Sean trusted they wouldn't harm him, and they deposited him shaken but whole at the base of the movie theater steps. Familiar architectural elements began to appear, and some sort of expansive marquee hung horizontally overhead.

When his turn at the ticket window arrived, Sean stepped forward, bumping his forehead solidly against the glass.

"Are you okay, sir?" An earnest teenager's voice coming from the booth. A girl's. It was startling to have someone address him directly.

"Oh, fine. Fine thanks. I'd like a ticket for the next showing of—" He stopped, embarrassed, unable to remember the title. "It's in outer space? Science fiction."

"*Ad Astra*," she replied. "That's a good one. Ten dollars for seniors."

Sean wondered if the staff ever said a movie they were showing was bad. He paid and she slid the ticket into his outstretched hand. "Will it start soon? Can I go right in?"

"Yes sir. Theater E, immediately inside and to your left. Refreshments on your right. Do you need any assistance?"

He did, of course. It must have been obvious. But he was embarrassed. "No but thank you."

He was hungry but couldn't imagine maneuvering through the crowded refreshment lines. He took an immediate left into a hall he knew from experience contained four theaters. He handed his ticket to someone at the entrance of the hall, then apologized fiercely as he knocked over two stanchions supporting a heavy rope barrier. He found the wall on the left side and stayed close to it. Memory told him the door to Theater E was the second on the left. He ran into a large someone, apologized again, and followed them inside.

The lights were up in the theater, but it was still relatively dim. He avoided the rows crowded with shadow and found a seat toward the back. He collapsed into it and wiped at the tears running down his face. He didn't know if anyone was sitting nearby.

The trailers weren't encouraging. Sean alternated between the three pairs of glasses he had on him and picked the one creating the least discomfort. Trailers were cut in a way to increase excitement, but these were jittery, the explosive transitions evoking panicked reactions and more stomach-dropping moments than he could handle. But he could follow the action more or less, his sense of anticipation providing a kind of continuity. He didn't catch all the titles, and he wasn't sure he could have told anyone what these movies were about, but he at least formed an opinion as to which ones he might want to see later.

During the first few seconds of *Ad Astra* Sean could tell there were large red letters on the screen, but he couldn't make out any of the words. He imagined an ambiguous message meant for him alone. A light show of shifting colors followed, then first sight of a planet, perhaps Earth, the Big Blue Marble, perhaps something else. He didn't recognize the actor, but knew it was Brad Pitt from what he'd read in the newspapers. Pitt's character recited a series of affirmations, words and phrases meant to ground him in the circumstance and the reality at hand. Sean understood the impulse. He did something similar nearly every day. The world was a complicated and slippery place. It was all too easy to lose your way. Sean supposed he himself was a kind of astronaut in a strange and alien world.

Sean sensed an expanding distortion, a buildup of fluid or a swelling of brain. He could make out little on the screen, a spreading of colors and shapes, a bleeding through from somewhere dangerous. When you can't see what's around you, words whispered from a seat close by, you must look inside. He could feel the unpleasant intimacy of someone's breath against his ear. He turned his head to see who was speaking. After a few moments the darkness returned a harsh "Excuse me!" and he rolled his head back to the screen. Perhaps one of the actors had said the line, but he didn't think so.

He was tumbling, falling out of space, then the parachute jerked him upwards. Sean wasn't sure what was happening on the screen, but understood it involved survival.

Next was a man's muddy face rising out of brown river water. Flashes of natives dancing, a firework sky full of explosions and Marlon Brando's swollen, brooding form.

This was *Apocalypse Now*, and it had absolutely no business being up there. Sean cried out and grabbed the arms of the seat, which meant grabbing someone else's hand, confirmed by their muffled complaint. Some child, perhaps. "I'm so sorry!" he cried. He waited for other complaints, about both his behavior and the wrong motion picture which had trespassed onto their screen, but there were none. An eddy of whispering, and the apparent family group sitting next to him moved, either finding safer seats or leaving the theater entirely.

A few minutes later a flashlight beam reached out to his row and lingered on his offending hand for an extended period. He sensed someone standing nearby. He sat still, knowing he'd earned this official attention, but dreaded the shame of being ejected. He stared at the screen pretending comprehension, until the presence left. When Pitt came back on the screen Sean was relieved. You always felt better when the hero arrived.

He thought it peculiar how none of the actors emoted in this film. Everyone seemed so suppressed, so flat in affect. At first he'd attributed it to bad acting, then decided this approach was crucial to the message. Pitt in particular had a scarily calm demeanor. Solitary men maintained this calm and rational exterior even as they ate the world.

A woman he'd loved in college suddenly entered the frame of the film. He recognized her from her voice, but even with his compromised vision her face displayed higher than a two-story building was hard to mistake. He'd lost track of her years ago. Recently he tried everything to locate her without success. Brad Pitt's thoughts were on the soundtrack. Was he speaking to her, or was this meant for him? "We do our jobs, we fulfill our roles, and then we're gone." The sound quality rapidly deteriorated at this point, and Sean lost his most coherent means for navigating the film.

There was a madness inherent in space travel, or perhaps there was a madness inherent in existence itself. He felt his skin crawl, and then saw it crawl. So much extraneous flesh. He felt the organs shifting around inside his body seeking an exit.

Sean sank further into the padding, the back of his neck rubbing against the top of the seat. He envied the no doubt normal family who'd made their escape. He closed his eyes to the unbearable, the indistinct whispers, the physical and mental effects of Zero-G, the psychological distress of being so far from home, the people he used to know now as distant as the stars.

He eventually lost the thread of the film. Pitt appeared to arrive safely back on Earth, but Sean had no idea how. Perhaps it was simply the magic of the movies.

He allowed the natural flow of the crowd to push him homeward. This meant a few missteps, a few unfortunate detours. At one intersection a boxy vehicle showered the mob with cascading lights. A squad of EMTs attended to the wounded, engaged in their usual activities related to aspects of the eternal.

But Sean landed safely in front of the closed library, and he knew his way home from there. He'd made the trip hundreds of times. His was the fourth house from the library, the "E" house if you counted the library "A," since the original A house burned down. Rumor had it the builder added this detail to help children learn the alphabet.

He couldn't see the fronts of the houses in the dark; they were set too far back, and few still had their lights on. He ran his hand along the fences and counted the gates. When he thought he'd come to his own house he opened the gate slowly, not wanting to draw attention to himself, or disturb anyone already in bed. But he stumbled on the front porch steps, almost falling, staggering forward and slapping his hands on the wall by the door. He searched his pockets for his keys, and unable to find them reached out and turned the knob. It opened—he had indeed forgotten to lock up.

He flipped on the lights and surveyed his world in its entirety, his vision unexpectedly cleared: the ill-fitting furniture, the cramped and tortured rooms, his life self-embalmed, an overwhelming supply of solitude with no room for anyone else.

The toxic reticence. The eerie quiet. The crushing isolation of space.

F is for the Farm

Andrew hadn't seen Beth in months, so when he received her note inviting him to the farm, he rushed from the apartment without telling anyone where he was going. He'd stopped being cautious with love. In his experience you seldom got a second chance.

He'd expected wide-open spaces, chickens, and cows, but the address was for a house in an older urban neighborhood with vintage bungalows, nearby schools and grocery stores, and a grand library at one end of the street. It was hot, so he parked under a large shade tree.

He checked the note again; this was the address Beth gave him, *#F Alphabet Row*. Above the house's dusty mailbox, a tarnished brass letter F was screwed into the brick.

The property appeared ill-kept. He stood on the stoop, a few fractured concrete steps rising from the failing yellow grass. Vines poked from yawning cracks in the foundation.

He knocked. He waited a minute and knocked again. An ancient woman in a stained beige dress opened the door. Her pale face was corrugated and mud-stained. "We don't welcome salespeople."

"*Mother*, he's here for me." Beth appeared and turned the woman around and nudged her inside. She embraced him fiercely. "I'm *so glad* you came."

He squeezed her gently. It scared him how much he liked this woman. "That was your mother?"

"We call all the older women here 'Mother.' Did you have any trouble finding us?"

"I thought you lived on a farm."

"You'll see." She grinned and pulled him inside.

The crowded mess in the front room initially made him think they were hoarders. Then he realized the trash was dead leaves and decaying flowers. The floor vanished beneath them. A muscular young man sat in the corner, reading under LED grow lights. He absent-mindedly, and blissfully, chewed on a plant. Torn blossoms spilled from his lips.

"That's Joseph," Beth said. The young man glanced up briefly and returned to his book without speaking.

Thick, woody vines covered the walls with broad leaves and those voluptuous blossoms. Vines grew into the bare brick. Multiple brick rows, around the windows, above the door, were distorted, pushed askew by the aggressive growth. Andrew doubted this structure was safe.

Beth caught him staring. "Aren't they great? They're all descended from the original plant Father discovered growing here when he bought the property." She squeezed his hand and led him further into the house.

The house was small, but packed with people, the furniture minimal and the interior doors removed. In every room a team tended not only the vine but several potted plants, pruning, watering, dropping bits into jars and bags.

The residents varied in age, although he didn't see any children, and many were quite old: seventies and eighties, nineties. They were all dressed in work clothes, nothing nice, and nothing clean. They paid Beth and Andrew no attention.

Beth kept moving, saying *Hi!* to various people, and *This is Andrew! Say hello to Andrew!* as she dragged him along. Despite her enthusiasm, no one said hello.

The kitchen was large, with two stoves and plentiful counter space. Industrial-sized pots kept the room steamy. An elderly woman wearing a headscarf stood at each pot, watching, stirring. Andrew couldn't have described the flavor. Just green—the air inside the kitchen tasted and smelled exceptionally green.

Beyond the back door a ramp led them down to ground level and a vista of plant rows receding into the distance, corn and peppers and tomatoes and a few crops Andrew didn't recognize. The omnipresent vines lay across the ground like fire hoses. People stepped over them carefully as they walked the rows with baskets, harvesting the swollen crops from the plants or off the ground. A high fence around the property shielded them from prying eyes.

An enormous antique plow hung from a pole nearby, the kind a horse or a mule pulled, with handles the farmer could hold onto. It was painted enamel black and had a giant shiny silver blade.

"That's so we don't forget how hard farming used to be. Isn't it *fabulous*? Father used it to create the first furrows, but we have a rototiller now. He bought the lot behind us so we could plant more rows."

A tall, black-haired man in filthy bib overalls stood beside the plow, glaring at them. "That's Karl. He's one of the originals. Don't mind him—he's a sourpuss. He doesn't like anybody, and nobody likes him."

A large man sat in a faded lawn chair with a glass of green juice. He was bare-chested and bronzed, had squarish white teeth, long white hair, and a wiry silver beard streaming with greenish stains. He looked up and smiled at Beth, glanced at Andrew, and nodded, returned his attention to his clipboard.

"Sorry," Beth whispered. "Father doesn't like surprises. I should have let him know you were coming. I'll introduce you later."

––––––––––

The farm had no proper bathroom. Beth showed him to the latrines at the far back corner, hidden behind plank walls and a rough-made roof. He was fairly sure this was illegal within the city limits.

"We've got three farms in one," Beth explained. "There's the house farm, and there's the field. Then we have a place underground. The Below Farm. I hear that's something to see, but you must earn an invitation. Even I haven't been there."

Andrew hadn't planned to stay long enough to earn anything. "Where does everybody sleep? I didn't see any beds."

She laughed. "You sleep wherever you can find a spot. Everybody gets tired eventually. They just lie down wherever they are. Most sleep somewhere out here between the rows."

"And if it rains?"

"If it's a light summer rain, and you're well-covered, it can be refreshing. When it pours, or when it's cold, everybody crowds inside, like a giant slumber party."

"Doesn't seem to be much privacy."

"But we're all family here, even the ones who weren't always."

He looked around. He didn't want her to see the doubt in his face. "You take showers?"

"Outdoors, when necessary. Father says modern folks wash too much. They scrub off their natural protective oils. I know you'll love it here. You can stay at least a few weeks, right? Tell me you have nothing better to do."

"Beth, you know I like being with you. But I'm not sure I can live like this."

She put her arms around him and kissed his neck, his ear. "I think you'll feel differently after you've stayed a while. We're the folk of the farm, of the plant and the vine. Soon enough you'll understand."

She had the same wide-eyed expression she wore when he first saw her at lunch that day, sitting on the ground just outside campus, feeding little green bits to the birds. When the birds became too many and too eager, he'd stepped in to rescue her.

She gave him some clothes to change into, battered old jeans and a faded T-shirt. "And your cell phone? I'll need that. I'll keep it safe. I promise."

"What the hell, Beth."

"Didn't I tell you before? I'm sorry. You can't have a cell phone here. We don't have wireless or cell phones. Don't you know those things give you cancer?"

Dinner was a vegetable, or plant stew, eaten from clay bowls. It had a bitter aftertaste, but it felt substantial. He became satiated, and sleepy. Andrew would come to hate the feeling.

He met more family members. Brothers and sisters, and more old Mothers than he could count. A few old men, who were reluctant to talk. No one said much more than a first name. The presence of the older people began to make more sense. Perhaps they had no family or income. They were taken well care of here.

Father walked among them as they ate, whispering, laying his hands on heads or shoulders. He whispered into Beth's ear, patted her on the head. He ignored Andrew.

After dark people wandered off singly or in pairs. She dragged him into the soft dirt near some tall corn and began pulling off his clothes.

"You love me, right?" she said breathlessly. "Tell me you love me."

"I am—I'm falling in love with you."

They made love and rolled out of the corn onto freshly plowed ground. There they slept curled together between the furrows.

Andrew never made the decision to stay, but after a few weeks he was still there. Every morning they ate a light breakfast—dry, chewable plant material—while Father, still ignoring Andrew, delivered a message or rambling reminiscence about living naturally, supporting the plant, and what the plant gave back. It sounded like poorly organized New Age mush, but Beth listened with rapt attention.

Each day, they tended plants. At first it was tidying up, trimming a few dead leaves away, smoothing out the ground around the crops where someone had been sleeping. Beth talked to the plants, and urged Andrew to touch them with tenderness, because it facilitated growth, and was the right thing to do.

When they worked in the house farm, it felt a lot like house cleaning, because the vines were always dropping bits and pieces. In between they sneaked kisses and grabbed opportunities for quick sex. Andrew could barely keep his hands off her, even though he often felt faint. This new plant-based diet, with the occasional offal added, was a challenge. He made frequent, exhausting trips to the latrine. He was sleepy but learning how to work through the drowsiness.

The entrance to the Below Farm was a low, crudely built masonry structure with a rusted hatch in the middle of the field. Two young men were always stationed nearby. Since Father still ignored Andrew, his going below seemed unlikely. That unpleasant fellow Karl supervised the Below Farm, so maybe it was just as well. Most workers with access were elderly, especially the Mothers, including the old woman who first greeted him at the door.

Those workers slept and took their meals below. Given the crowded conditions in other parts of the farm, it made sense. Andrew rarely saw them after they went down.

Andrew frequently tripped over some bit of the vine, and he had to be incredibly careful not to nick or damage it in any way. Eerily quiet most of the time, these people became loud and irate when such mistakes occurred.

At the end of Andrew's fourth week, Father came and sat with them both and addressed Andrew directly:

"Once this land was forest, then farmland. Then the farms were abandoned, and nature took them back. Human beings in their ignorance plowed it all under again, building industries instead. When these industries failed, as all human activity eventually must, they scraped them off the land, and they built these houses.

"But something persisted, hidden within layers of time. A generous plant, unlike all others, a plant willing to give back to those who gave it care. If you are to stay here, you must honor this plant and our ways."

With Beth watching, Andrew felt he had to agree. But he was hardly a convert. He distrusted most religions, including societies, parties, clubs, whatever they called themselves. They were always trying to recruit you. He was content if he could spend more time with Beth. Life here wasn't exactly unpleasant.

It reminded him of long camping trips when he was a kid, but with sex involved.

"Do you believe everything your dad says? I moved out of my parents' house years ago."

Beth looked unhappy.

"First off, he's not my dad. We call him 'Father' to honor him. I did move out of my parents' house. I was sixteen and I haven't seen them since.

"I used to fantasize having an apartment downtown, coming and going as I pleased, but I outgrew it. This land is more important than we are. The vine is more important than we are. We are temporary. But the land and the vine are not."

Andrew stopped asking questions. He would have to watch for an opening, then somehow talk her into leaving with him.

After several months, Andrew realized it had become a voluntary incarceration. Beth was perfectly happy here. If he said anything negative, she became cold, and he became isolated and alone.

He'd been assigned the nastiest chores: maintaining the latrines and filling the giant organic compost vats, which often included the dead animal remains. He himself tossed in a dead fox he'd found by the fence.

This was their way of testing him. There had been other newcomers since Andrew arrived, and as far as he knew, all remained. One or two were given the right to represent the farm at various farmers markets around the city, where they sold their potent green juice. This was a major source of the farm's income. Several had even made it to the Below Farm. This offended him. Hadn't he done everything they asked?

The other major income source was the "endowments." Some of those old people hadn't been destitute. They'd had resources, money, property, which they signed over to the farm.

"They believe in what we're doing. We're they're family now. They either don't have kids, or their kids don't appreciate them. You would do the same, wouldn't you?" Beth was enthusiastic on the subject.

"Sure. But I'm broke. I've left school. At this point my roommates probably think I'm not coming back. I don't even have a place to live anymore."

She smiled. "Then you'll just have to stay here with me."

Andrew closed his eyes. He was so tired. And maybe Beth wasn't who he wanted after all.

During Andrew's first month, one man accidentally cut deep into his palm with a harvesting knife. Such accidents weren't uncommon. The knives were sharp, and they were encouraged to be more productive. Sometimes they rushed. Andrew was nearby and grabbed some rags to bind the wound.

The fellow pulled his hand away angrily and ran to the nearest vine and allowed the blood to flow generously over it. Then, staggering, and pale, he came back to Andrew and presented his hand for bandaging.

Andrew witnessed this ritual several times. Giving the blood to the vine was always the first step, before any medical aid was administered, usually by the Mothers. As far as he knew, no one was ever taken to the hospital, although sometimes it appeared necessary.

The Mothers intentionally bled themselves. Numerous times he saw them gather near the crops, and one would enter and hide herself and come out bleeding, or the other Mothers had to go in after her because she'd done too much with the knife and passed out. They'd carry her away, with bloody bandages wrapping both arms.

He pointed this out to Beth.

"We have to show respect," she said. "The Mothers will do anything for the plant and the farm."

At the end of every month, they held a festival, a party, meant to blow off steam. Father would deliver a speech, enumerating their accomplishments that month, items harvested, and bottled juice sold, and then the drinking and dancing began.

The drink was an alcoholic version of the farm's green juice. He didn't know where they got the alcohol. Maybe they brewed it in the Below Farm. After two drinks, even the quietest were singing, dancing around half-dressed, couples dragging each other off into the darkness.

But what was unique was the chanting, the rhythmic recitation of sounds and words in a language he did not recognize, including lots of odd, painful throat sounds. It sounded like the Appalachian Holy Roller speaking in tongues.

Several times he interrupted Beth's dancing and asked her if she was okay. She certainly didn't look okay. He stopped when she became angry and turned her back.

He didn't feel the same euphoria. Maybe the alcoholic juice hadn't been in his system long enough. He felt a slight fuzziness, a pressure in his head which went to the edge of a headache without crossing over, and everything appeared darker and further away. He sat for a while, watching Beth dancing, listening to the non-words she spoke. Finally, he risked asking her, "Did Father teach you this language?"

She turned around, laughing. "Oh, we don't *learn* it. Over the years it comes into us, and we let it out in speech. We know if we don't let it out periodically it will build up in our flesh and make us ill. You'll discover it, too, when you've been here long enough."

The celebration went on all night. Andrew didn't remember falling asleep, but he was swallowed up and smothered within a cloud of sound. For a time before sleep, he forgot his own name, her name, and where he was.

———

One morning, a few days later, Karl rousted them awake. "Come with me. Congratulations. We've assigned you both to the Below Farm."

The two guards beside the hatch were sleeping and Karl wordlessly kicked them awake. He guided Andrew and Beth below.

From its first details the Below Farm filled Andrew with dread. Overly bright halogen bulbs hung from the ceiling casting a harsh white light and generating much heat. Compacted vines lined the walls. The vine had coiled around itself repeatedly to create a support system for both the slanting entrance tunnel and the multiple chambers which followed. The staircase had vines trailing beside and underneath it. An old man with an acetylene torch was stationed near the stairs. Periodically he burned a flame near any vines threatening to grow where they were not wanted, such as over the steps or other apparatus. Vats and drums, some connected to hoses and pumps and other equipment, were arranged throughout the space.

A forest of roots and vines hung from the ceiling. Mothers and elderly men were scattered throughout, tending to these roots and vines, cutting some and dropping them into the carefully watched vats, preserving, and protecting other sections, tying them back to get them out of the way.

None of these older folks looked at all healthy. Andrew wondered when they'd last experienced daylight.

A few workers were Beth and Andrew's age. They were used for the more labor-intensive jobs. Karl put them to work rolling fresh vats into place, stationing full ones to be hauled up the stairs. Other workers were in the far reaches of the Below Farm, digging and rearranging vines, extending the farm's reach, but Andrew never saw them.

Andrew had a fear of enclosed spaces. His impulse was to run back up the stairs and leave the farm. He controlled his claustrophobia for Beth's sake, but his hands were shaking, his throat dry as bark.

A yellow liquid skim lined the floor of the Below Farm. Drainage from the irrigation system, juices dripping off the vine and from the various dangling roots. They stood in this liquid all day, every day. After a few weeks, the bottoms of their feet were furry with fibrous growths. They shaved them off using disposable razors, but they came back.

He felt for the oldest Mothers, none of whom seemed fit for this environment. He tried to talk to them and see how they were feeling, and unlike in the farm above, down here they didn't seem to mind talking.

Beth, on the other hand, went quiet. She seemed depressed, and they rarely had lengthy conversations anymore. She was still affectionate, and at night hugged him even more tightly than before. But he felt a desperation in it. She seemed defeated.

Andrew had assumed the Mothers weren't to be trusted. They were watching everyone else, and he frequently saw them in conversation with Father. But here they were more relaxed, even eager to chat, although sometimes the relaxation seemed more like fatigue, and the chattiness more like delirium.

Hatches had been placed here and there on the floor of the Below Farm, and once he'd seen some Mothers open a hatch and descend. So, there was another, lower level, and who knew, there might be levels even further down.

Usually, a Mother was stationed at each hatch, but not always. Rules below were more relaxed than rules above. Or they thought no one wanted to go deeper into a place which was already wet, unpleasant, and barely tolerable.

Over time, the population of Mothers in the Below Farm dwindled until there were only a few. Andrew assumed they'd been reassigned upstairs. The ones who remained were a listless bunch. Beth said they needed more older women to join the family, and they had members out in the city recruiting. He'd never heard her use *recruiting* before.

"Is that why I'm here? You recruited me?"

She looked embarrassed and couldn't look him in the eye. "Of course not. I *liked* you. I *wanted you* here with me. You've been good for me."

"You could have been sent out recruiting, and still liked me. Those two things are not contradictory. Now maybe you're a little less interested now I've been here a while? Is that what's going on?"

"Andrew! No!" She became weepy. "It's just this *place*. Everybody has talked about the Below Farm as if it were something special. I thought being assigned here was an honor. But it's *awful* down here! I'm *miserable*."

"You can talk to Father. Get him to reassign us. He likes you. It's obvious."

"I can't disrespect him like that, asking for special favors."

He put his arms around her. "Maybe if we do a little more exploring into how everything works here, we can figure something out. Maybe starting with this hatch." He pointed to the one he'd recently seen Mothers access.

She wrinkled her face. "Are you kidding? It's terrible enough at this level."

"If it's too bad we can leave, but maybe we'll find out something useful."

They lifted the hatch and slipped in, trying not to make any noise. There was plenty of light. But also, an overabundance of vine. Stepping off the stairs they were confronted by thick vines leaving a narrow passage through. A loud thrumming noise pulsed ahead of them.

They found the first body ten yards in. Andrew had no idea what it was at first, a swollen vine, like some sort of plant tumor, with a mass of filaments on one end of the bulge. His eyes wouldn't quite focus with the gloom below, the scattered bright bulbs above. Then he saw the facial pattern in the bark of the tumor. A woman's wrinkled, disintegrating face. And those grayish, fragile-looking filaments was her hair. He touched it. It fragmented and dissolved like cobwebs in his hand.

He walked a little further. He couldn't quite figure out where the corpse stopped and the plant began. There were many more in diverse sizes, more than a dozen. Many more. Besides the vine, the bodies were connected by a fatty-looking fungus, and it was the fungus making the thrumming noise. The fungus was overwhelming, yards long and wide. He froze, unable to move further. The corpse plant writhed with bugs, many flowing over the dead faces. He reached down and scraped them off a face. It was the Mother who'd answered the door when Andrew first arrived.

"You have to understand." He realized Beth had been speaking behind him. "Some of these people were already dead, and the rest were going to die soon. They gave their bodies willingly. That's why we need the older ones in the family. There are never enough. The vine—"

"You *knew* about this?"

"I've been told. I've been told how beautiful... I've never actually *seen* it."

"What *else* haven't you told me?"

The alarm went off above them, sounding like overlapping screeches of pain. They hurried back to the ladder and climbed.

Workers were running toward the exit. Andrew wondered if there was a fire, or flooding, but he didn't see anything obvious.

"The plow," a Mother said nearby. "The plow." Several others repeated it.

Behind him, Beth said, "Our presence is required, but Andrew, you're not going to want to see this. Just do what they say, but keep your eyes shut. That's what I always do."

People had gathered between the house and the rows of plants. Several young men were taking the plow down from the pole.

"We live on fertile ground. When our income falls there must be other reasons!" Father was walking back and forth before a naked figure staked to the ground. "This man has been with us since the beginning, but all this time he has betrayed us. He has stolen from us, and he has stolen from the vine. He has behaved not as family, but as one of the strangers who lie, cheat, and steal beyond these walls." Andrew and Beth pushed closer. The man on the ground was Karl. He'd been severely beaten. His mouth moved sloppily, but no sound came out. Father spat. "Bring up the plow."

The crowd separated, a few stronger men grabbing the plow handles and positioning the blade between Karl's squirming legs. The rest formed a line on the harness end, which had a long rope attached. Family members latched on to the rope. A couple of the Mothers pushed Beth and Andrew toward the end of the line.

Beth waited until the Mothers found their own place, then dragged Andrew away toward the house. "You don't want to be a part of this. You don't belong here. Joseph's one of the plowmen so there won't be anyone guarding the front room."

They made their way along the fence behind some tall plants, then to the back door. Everyone was focused on Karl and the plow. Father shouted "Now!" and Andrew turned his head.

As they entered the house, he could hear the huffing and the laborious grunts behind them, as if from a giant beast. "I guess Karl will soon be below feeding your precious vine."

Beth jerked his arm urgently. "Forget him. His bits go into the compost."

"You've seen this before?" She didn't answer.

They reached the front room. She opened the door and pushed him onto the threshold. "Go! Before someone notices!"

"Come with me!"

She dropped his hand. "I can't."

He stared at her. "So, I was just a recruit, right? That day in the park you were waiting for someone like me."

"It was my assignment. I waited until the right guy came along. We need new young guys, just like we need old women, Mothers. They fit the plan. But I liked you. I *really* did. Better than anyone—"

"Anyone you'd recruited? There were more like me? This Joseph, was he one of yours? Is that why he seemed so standoffish when I first showed up?"

She looked up at him. "You must *leave*, Andrew. They're my *family*."

He turned and went over the threshold, almost falling as he stumbled down the concrete steps. He heard the door slam behind him. The house's exterior looked the same as it had the day he arrived. He crossed the quiet street. His car had been towed, probably some time ago, but he'd expected that. There were kids on bicycles, teenagers with books headed toward the library at the end of the street. Everything possessed this strange, bright normalcy. He was embarrassed by his slovenly, dirty appearance.

He passed three black parked cars. Two men in ties and jackets sat in the front seats of each. One had a cell phone, talking as he stared at #F.

Andrew wanted to tell them what was happening inside that house, but guessed they already knew.

G is for Ghost

The architect engaged Lewis to gut a house near the middle of Alphabet Row. The clients were young marrieds, double-income with no kids. Dinks. He'd done a number of these: the couple would buy some old Victorian because of the glamour of it, the grace, but before moving in they'd have the interior scooped out and hauled away, then replaced it with a condominium-style decor, probably not much different from the one they lived in now. It was crazy, but Lewis got paid for demolition, not psychiatry.

The house had twin gables out front and ornamented gutters. The outside lights and the lightning rods up on the roof had filigree work around the bases. Finely detailed gingerbread braced the eaves. The paint had been kept up: there was very little chipping, and the shingles looked intact. A couple of clapboards showed some splitting, but there didn't seem to be any water damage. The garden around the side still bore flowers, and the driveway leading up to a separate, finely-kept garage, was a smooth, unbroken stretch of clean concrete.

The other houses on the block were not as well-kept. Ragged grass, lopsided hedges and shrubs, lots of dead spots. Garbage cans exposed, some of them spilled. A bunch of ugly sisters for the most part. There wasn't much home improvement going on. Lewis usually didn't find much work in neighborhoods like these. He wondered if the well-to-do young couple would be welcomed here.

If they actually moved in, of course. In more than one of these projects the young couple backed out. If they had the money, he supposed they felt they could afford to be fickle. But usually not before the house had already been autopsied, all its insides gone forever.

The architect had given him a plan and a grocery list of what had to go. That was the common procedure. Sometimes the buyer would come by to watch some of the demolition, but that usually wasn't the case. Most didn't want to watch; they kept their distance, dealing exclusively through the architect or some contractor. Lewis dealt a lot with people who liked to maintain their distance: chief architects who didn't even want a glance at the property until the greater part of the dirty work had been done; young buyers whose interest stayed remote and general until he'd removed a ton of old plaster and lathe from the place, all kinds who didn't like the grime of what he had to do to someone's grand old memories. And maybe memory was part of the key. The houses they had bought, and he had to gut, were so like houses remembered from childhood, or from dreams of childhood. But now all the cozy furniture's been moved out and the people have died or moved away and only the grizzled memories remained.

It reminded him of those old-fashioned ghost stories where the storyteller keeps you at a supposedly safe distance by telling you that he heard the tale from a friend of a friend, or read about it in a letter or in a diary written by someone who lived a century before. And it does make you feel a little more secure for a while, until the very distance of the telling makes you think terrible things might happen to just about anyone because you're too far away from the ghost to see the wires that make it glide, and then you begin to wonder if the author feels he *has* to tell it to you at such a distance because your nerves might unravel if exposed to the awful manifestation close up. The ghosts in such stories were like most people's memories: in order for people to function normally these specters had to be kept at a distance, but keeping them at a distance made them all the more awful, still more awful because they began to seem less and less a part of you.

Lewis understood the need, all right; it was always a gamble. He'd lost a mother, a wife, and a daughter not yet three in a house very much like this one, his whole life burned to smoke the shape of his memories. After ten years and the pain of the grief being no better his doctor had him write down the most important of these memories on separate sheets of paper, then burn them one at a time in an ashtray. It had seemed an atrocity at first, until he realized that the memories were still there. The act had just made it seem possible there was room for the new as well. Like these houses. He might scrape them clean to the outside walls like some crude gynecologist, but the gray phantoms of the lives that had begun and ended there would still be present, in <u>his</u> mind if in no other's.

Not that he'd ever believed in ghosts, at least not in the way people talked about them. Gnomes or gremlins or goblins or green gases guiding you through the hallways or something similar. He didn't understand any of that, none of it at all. He just knew that death wasn't as any of us had imagined it. Death was something we didn't know at all.

Maybe there was just too much of the grave in Lewis's work for the people who employed him. He'd stopped trying to figure, or to argue, or to suggest. He just did his job. He used to be a builder, back before he got the tremble in his hands. Now he was a destroyer. He did it quickly and efficiently, and always by himself. The fact was, he didn't like people watching him while he did what he was paid to do.

He left the fancy gate wide open: he'd be going back and forth a lot and he didn't want to scratch it up. He could already feel the gazes on his back, the gatherings at windows up and down Alphabet Row. He wanted them all to know he was going to play the good guest on their block, and show this house the respect it deserved. If he was careful bringing the materials out to his truck, they'd hardly know what he was up to. Guilt warmed his face. Suddenly he felt like a ghoul.

The air inside the house was dry and slightly dusty. The electrician had left the power on to the main entrance hall--a bare bulb hung incongruously from a Gothic arch. Similar bulbs hung from strategic locations around the house. All remaining circuits had been cut, lifelines severed so that internal supports and sheathings could be safely removed. The shadowed walls had the serious, grim faces of corpses.

Lewis gestured vaguely to the house, as if delivering the last rites. He pulled his reciprocating saw out of its case, plugged it in and turned it on. Its high whine was like the garbled arguments of a thousand angry bees as he used it to gnaw through old plaster, lath, and timber.

Lewis loved his houses and hated to see the old interiors go, but he had achieved enough distance through a range of demolition jobs that he always found things to appreciate as he unmade the house a nail, a board, and a wall at a time. Once the dropped ceilings and floor coverings were taken away it was possible to trace the locations of older, non-bearing walls which had been removed during some previous remodeling.

The walls themselves most often clearly indicated the course of a house's evolution: layers of wallpaper and wallpaper borders tracking the changes in taste over generations, gas fixtures chopped off and their gaps plastered over, wires leading to a servant's bell, the shaft of an old dumb waiter, the pipes for a radiator system, knob and tube wiring, lost coins, lost toys, lost letters.

He found the yellowing sheets of paper wedged behind the baseboard of a small room at the back of the first floor. It had been a child's room several times during its lifetime; the third, fifth, and seventh layers of wallpaper all had a child's icons: teddy bears, dolls, toy soldiers. Even the original layer of plaster bore the crude, faded stencil of a hobbyhorse.

He unfolded the sheets carefully and settled down into a thin layer of plaster dust to read, gingerly—and eventually reverently—turning the pages.

I thought the very casualness of it was going to push me over the edge.

Every day Jimmy did his usual things--getting up, getting dressed, eventually, fooling around before and after breakfast, disappearing until school was out. After that, I could hear him outside, or in his room singing to himself. Occasionally, looking out my study window, I would catch a glimpse of his bright green jacket, his favorite piece of clothing.

But Jimmy had been dead just over a year.

I thought the very casualness of it was going to push me over the edge. Carol would just be talking about him, about something he had done or said that day, or talking to him, telling him he needed to clean his room before dinner or something, and I'd just have to get out of the room, I'd run crying out of that room, and Carol would just sit there—I thought—wondering what was the matter with *me*.

Today we were getting ready to drive up to Lookout Mountain. We were going to visit that spot near the top where Carol always piled oddly shaped and colored rocks in memory of him—he'd always loved rocks—his room was full of them and for days we kept finding them there and in odd places around the house when we finally faced the task of gathering up his things and cleaning out his room, scraping it hollow, to the very walls.

I didn't think we should take him up to the mountain. It seemed perverse. Carol was telling him to get that damn green coat on, to go get ready we were leaving soon. And damned if he didn't leave the room singing, like we were all going on a picnic.

And I started crying. I never could cry right, and it leaked and spilled out of my eyes and all over me like a slow rupture of my head. She looked at me as if she were surprised. "What's wrong?" she said. For the first time since I'd known her, I could have slapped her.

"What if he doesn't *know* he's dead?" I cried, "Or if he's just a memory, and we're both crazy? Carol, don't we *need* to tell him? I don't know *how* we're going to tell him. I feel like I've *failed* him!"

She didn't say anything, and that infuriated me. She just gave me a quick hug and left the room. Maybe she didn't want the illusion, the glamour, spoiled. I don't know.

Suddenly Jimmy came into the room. I realized then I had never looked *directly* at him. I'd been too uncomfortable. And always before he'd appeared when Carol was with me, as if this were *her* experience, not mine, that she was the one responsible, and it was something I could only be embarrassed about. And underneath that feeling of embarrassment, such a terrible jealousy. But now my son had come to *me*, and so I thought I should look at him directly, look him in the eyes.

He was pale, whiter than I remembered, and gray when he stepped through shadow. But not *so* pale, not so pale after all.

My own skin had taken on this alabaster color. In the past year I'd hardly been outside the house.

I made myself pick him up. I made myself hold him. That peculiar warm, clean smell of his hair filled me — it was a smell that would be with me, I knew, forever. I thought about how we were going to tell him, finally, how the bedtime stories might be changed, altered slightly, to prepare him, how a bedtime story might be the best way to tell him that he was dead, to tell *us* that he was dead.

I squeezed him tighter to me, then held back, suddenly afraid I might squeeze right through him.

"I love you," I said, and began to cry. "I love you ... very much."

After a time of holding, and kissing, and whispering secrets I'd almost, but not quite, forgotten, I felt the gentle outline of his small hand pressing into my back, holding me.

And passing through. And passing through. And passing

The words trailed off the edge of the page, as if the paper couldn't hold them within its bounds. Lewis wondered how many families ago this family had been, how many lives ago. He wondered where that mother was, and what had happened to that father, and if the son still played here on long hot summer afternoons, and if he were warm enough when ice caked the windows, and the cold was a snake looking for a gap in the framing for its slow passage into the house.

The dust rose and settled in the room, sunlight making it glitter as it drifted past his face and out the door. And when he finally stood with crowbar in hand and swung it in tight arcs into the walls, a smell of warm hair and a grin the length of a boy's forgotten name came up to greet him.

H is for the Hunt

The first thing she did after moving in was to begin a new painting. She set up oils and easel in one corner of the bedroom so she could work on the canvas before sleep, gaze from her bed at the work in progress illuminated by moonlight through the window, and if inspired add bits first thing in the morning when she crawled from the covers fresh from a dream.

The painting evolved with a much gloomier style than Bella planned, hues shifting darker even as the paint was applied, shadows appearing almost by chance. Still, the developing portrait captured her sense of the figure in her dreams, particularly in the eyes, heath brown with red undertones, a fragment of Hampshire green, bark and moss, small flecks of iron, the whites half milk and half cream. A hunter, but was Bella its companion or prey?

She didn't have her new sanctuary exactly as she wanted it. Despite daily adjustments, that goal was never achieved. But she enjoyed covering the walls with paint and fabric, lighting the space with bulbs and candles scented with lavender, rose, and cinnamon. She hung jewelry, family heirlooms handed down from both grandmothers, from lamps and window latches and cabinet knobs. Bella kept herself aroused with smells and colors, books and music, and fantasy. She created intimacy and the illusion of protection. She stopped watching the news.

She couldn't sleep her first night in the new house. Ideas kept intruding: a different arrangement for the mantle, a new color for an accent wall (Han blue, brighter than Royal), a furniture arrangement with better flow. A battered guitar went into one corner, never played. She returned again and again to the canvas, adjusting the figure's profile to reflect her ambiguous and ever-changing desire, making the lips softer and suffused with blood. The background began to fill in: corrugated ridges of trees and highlighted mist, fronted by a gathering crowd of uncertain shapes.

The next day, too tired to do anything, she lay on the couch, sat in different chairs, assessed a range of views. She replaced and rearranged the objects on the mantle. Mysterious origamis. A small rooster figurine with a bright red comb. Multiple incense burners. One of her mother's old dolls with large, startled eyes. A heavy metal statue which was either a youth or a fawn.

The next few days it stormed every evening. She hoped the roof didn't leak. Hail pounded the house. She prayed the windowpanes held. Having a partner, someone who cared what she felt, might have helped her confidence, but partners always came with a price. She would wake from dreams out of breath, her heart galloping. She imagined she could hear the last trailing notes of distant hoofbeats.

Built during the late twenties, the houses on Alphabet Row each had a large letter by the front door. Children walking to the library would have the alphabet pressed into their malleable little brains. Hers was #H, a modest brick cottage with a small front lawn. She had to save for years to buy it. She had a lovely wooden H custom-made in a vintage Victorian font which she mounted herself. The porch needed work. She hired a man to replace the rotted boards. He said he'd charge her less if she would only smile. She said she'd gladly pay the higher rate if he just did a decent job.

She was in her early forties, never married, and not sure she wanted to be. Maybe if she met the right person, man or woman. So far she'd had difficulty imagining that figure. She knew she wanted someone kind and passionate, someone who loved the skin Bella came in, and needed no alterations made.

———

Lightning, hoofbeats, a thunder of hounds baying. Hints of a catastrophe, an atmosphere of havoc. Hoof and claw and mangled paw, fur and scale and gleaming, naked skin. The farther away the baying the more seductive its harmonies.

Bella was awake again. She remembered few specifics from these dreams, the impression of impending doom, past destructions echoed in the failures of the present. People never learned. She peeked outside her bedroom window. A waxing crescent moon hung like a threat. The night sky had exploded into dark blossoms. She saw nothing to be gained by fighting for sleep and ran a bath.

She had a week's vacation left, then it was back to a barely tolerable office job. She needed to find something more fulfilling but hadn't yet mustered the energy. Her home was almost how she wanted it, but her enthusiasm lagged.

She grabbed some random candles off the bathroom shelf, arranging them around the tub. She slipped in. Her body drew in the heat. The deadness began to thaw. Her fingers wandered over her breasts and down between her legs. She'd never found the right words to tell someone what she needed. Too many of the words came from men and they sounded like wounds, like something hunted, torn, and killed, and she wouldn't use them.

Bella thought back to the time when she and her girlfriends were young and beautiful, although they certainly did not know it. In their heads they were ugly and unbearable and convinced they would always be alone. Some couldn't wait to get married to young men who would one day view them with disappointment.

Tension arched her back. Her mother used to say, "It's your hormones talking." Her hormones never talked, they screamed. She didn't know how long she'd been in the water. She heard the approaching gallop and it terrified her, the rage and the threat of the thunderous chase, now matched by her heart and lungs, and a distant moan which didn't sound like her own voice.

She needed to get out. If she fell asleep she might drown. She watched the candles burn into nothing. She'd forgotten what flavors she'd chosen. A hint of lemon, some pumpkin, which she rarely used. She opened her eyes. She'd lost track. The night to come was Halloween, and she was unprepared.

———

Bella didn't have time to arrange anything elaborate, but it would be her first Halloween here and it had to be at least inviting. From the boxes of miscellanea she'd been loath to throw away, she pulled out some long strings of beads, dark cloth streamers, a couple of stuffed black cats, and tried to arrange them artfully. She didn't know how young the children might be, so she opted for spooky over scary.

She painted a cardboard box to resemble a headstone and propped it by the front door, its epitaph, "Ghoulish Treats Inside!"

She hurried into the bedroom to change. She stopped short at the painting. She hadn't realized she'd completed so much. The hunter stood in front of a crowd of shapes on horseback, with other figures on the ground on all fours, leashed, chained, and muzzled. She couldn't quite tell the species of these creatures, or even the approximate layout of their features. The androgynous hunter, however, held her with a disconcerting depth of gaze.

She found a long piece of red trim and braided it through her hair. She changed into a puffy black blouse and a voluminous red skirt with a vintage black nightie underneath.

The smaller children came first, before dark, their smiling parents watching from the yard. Some wore plastic, unbreathable costumes, their masks off, hanging from their hands like flayed faces. One child carried a spinning toy creating a loud cracking noise. "That's my bones breaking," he whispered.

When the older kids arrived, the costumes became more elaborate, involving paint, makeup, feathers, and jewelry. A few didn't care about the candy—they carried small bags and only took one piece. Others were all about the candy, the openings of their bags thrust toward her like ravenous mouths.

The weather began to turn, the wind turning the trees into swaying, disintegrating heads. It made her sad to watch the kids hurrying home. A gang of teenagers appeared in front of the porch, collars up, caps and hoods obscuring their faces. They hadn't bothered with costumes or treat bags. It began to snow. Although not unheard of, snow on Halloween was an insult.

"Can I help you?" she asked, one hand ready to slam the door.

"Trick or treat?" one said, maybe a boy. The others snickered.

She still had some candy, and she figured the younger kids were done for the evening. "Sure. You can have what's left."

Only one came forward. His hand darted from his sleeve snake-like, clamped on a handful of treats, and withdrew. His head shook and the hood came off his face. He wore white makeup, or maybe he was naturally pale. One eye was stapled shut. "How about a kiss, too?" His tongue came out. She slammed and locked the door.

"Old hag!" came muffled from the other side. She didn't feel insulted. It meant she'd lived long enough not to put up with crap.

She watched from the window as they faded into the shadows beyond the street. The snow was heavier, and it was difficult to distinguish details, but it seemed the houses there had become ragged and tree-like.

A cluster of silhouettes emerged from the shadows. She couldn't say with certainty, but some appeared to be on horseback, others scrambling low to the ground, their chains clinking amid the general din of shouts and growls. They discharged violent explosions of breath. The windowpanes rattled.

Long spears and pikes rose above the throng and the forms became more distinct: a wild gang of diaphanous outlines, beautiful men and women but with something off about them, and the tallest on horseback, so handsome, and in charge. Bella was drunk with the possibilities.

But it all faded into obscurity again, into a snow-covered street and lawns, the murky houses beyond. She walked away from the window, thinking her imagination had finally gotten to her. It had been a long day, and she'd eaten little, and those teenagers had unnerved her.

Bella went into the bedroom and stripped down to her black nightie, wrapping herself in a worn, loose robe which once belonged to her father. There was no moon as far as she could tell, and in the reduced light the painting had become a morass of shadow, with little detail distinguishable.

She went back into the living room and lit a fire, the first in her new home. She'd paid a lot to have the fireplace and chimney cleaned and repaired and been anxious to use it. She settled down with a glass of wine. Soon the fire suffused the room with a red glow, the heat building until she had to slip off her robe. She spread it over the floor and lay down, imagining burning forms in the flames.

———

A pounding on the door broke her reverie. Some late trick-or-treaters or maybe those nasty teenagers come back with more insults. She didn't know the hour. She didn't wear a watch and had no idea where her little clock was. She'd lost it in the move.

She climbed off the floor and staggered over, ready to send them away with anger or regrets depending on who they were. It was only as she slung open the door did she remember she was in her negligee.

The man looked familiar. He appeared ill, bags under his eyes and jowls drooping. He leaned against the doorframe for support. "Bella."

That voice. "Roger? Is that you?"

He smiled weakly. "It's been a minute."

It had been ten years. She almost said, *I thought you were dead*. That had been the gossip, and she'd cried and cried as a result. Although things had ended unpleasantly, he'd been her first real boyfriend, her first lover. She'd never known his exact age, but knew he was older. Now he looked *much* older. "Come inside! This weather, and you're not even wearing a jacket! I have a fire—" He didn't let her finish. He slouched past her, trailing drips and splashes onto her polished wood floor. She noticed he wasn't wearing socks or shoes. "Please, sit in the chair. I'll grab some towels."

She could feel herself blushing. Her heart pounded so hard she felt dizzy. She focused on gathering towels. He hadn't been the best boyfriend. She always asked him to hold her a little longer, but he never would. The last time she saw him he said she was getting fat and she needed to do something.

Bella rushed back into the room. He'd taken off his shirt, now a soggy lump by his rough looking feet. His pants were unbuttoned. Water dripped everywhere. The seat cushion was soaked.

"We need to find you some dry clothes." She dropped to her knees and began rubbing his feet, his ankles and calves. She glanced up at his sad face. "What happened to you? I haven't seen you in years."

He grimaced. "After you, not so well. I got reckless, and there was no one who wanted to help me. If you hadn't—you could have been more patient. But don't let me take it out on you."

She stood up. "I have some sweatpants that might fit—"

"Don't leave." He pushed himself upright and let his pants drop. He kicked them out of the way. He wasn't wearing any underwear.

"Christ, Roger." She didn't move. She was both insulted and excited. He stepped a little closer and she lowered her eyes to the matted hair on his chest. Her palms itched. She wanted to hold on to something. She let her hand graze his belly. That sound in her ears again. A distant rumble, thunder. It was hard to hear anything else.

His lips tasted harsh. What had he been eating?

Inexplicably, his damp body generated heat. He held her tightly and it felt as if she were being burned. She pawed at the back of his neck, but didn't want him to let go. Her nightie rode down on one side and a nipple fell out. His mouth traveled there and began to suckle. She slipped out of the rest of her garment and kicked it aside.

She stepped back. "Just let me—" She was surprised when he leaned over and brushed her neck with his teeth. She gasped when he began nibbling on her breasts.

She stepped back again. She was aware how her belly jiggled. This happened so quickly she hadn't had time to worry about the parts of her body she liked, the parts she didn't. She hoped he'd changed. She wanted sex to be different this time. Something delicious.

He crouched on the rug in front of the fireplace, pulling her to her knees. Changing shadows obscured a lot of his body, but she could tell he was much thinner than the man she remembered, his ribs more prominent, his belly flat, receding into his crotch, where his member was almost lost in all the hair. He wasn't that attractive. She thought she smelled blood on his breath. In some ways he seemed more dog-like than man. That was a terrible thing for her to be thinking, but it didn't discourage her. She lay down beside him. She shivered, feverish, yet could feel the sweat running across her skin. He hovered over her, kissing her neck and breasts, running his fingers down her ribs. It felt as if a layer of her skin were being peeled.

It embarrassed her how ungraceful she was, raising her legs at an awkward angle, struggling to rest her ankles on his back. She was afraid to see whatever was in his face.

She could not catch her breath. Her chest was full of pain. She rolled her head back and her eyes took in a distorted sample of the room. High up on the mantle, her mother's doll watched. They locked eyes. The heavy statue of the fawn, or was it a boy, rocked on the mantle and fell. She didn't hear it hit the floor.

His head drifted close to hers and to her surprise she bit his neck. She felt herself fading, shriveling along the edges.

He threw his head back and his neck seemed too long. His mouth distorted around a snarl. He paused, bent down, and kissed her gently on the lips. The sudden tenderness made her want to cry.

He moaned so deeply she felt him vibrating through her body, then the moan expanded, became a howl and she wanted to escape, but he was too heavy. For a moment she thought he was going to eat her. She looked up and saw that his lower face was more snout than mouth and nose. "Get off me!" She felt around and grabbed the statue, swung it into his face as hard as she could. With a bellow he jumped off.

He dropped his head back and loudly sucked in air. She scrambled away from him. He hunched over on the floor. It sounded as if his bones were breaking. A swelling began in his shoulders, his skin rippled, slid away from the underlying muscle, and tore. His jaw dropped and kept dropping. More teeth came in.

He turned to her and slid closer, a hideous semblance of human plaintiveness inching across his features. She hammered him with her fists until he slinked away. He left a husk of nasty skin behind him on the floor.

He raced around the room on all fours. His movements were sloppy and uncontrolled, knocking over furniture, running into walls, leaping up and sending all her precious things flying.

"Get out! Get out!" Naked, Bella grabbed a broom out of the corner and attacked. She hated the sight of him now and was desperate to have him out of her home.

She ran to the door and jerked it open. "Out!" Much to her surprise he obeyed, but she ventured a few steps after him to make sure.

He sprang across the porch and onto the slick, snow-and-ice-covered grass, skewing sharply before he righted himself and joined the rest, the ones who were chained, huge dogs with vaguely human heads. They'd moved into her yard, looking half-starved, dragging their hindlegs behind them as if their backs were broken, their long pale tongues licking the ground.

A horse broke from the horde and crossed the lawn to her porch. A halter of liquid flame flowed from its head and turned the snow into steam. The horse itself was so black it receded into the dark, leaving the rider floating in air.

The hunter jumped down and stepped onto the porch, stopping a few feet away. Bella began to shake. The tall creature moved forward and handed her a piece of rough cloth, more like a horse blanket than anything a human woman might wear, enough to cover her breasts and little more. Bella felt dirty, and noticed all the dried blood across her skin, whether Roger's or her own she could not tell. She held the puny rag in front of her.

This close, Bella could see the figure wore a metal helmet so sheer it was transparent. The eyes peering through the helmet were hypnotic, heath brown with Hampshire green, bark and moss, half milk and half cream. The hunter slipped it off. Bella glimpsed the shine of two antler nubs peeking from a mass of pale, translucent hair.

She couldn't have identified with any confidence the sex of the person gazing at her. The long hair was pulled back to reveal a delicate neck and facial features. The brows were bushy over those startling eyes, the lips red. The hunter took her hand, leaned over, and kissed her, then attempted to lead her off the porch.

She resisted. "I'm confused."

The hunter spoke softly. "Pardon me, but I do not believe you are confused."

"Wait, are you telling me it's my time? I'm only, I'm not ready..." Her voice trailed off.

"We do not choose. It chooses us."

She gestured weakly toward the others waiting. "You want me to ride with those?" She heard the clash of the heavy chains.

"The chains are not for you. I have a fine steed waiting. You can name it anything you like."

Bella shook her head and slipped out of the hunter's grip. "I'm saying no. Has anyone told you no before? Come back later. Much later."

The hunter stood for a moment as if surprised, saying nothing, then mounted the horse again. Something more might have been said, but Bella had already gone back inside to begin cleaning, and did not hear.

I is for Infestation

"I love you to pieces," Eric told his daughter. Abby had been missing her mother, and old enough to understand her mother wasn't coming back. He didn't know how to comfort her; the wrong parent died. His late wife had always known the right thing to say. He kept telling Abby how much he loved her. He didn't know what else to do.

"How many pieces?" She looked dead serious. This was back when his eyes were still working properly, and he could see her so clearly it hurt.

"A million. People have at least a million pieces in them I suppose, depending on how you count."

"I love your million pieces too, Dad."

Abby helped him choose his new home. Because of his deteriorating eyesight Eric needed his daughter to steer him away from anything having serious accessibility or condition issues. He told her the house would be hers soon enough, so she should choose whatever she liked. "Don't talk like that," she said. "You're going to live forever." He didn't contradict her.

It was a one-story cottage. A bungalow. An "adorable chalet in the American Craftsman tradition." Eric had no idea what any of these terms actually meant, but Abby promised the house was plenty big enough for a single person, without being so big a progressively blind person might get lost or confused. There was even a spare room for a live-in nurse, or for Abby when she visited. He wasn't ready for a caretaker just yet. He expected he never would be. He hoped he would have at least some say in the decision.

Abby said the brick work was impeccable. Not that it mattered to him, but she seemed inordinately pleased by this statement. Sometimes, in certain light conditions, he could barely make out individual bricks, but most of the time he could not.

"Dad, I'm afraid there's a small infestation. Nothing that serious. I've made an appointment with the exterminators, but they can't come by before you move in."

"What *kind* of infestation? Bears, willow trees?"

"Insects, funny man. I don't know what kind. Beetles of some sort I guess, hard, nasty-looking things. Their shells turn color in the light. Camouflage, I suppose, to protect them from their natural enemies, whoever or whatever they might be. No severe damage though, according to the inspection. More of a nuisance than a threat. They've chewed a little on the west wall of the living room, around the baseboard. I don't think it has to be replaced, just spackled and repainted."

"Sigh. I used to love to spackle." He joked to cover his nervousness. Eric didn't like the idea of bugs, some invisible enemy, feeding on his house, but Abby didn't sound concerned. He would wear shoes inside, or at least hard-soled slippers. The idea of experiencing a crunch beneath one of his bare feet horrified him.

Abby completely supervised the move. His job was to sit quietly in a chair. She had the movers arrange the furniture exactly as he'd had it in his old apartment. That wasn't necessary but he appreciated the thought. The only significant difference was the distance between various items, which did trip him up at first.

"Dad! Are you okay?" When Eric sat down on air instead of his bed Abby was there instantly.

"I'm fine. Stupid mistake. I'll practice and map it out in my head so it won't happen again." She raised his shirt looking for injury. "Please don't do that. I'll let you know if anything hurts."

"Sorry. I should have asked." They sat for a moment. He figured she was as embarrassed as he. "Dad, I've locked the door to the cellar. It's on the north wall of the kitchen. We don't want you opening that door by mistake. But I've left the key in the lock for the exterminators."

"Thank you for that. I'm not a fan of stairs."

She called him every day at first and dropped in every other. But then she had to go away on business. "The exterminators promise they'll be there next week. You have all the emergency contacts in your cell, right?"

"That I do, and it's been charged. I wouldn't know what to do without it. Enjoy your time away."

"I could always cancel. My boss would understand."

"Don't you dare. That's your career. You weren't like this when I lived in the apartment. I got along fine then. I'll manage even better here."

"I know. I just—"

"Have a little confidence in your old man. If you don't worry I won't."

It was a smallish fib. Eric worried all the time. His was an unstable world. He was not a good blind person, not that he was completely blind, but significantly impaired, some days more than others. The unpredictability was a major issue.

People came to the door several times a week trying to sell him things: siding, better windows, a new roof. He had no idea if he needed those things, so he assumed he did not. Abby would have told him.

Once it was a little girl and her mother selling Girl Scout cookies, at least that's what they said. On the porch they were a short shape and a tall shape, but every few seconds he caught a clear glimpse of a face, a sweet smile.

"I love your *I*," the mother said.

"Pardon me?"

"Your big letter *I* by the front door. We noticed some of the houses have them and some don't. They're from when the neighborhood was built, aren't they, to help the children with their alphabets? Such a charming idea. You know, I can't think of another street that uses letters instead of numbers for the addresses."

When Abby explained this to him he couldn't get over the fact he now lived in the *eye house*. He gave them a twenty for two boxes and told them to keep the change. It was the only denomination in his wallet.

"You have bugs," the little girl said.

"So I'm told. Why, are some of them out here?"

"There's one on your leg. It's pretty."

He suppressed the urge to beat on his pants. "Well, at least it's pretty." The mother laughed and they left. Eric waited a few minutes then began shaking his legs. He had no idea if he got rid of it.

He sat in his living room all afternoon listening to music and eating cookies. He kept hearing a low buzzing. He thought it might be his radio, but after turning it off the buzzing was still there. It might be his hearing. If so, he didn't want to know. One sensory deprivation at a time was all he could manage.

He took a long nap. Eric looked forward to his daily naps. He had a nightmare about earwigs. Weren't those the bugs who crawled into your ears and chewed through your brain? Maybe he was thinking of something else.

———

He woke up disoriented, feeling old and infirm. He shouldn't have eaten all those cookies. Abby said too much sugar was bad for his eyesight. Some people had bad hair days. He had bad eye days, and this was one of them.

The light from the windows seemed overly bright. How long had he slept? He staggered into the kitchen and grabbed a can of juice from the fridge. He didn't know what flavor; it was going to be a surprise. But he couldn't find the kitchen chairs. Had they all been moved? Eric worked hard to make his world work for him. Now, overnight, he was inept. He threw his juice in the sink and went back to his bed.

He enjoyed listening to his recorded books, but now he was afraid of whatever sounds they might be masking. The ceiling momentarily came into focus. Millions of cells of color. It made no sense. Suddenly they broke apart and were everywhere. Afraid the ceiling was about to collapse, Eric climbed out of bed and made his way into the living room. The walls appeared slanted, unmoored. He moved in tiny increments, afraid to fall. If he fell Abby might insist he could no longer live independently.

He sat in a comfortable chair and tried to calm himself. He was just having a difficult day. This would pass and soon he'd feel comfortable in his new home again.

Abby said the infestation was evident on the west wall. But which direction was west? He turned his head until he detected signs of movement. A large blank space, a wall, bubbling with activity. The wall appeared to be melting. Then all motion stopped. He felt immediate relief. But did the motion cease because they could tell he was looking?

He hadn't eaten enough, and what he did eat was mostly sugar. He got up to go into the kitchen again. Whether he could find a chair or not, he would eat some real food, some veggies and a little of the leftover chicken, and water. He would drink lots of water.

But he went in the incorrect direction. He felt himself falling into bed again.

The following morning Eric woke up refreshed. The house's geometry had returned to normal, and he felt oriented in both time and space, calm and ready to meet the day. A good rest made so much difference.

The exterminators arrived an hour later, seemingly without warning, but Eric couldn't be sure. He might have missed their call. He sat at the kitchen table while they worked around him, talking among themselves, using words he was unfamiliar with, including the names of various species and their feeding habits. He tried to tell them about the infestation, but they didn't seem interested. Their faces were mostly a blur. He had a tough time focusing, touching the chairs repeatedly, reassuring himself of their presence and wondering about their disappearance the day before.

They talked around him and rarely to him. He was used to that. He didn't feel insulted by their behavior. But Abby would have been, on his behalf.

He imagined he was ill-kempt, and it embarrassed him. He couldn't see himself clearly in the mirror, so could only wash himself as best he could, and feel his hair and skin for clues.

"The key to the basement door should be in the lock. At least that's where my daughter left it." A few minutes later he heard their steps tromping down.

He couldn't hear them in the basement. For all he knew they were down there gossiping and eating lunch. Eventually they came back upstairs. He didn't know how many of them there were, four or five? There was an awkward silence while Eric waited for someone to speak.

"There are definite signs of infestation, and we'd recommend some repair and replacement for the sake of structural integrity, but honestly, we couldn't find anything active," a man said. "Nothing at all."

Eric was astonished. "But I've seen, well obviously I can't rely on what I've seen." There was another awkward silence. He could hear boots shuffling. He felt like an idiot. Finally, wanting to get them out of the house, he said, "Just send me a bill, and a summary of findings if you don't mind. My daughter will send you a check."

After the exterminators left, Eric half-expected to have no more issues with bugs. When his eyes failed him his imagination often intervened, filling in the gaps. But the experts had just told him there were no bugs, and he expected his imagination to believe them.

―――――――――

Next morning Eric felt warmth on his eyelids, spreading across the rest of his face. He reached for the wall and was relieved when he felt its coolness beneath his hand. Then portions began to disintegrate, bits clinging to his fingers. He opened his eyes and shook his hand. Small, glittery things went flying, and he couldn't say for certainty if these included fragments of his fingers. Some new insanity.

He sat up in bed and twisted around for a better view. The wall possessed thousands of tiny moving parts. Collapse seemed imminent.

The wall leaned dangerously close, ready to topple. He covered himself with his blanket. It made for imperfect protection, but it was better than nothing. He had to call Abby or whoever he could reach. They'd hospitalize him with some mental diagnosis, but what choice did he have?

He reached for his cell on the bedstand, but his bedstand wasn't there. He slid out of bed and went down on his knees and felt around and he found, once again, bits and pieces, scattered and moving. He didn't know if they were from the bedstand, his cell phone, or both. A loud buzzing filled his ears.

Something swarmed across his hand. Panicked, he struggled to his feet and stumbled into the bathroom. He was surrounded by great pulsing blobs of white. One of those blobs was low to the floor and directly in front of him. He began to pee and hoped he wasn't splashing it on the floor. For a moment he thought he saw trees through the wall, as if all the plaster and stud and exterior brick had evaporated.

He left the bathroom hoping to make his way out the front door and across the porch and into the yard, to the sidewalk if he was lucky. He would cry out and his neighbors would come and help him. But something was trifling with his feet.

Eric wasn't wearing his slippers, at least he didn't think so. The floor was in constant motion, sending out tendrils across the bridge of one foot, around the heel of the other. He tried kicking at the movement. The phenomena bent around his kicks. He ran into a wall which went spongy then flowed around him. He was immersed, but not drowning. Could he swim through this?

He wasn't sure where he was in the house, or if he was headed in the right direction. He thought a person of incongruous form might be standing in front of him. "Hello?" he said, but in a blur of movement it went away, perhaps to avoid confrontation.

These *bugs* were inhospitable to his presence, separating as he approached, then gathering to block his way. Their movements were alternately calm and then irate as they crowded around him. He could no longer speculate which patterns suggested specific furnishings in his home. The bugs appeared to have installed themselves into every square centimeter of the house.

At one point Eric thought he might have reached the front door, but he couldn't find the knob, and the doorway itself was impossible to negotiate. It kept altering shape and shrinking into an opening too small for him to access. He stumbled around attempting to acquire a different perspective, but the room remained inchoate, its pieces unsettled. He could have been anywhere. The borders were inexact.

He wasn't sure when it began, but he realized the individual pieces had begun to bite. Once he was aware, the nibbling felt constant. However, each succeeding bite seemed less painful. Perhaps he'd developed a tolerance and would one day become immune. But he was sure he was missing pieces, and some of his pieces weren't him.

He leaned against something. He thought it might be the kitchen counter. He felt around, found a drawer, reached in, and foolishly brought out a knife. He made short, vigorous swings into the surrounding space, but as he stepped away from the counter his legs failed, and he fell. The impact knocked the breath out of him. He screamed. He had impaled his own hand.

He could feel them crawling over the injury and it felt better. When he held his hand up to the light, fingers spread, it looked unusually fuzzy, with pieces of the blurred silhouette falling away. He found the sink and thrust both hands beneath the faucet, letting warm water run over them. The water soothed until his hands felt normal again.

Around him, the house's infrastructure looked seriously compromised. He felt responsible. This was supposed to be Abby's house eventually. He might not have anything left to give her.

He collapsed into the floor, triggering a scatter of movement radiating across the room. He didn't have the energy to pick himself up again. He'd been spread too thin.

This was what dying was like. Fragmentation awaited everyone. People ended broken into their component materials, consumed by natural processes. All the small failures in anatomy and mentality which came with age were meant to prepare you for these final moments of decomposition.

A large shape loomed in front of him, a swollen head, a long body, moving arms and legs. *So, are you the insect queen?* He could only think it. When he tried to speak the question, his tongue didn't seem to be there anymore.

————

When Abby next visited she pounded on the door for several minutes with no answer. She knew her dad wouldn't like it, but she used her key to let herself inside. She scoured the house looking for her father, but she couldn't find him anywhere. There were no signs of a struggle. She hoped he hadn't gone out walking by himself. It wasn't safe. Usually when she visited her dad she'd find at least a small mess: a jar of jam left out of the refrigerator, some books knocked off a table, clothes on the floor. She expected these small disorders given his poor eyesight. But if anything, the house appeared to be in perfect order.

Except for the bugs. The exterminators must not have come. She saw the beetles crawling over the walls of the living room as she came in—many more than had been there before. In the kitchen they squirmed out of the wallpaper seams. In her dad's bedroom they were invisible, but she could hear them— what?—eating? She detected movement in her peripheral vision, but nothing revealed itself when she turned her head.

"Dad!" He didn't answer, but if she wasn't mistaken there was a slight increase in the volume and intensity of the noise.

J is for Jolly

Green and red pleated paper balls hung from the store's ceiling, white plastic garlands wrapped the columns, shiny mylar balloons floated free and unmoored. Candy canes adorned the walls like a spray of upside-down J's. Over the intercom system Bing Crosby sang *Silver Bells*. A large banner suspended over Wallace's head said WELCOME TO THE NORTH POLE!

Wallace needed to remember so many things: to call them "children," not "kids," that Ho's always came in threes, and to never promise what he could not deliver. *It'll be a surprise and you're going to like it.* He practiced these words in his head again and again.

On Christmas Eve the line of kids and parents waiting to see Santa wound through the toy department and out into appliances and bedroom furnishings. Wallace thought it might be the longest line in his thirty years playing the part. He wished he could say it was because of his skillful portrayal, but his best years as Santa were long behind him. These days his biggest concern was masking the booze on his breath. He switched to vodka days before the job began—clear liquors were the least detectable—and he had a strong curry for breakfast. He chewed on garlic and mints all day, and after dinner he gargled cider vinegar. He'd pay for all this contamination tomorrow, of course, but his usual Christmas Day was spent alone, sleeping until noon, and watching TV the rest of the afternoon. *Not such a sad way to spend a holiday. I prefer it that way.*

A lot of the smaller kids were tired and anxious, barely holding it together. He knew the feeling. Too much wanting, too much excitement, hurt. No child should be crying on Christmas Eve. He always tried to whisper something consoling when he had them on his lap. It rarely helped. So many were terrified of the jolly old elf. He understood that. Santa wasn't human, but he had to pretend to be. Kids sensed that, and it made it worse.

The skinny elf behind the camera glanced nervously at the line, no doubt wondering if they were going to get through all these children by closing. They hadn't been prepared for so many. Last year the store cancelled because of the pandemic. That made for a meager Christmas. Santa and his three elf helpers all needed the extra cash. Wallace got by on a small pension plus social security. Since retirement this was his only consistent part-time gig.

Some of these kids had been in line for over an hour. Jackson, the store owner, liked to overbook the Santa line. He wanted that twenty-five bucks per photo with Santa. Children got to sit on Santa's lap and spill their guts for free, but if their parents wanted photos—and many did, even if their child was bawling—they had to pay the fee.

Those steps up to the gold and red Santa chair were harder to negotiate with each passing year. Wallace had bad arthritis, and if he was inebriated he required at least two elves to help him make the climb. He knew the teenagers who played the elves hated that part of the job. *I'm sorry, I'm sorry. I know I'm just an old drunk,* he thought but never said.

Wallace went back to "Santa School" every few years for a refresher. They taught you things like executing a proper ho-ho-ho and how to maintain a curly and super soft beard so that when the little tykes grabbed it their stubby fingers slipped through without pain. Recently the course added instruction on handling active shooter scenarios.

Every two hours the crew got a ten-minute break, enough time for Wallace to take a leak and fortify himself with some liquid Christmas spirit. "What's in the bottle?" Jack, the new elf, asked. Jack's costume was still pristine, a sparkly green. He asked lots of questions.

"Eggnog. It's good for you. It's got eggs in it."

"Doesn't look much like eggnog."

Annoyed, Wallace wiped his mouth on his sleeve. "It's a special formula for my ulcers. You're not planning to aggravate my ulcers are you?" Jack was smart enough to walk away. When his break was over, Wallace tried to hurry back, in his rush knocking over a large stack of jigsaw puzzles. He overheard Jack make a jeering noise.

Back on the Santa chair he tried to maintain his standard of giving each child focused attention, but the parents were getting antsy, and they were the ones rushing their children through. Kids were giving him a couple of sentences and then leaping from his lap. He was supposed to give each kid a lousy packet of four jellybeans when they climbed up. He usually gave them two or three of those packets. The candy would be stale by next year anyway.

His Santa suit stank. The kids who scrunched up their little faces obviously noticed. *Sorry kids.* It was worn almost to transparency in spots. Every day on his way to work he froze waiting for the bus. It wasn't leather, or silk, or any material he imagined the real Santa suit was made from. But he was required to supply his own, so it had to be one he could afford.

Wallace no longer needed a padded suit. Now he had his own bowl full of jelly. His jiggles were getting a bit out of hand, and some days his face was as red as his suit, his jaw, and cheeks sore from all those forced ho-ho-hos. By the end of the shift his knees and finger joints would be swollen, and he'd be breathing hard from the pain.

When the next kid plopped down hard onto his lap Wallace farted. The hardest part of the job some nights was trying not to fart. "Don't worry, that was just Rudolph," he whispered. The little boy giggled. Wallace prided himself on his relationships with children. This was perhaps unjustified.

It appeared someone placed an ugly doll at the front of the Santa line. Wallace looked for Jack, thinking he must have been the prankster. The doll didn't move, and the children stuck behind the figure were beginning to complain. "Do we still get our turn?" said a small child near the back of the line.

Wallace had no idea what this toy was intended to represent. He didn't keep up with the latest TV shows and he couldn't afford to go to the movies. He couldn't quite make out its features. It was late, he was tired, and he'd had too much to drink.

The doll appeared to be naked or wearing some sort of tight red outfit. Its face was covered with scruffy, dirty-looking fur. An ugly, awful thing—what child would want such a toy for Christmas? Wallace wouldn't have allowed one in his house.

"Psst, Santa. Are you awake? We're getting short on time."

Wallace looked up at the Jack elf tugging on his sleeve. He realized there was another moppet sitting on his lap, staring up at him with big green eyes. "I'm sure you'll get everything you want, sweetheart," he said, and kissed her on the forehead.

"Hey! You're not supposed to do that!" Jack exclaimed, but the child was gone and another, almost identical youngster had taken her place. This rotation continued unabated for another half hour, Wallace performing exactly as he'd been trained. Now and then he would scan the crowd, looking for the ugly doll.

It occurred to him then that it might not have been a doll at all. Sometimes there were children with disabilities. Although they were often moved to the front of the line, they or their parents sometimes insisted they be allowed to queue up like everyone else. Wallace felt ashamed the word *ugly* had popped into his head. He'd been tired and the figure had caught him off guard. He hadn't looked at it the right way. There was no such thing as an ugly child.

An older boy slid onto his lap, poking Wallace in the belly with his sharp elbows. He had a list in his hand, a long one. He began reading it. The kids weren't allowed to do that. To save time they were supposed to tell Santa their top four or five. Both Wallace and Jack tried to interrupt, but the boy wasn't having it. He talked over them. It was the usual wish list of outrageously priced electronics. Wallace gave up, looking around the store, not bothering to listen.

That different-looking doll child, now lively and quick, was bounding about the Christmas displays and eventually landed on top of a toddler's head, ripping off the kid's red-and-green-striped stocking cap and running its gnarled fingers through the kid's blond hair, picking things out and eating them. The poor toddler began to wail.

Wallace screeched and leapt to his feet, dumping the older boy from his lap. The boy rolled down the steps screaming, his alarmed parents running to his side. There was blood. Wallace tried to explain about the strange child, or doll, or whatever it was, but it was nowhere to be found.

Dash away dash away, all.

It had snowed quite a bit during his shift. Wallace shivered waiting for his bus to arrive. He wished again he'd brought a change of clothes, or at least a heavy coat. Jackson fired him on the spot, making a big show of it, perhaps thinking that might avoid a lawsuit. Adults were screaming at him, and all the children were crying—that was the worst part. How do you comfort a child who's seen Santa fired on Christmas Eve?

His Santa career was over. The bus was late, and Wallace was convinced he would die if he didn't get out of the cold right away. When it finally arrived, he jostled past the people in front of him and climbed aboard.

"Hey, Santa isn't supposed to be a jerk!"

Wallace didn't bother turning. "It's the twenty-first century. *Anybody* can be a jerk."

There were two other Santas already on the bus. Wallace wondered if they might have heard about his firing, but they didn't acknowledge his presence. He understood. When you were in the role you needed to convince yourself you were the real one.

As the bus passed the downtown shopping centers he saw several late-night Santas ringing their bells beside cardboard chimneys. Maybe he could still get one of those jobs.

The neighborhoods proclaimed their joy with colored lights and huge displays. Quite a few houses had Christmas lights along the edge of their roofs, the colors racing. More suitable for a used car lot than holiday decoration, in his opinion. There would be fewer tomorrow night, and many fewer by the weekend, although there were always people who kept their lights up until mid-January, which always felt a little desperate to Wallace.

He saw increasing numbers of Santa Claus inflatables in the yards with reindeer, a giant Frosty the Snowman, an elf or two, beginning to collapse under the weight of the fresh snow. Most would be a sad pool of vinyl by morning.

One of the other Santas had fallen asleep and was now snoring. Wallace had never allowed himself to do that in public while in costume. It didn't matter if you were a fat Santa or a skinny one, a solemn one or a crazy one. But a certain air of mystery had to be maintained. Santa's alienness was key. Whether you considered him an elf, a supernatural being, or even a demon in disguise, the one thing he was not was human. Could a human being deliver toys all over the world in a single night?

Wallace was beginning to sober up. That was quite an achievement for him on Christmas Eve. He heard a persistent tapping on the roof of the bus, then scrabbling as someone, or something tried to hold on. Maybe it was a squirrel attempting to hitch a ride. There were lots of squirrels in this area. His neighbor called them tree rats. He heard the noise again, followed by a thump. It was probably just a low-lying tree branch scraping the roof as they passed beneath it. People didn't trim their trees adequately.

He'd have a drink or two when he got home, sitting in front of the Christmas tree. Maybe he'd start a fire in the fireplace. He hadn't done that in a couple of years. Liquor and a warm fire, maybe Christmas music on the radio. He'd feel better, at least better than this.

He managed to get off the bus and halfway down the block without slipping and falling. He counted that as a victory. Wallace felt two snowballs hit him squarely in the back. It ought to have annoyed him, but he thought it funny, given the evening he'd had, and he admired their aim. He'd fire back at them if he weren't so tired. "Damn street urchins!" he shouted and began giggling uncontrollably. He had to be careful. If he fell over and they ran away he might not be able to get up and he'd freeze in place. But that sad mental image made him giggle even more. What were those kids doing out anyway? It was late to be throwing snowballs.

The squirrels were active this evening. He could hear them jumping from tree to tree. They were having much more fun this Christmas than he was. Snow fell from a branch and onto the back of his Santa suit, sliding down his neck. The sudden chill made him shake uncontrollably.

He recognized his house by the decayed string of lights wrapping the bush by the sidewalk. They hadn't worked in years. At least it saved him money on electricity. He kicked his way through the snow and lifeless vegetation covering the flagstones, his yard a frozen dead jungle.

He struggled to climb the steps onto the porch. A big letter J hung by his door. He used to paint it every year to look like a candy cane. Now it was striped in different shades of gray. When he was a kid he made a wreath out of painted popsicle sticks and pipe cleaners. He still hung it on his front door every Christmas.

He juggled his keys, dropped them into the snow which had blown across the porch. "Shit!" He bent over, freezing his fingers scraping them on the boards until he found them.

Someone snickered behind him. He turned around, imagining himself jumping off the porch and giving chase. Of course, that wouldn't happen, and he didn't see anyone. The squirrels raced across the porch roof, their chatter sounding like laughter. *To the top of the porch, to the top of the wall.* Next week he would buy himself some rat poison, or maybe a handgun. Call it a Christmas present.

A foul smell hit him in the face as he entered his home. It had been there awhile, but so far he'd been unable to track it down. A dead animal, or maybe just food spoilage. *You get used to it.*

His little Christmas tree leaned far enough to the left the ornaments on that side kept falling off. It was a terrible tree, but he felt sorry for it and couldn't bring himself to take it down. He'd left it up, with its handful of ornaments, for years. Of course, it was long dead. But at least there weren't any needles left to shed.

He'd left that plate of lime Jell-O he'd had for breakfast out on the table, a spoon still in it. It now had a couple of bugs stuck to the surface, but he could eat around those. He sat and took several bites. He loved the lime taste, and green was his favorite color. He'd come to hate red.

He glanced around the dining room at his collection of snow globes, displayed on narrow shelves attached to all four walls. They were the nicest things he owned.

He could hear Christmas carolers out on a sidewalk a few houses over. It was kind of late for them, but he liked hearing the music and their failed attempts at harmony. They'd skipped his house ever since the scene he made five years ago. For some reason he'd thought they were trying to break in.

He'd always wanted a Christmas village with tiny figures of Victorian shoppers their arms full of packages. But the good ones were so expensive. He'd been saving up, but after tonight that dream was probably out of reach.

He made a jam sandwich and placed it on a table by the fireplace along with a warm beer. He scrawled FOR SANTA on a piece of paper and stuck it under the edge of the plate. It was ridiculous, of course, but he did this every year. At least Wallace now had a snack ready for the morning, assuming the mice didn't grab it this time.

He took off his wet socks and hung them from the mantle. He needed to remember to take them down. He'd burned up quite a few pairs over the years. He looked for matches to light a fire but couldn't find them anywhere. Realizing he was too tired to engage in a lengthy search and still a little intoxicated, he sat down in his greasy upholstered chair and stared into the cold, blackened firebox.

He heard the squirrels clattering on his roof again. Or something larger than a squirrel, a racoon maybe—some of those thumps were loud. A narrow stream of soot and ash drifted down into the firebox. Whatever it might be was messing with the chimney. It would regret that. Every couple of years Wallace used brushes and a vacuum to clean off the smoke shelf above and behind the damper. There were always a few skeletons, birds and squirrels and remains he could not identify.

He used to watch his father perform that chore when he was a kid. That's when he realized Santa couldn't possibly be human. Not only was the flue too narrow for a jolly fat man, but how did he get past the smoke shelf and the damper? Santa was either the greatest contortionist ever or some sort of alien.

Wallace fell asleep in his chair before midnight, as he did every year. In his dreams he was the real Santa, traveling through both time and space in his mission to save every single child the pain of disappointment. Santa's bag was depthless, with room for everything. At one house he pulled out an eight-by-ten-foot swimming pool. Chimneys were no obstacle. All he had to do was touch the side of his nose and he became thin as a worm, and so long his head was poking out of the fireplace while his boots were still on the roof.

Wallace wasn't awake when Santa came.

Much to his surprise there were presents beneath his dead tree for Wallace to open Christmas morning. He usually didn't have any Christmas presents unless he wrapped something for himself. Even more surprising, the jam sandwich was gone. So was the can of beer. *Well, God bless us everyone.*

He fell to his knees beside the tree, overcome by the memory of childhood excitement. The packages were haphazardly wrapped using pages of old newspapers, magazines, and random trash. He felt jittery opening them, but he was too curious not to. Inside the first was a delicate bird's nest containing a small skeleton. In the next one he found one of the fake candy canes the store used as part of its decorations. In the final package was a red-and-green-striped stocking cap, the right size for a tiny child. Wallace remembered it from last night's Santa line, and the terrified toddler who'd worn it.

He got up and walked around the house looking for any other indications of stirring creatures. He thought he heard a sighing, wheezing noise, and entering the dining room he saw the large feet sticking out from under the table. They were blocky and covered with black hair, the toenails yellowed and untrimmed. He got down on one knee and peered under the edge of the tablecloth.

All tarnished with ashes and soot. The creature was the one he'd seen in the store the night before. Its head was large and bulbous, covered with dirty, knotted white hair. *No rosy cheeks here.* Its thin lips were barely visible beneath the mats of hair. At first glance Wallace thought it was wearing a red jacket, but upon closer examination he was convinced it was the figure's leathery crimson hide, although it was possible body paint was involved. There were spots, creases, where the redness faded into dirty gray, particularly under its arms and little round belly. Lying crushed in one of its simian paws was the beer can.

It kept its genitalia tucked between its legs. *As all decent Santas should.*

Its eyes snapped open. They were like green jewels. It jumped to its feet, and immediately Wallace understood this was no jolly old elf.

It rotated its head as if looking for an escape route. It leapt up on the table with a single bound, and there began the most amazing transformation, its belly spreading, ballooning into a huge sack with a mouth-like opening. *Do I really have nothing to dread here?*

This vision of Santas gone bad reached out and grabbed what it could, sweeping Wallace's collection of snow globes off their shelves and into its moist fleshy bag. Wallace tried grabbing horrible Santa's feet, trip him up or pull him down, but he was too slow and clumsy and Santa too quick. Once the snow globes were gone Santa bounced through the rest of the house, snatching what it could and shoveling Wallace's things into its sack. By the time Santa returned to the fireplace it was practically waddling.

Santa turned to look at Wallace, opened its mouth, and emitted a mournful noise, reminiscent of foghorns and ships sinking into a watery grave. At the end it inhaled deeply and was sucked backwards up the chimney.

Wallace moved as quickly as his unhealthy body would allow, stumbling out the door and down the porch steps. He kept looking for Santa on the roof or Santa in the trees but could find no trace of him.

Three kids on bicycles raced by, almost running Wallace down. He spun like a top and attempted to give chase, shouting curses when he could not keep up. In his exhaustion he began to laugh, and although he tried his best, he could not stop.

K is for Killer

Kevin was convinced he was going to suffocate. He'd never been inside a car trunk before, but it seemed like a likely place a person might asphyxiate. It smelled strongly of dog, dirty clothes, and rotting leather.

He'd taken a shortcut through the alley after visiting his girlfriend. A powerful man crept up behind him with a knife and forced him into the trunk of an older model car. Kevin's brother took karate when they were kids. Kevin didn't. He wondered if it would have made any difference.

Kev's girlfriend believed in karma. At least she was always talking about it. She was very spiritual. He was not, but he had to wonder if he had done something in a previous life to deserve this. He was forced into a fetal position. His knees throbbed. His knuckles bled from futilely knocking on the inside of the trunk lid. No one came to save him. No one knew he was there.

They must have driven halfway across the city. A lot of turns, speeding up, slowing down. He felt sick to his stomach. No stop until he heard the garage door opening, the car pulling inside. The man blindfolded and gagged him before helping him out of the trunk. But not before Kevin saw his face, the green knapsack on his back. He shouldn't have looked. Now the man would have to kill him. Kevin had always been a klutz. He couldn't even act like a proper victim.

The kidnapper led him down an incline, then through a space smelling strongly of earth, some area underground maybe. Then through a rough wooden door (Kevin got splinters in his hand when he fell against it), then stepping onto concrete, and the man sat him in a sturdy chair, tying down his arms and ankles. Kevin was in full panic but didn't speak. He strained to listen for clues. That's what the victims did on TV. You might survive if you paid enough attention to clues.

———

"Welcome to my home. Now yours, temporarily." His kidnapper removed the kerchiefs from over Kevin's eyes and mouth.

The man hadn't bothered to put on a mask, so yes, this fellow was going to kill him. A long keloid scar ran across the guy's neck, which would make him easy to identify in a lineup, not that there would ever be one.

The fellow wore baggy khaki pants and a worn-out lumberjack shirt. So, no fashionista, this one. He held a stretch of rope in one blocky hand. Lots of big knots, which made Kevin's stomach churn, wondering how the rope might be used. The guy had dark blue eyes. Those were rare weren't they? Cold, sunken. The rest of his face was puffy, pale, nondescript. A face from any crowd, except for those eyes.

———

They were in a small room, made smaller by the surrounding shelving. The shelves were full of small bits of junk, what his mother called tchotchkes. Little nonfunctional figures, some of them grotesque. A dog with three heads. Others definitely phallic. Fertility figures. A statue of Kali? So, his kidnapper was a little cultured, perhaps. Also purses, watches, bracelets, rings, earrings. Was that a swatch of hair? And there was another one, and over there three more. Keepsakes. No. These were the kidnapper's goddamn trophies.

"I see you're admiring the collection. Maybe I'll tell you a little about them if there's time. I don't keep body parts, not anymore. They stink after a while. I call this the throne room. You're sitting on it, actually, but you're not the king. I am. But I've got no queen, not now. And that's because of assholes like you. Pretty boys."

Kevin had never been called a pretty boy before. What was this guy going on about?

There was a black iron barred door centered in the wall in front of him, keys tantalizingly dangling from the lock, a staircase visible in the dimness beyond. The wooden door through which he'd entered was to his left, hiding what he thought might be an underground tunnel to the garage. To the right lay a short hallway with a row of four narrow doors, a sliding panel at the bottom of each, maybe for food trays. Cells? Dark stains on the concrete floor: oil or paint, dried blood maybe. If blood, there had been a lot of it. The air. It stank of bleach and something foul underneath. It reminded him of a kennel.

His kidnapper kept moving from foot to foot as if he needed to pee. Speaking of, how was Kevin supposed to relieve himself? Thinking about the question brought on the urge.

"Like my kit? In the profession we call this a murder kit." He emptied the knapsack at Kevin's feet: handcuffs, duct tape, claw hammer, rope, gag, garbage bags, rags, a little bottle of something. Everything a serial killer needed for an exciting weekend ahead.

Would Kevin be here longer than a weekend? Alicia would wonder what happened to him. They had plans. Maybe she'd call the police when he didn't show up or answer the phone. Or would she give it a day or two first? No, Alicia was impatient, and quick to anger. She'd drive to his place and beat on his door, yelling and cursing. Then she'd regret that for a while. Then she'd call the police. But what could lead them to this basement? If this were a movie Kevin might have found a way to leave a trail, or at least a message. But Kevin had never been clever.

He didn't have his Klonopin with him. Without his medication he had no way to control his panic. At least he didn't think so. It had been a while since he'd tried.

"Let's get to know each other a little. Tell me how you met your girlfriend. Something made you keen on her, right? What was it?"

Kevin wasn't about to tell this killer anything about Alicia. "I don't have a girlfriend yet. I just moved here from Kansas."

An explosive blow snapped his head to the side. "That's a lie. I watched you leave her house. First warning. You don't want to lie to me. You start out lying and it's kaput for you, Kevin. What attracted you to her?"

How did he know his name? So, he'd been watching Alicia's house. Did he know her? The possibility chilled him.

"She has a killer smile. I ordered coffee. She smiled when she gave it to me. I was dazzled. I asked her out. Spur of the moment."

"Thank you kindly for answering truthfully. She works at that coffee place on Main. Yes, I agree. Killer smile. So, you asked her out, just like that? I couldn't do it in a million years.

And even if I did a woman that pretty would never go out with me. What makes you so special, Kevin?"

"Nothing. Nothing at all. I just asked the woman out. You ask enough times, and one will eventually say yes."

Another blow. Kevin thought his ear might be bleeding. The guy was wearing a big ring. It looked like a woman's ring, a cluster of pearls, some sort of purple stone at the center. "Not in my experience. But we live different lives, don't we Kevin? You get what you ask for. I don't. She won't even speak to me, your Alicia. She calls the manager over and he throws me out. All because I gave her a little compliment about her ass and what I'd love to do to it. Nothing kinky, mind you. Just straight sex. I'm straight, Kevin, in case you were wondering."

Kevin was not. So, his kidnapper knew Alicia's name. Damn right she had him thrown out. She was a strong woman. She knew what she wanted. She didn't put up with crap. This was very bad. What could he say to this guy that would make things better? What could he say to make him leave her alone? Alicia already thought Kevin was a little weak. This was his chance to prove otherwise.

"Is she a good kisser? I bet she is, those lips. I'm betting she has a knack for it. She'd be a great queen for me, your Alicia, but it wouldn't be voluntary, not with that stuck-up bitch. Pretty women don't go for guys like me. They won't give us a chance. They don't want a nice guy, so I stopped being a nice guy a long time ago. All I ever wanted was one reason not to hate the world, and they won't give it to me. The only thing keeping loneliness away is I keep myself busy. I have … *interests.*"

Kevin glanced at the trophy shelves, then back at the ring. He didn't want to be hit again, but he didn't know how to prevent it.

"You like the ring? It was my mother's. She was a bully, until she got old, and I got big. She gave me this beautiful necklace when I was a kid." He pointed to the scar on his neck. "I was glad when she died. I'm just sorry I didn't kill her myself." He stopped and gazed at the ceiling. "Did you hear that? Somebody at the door? I hate it when people come by unannounced, don't you? They have no business here. No need to interrupt our time together, mind you. Eventually they'll go away. They always do."

Kevin had heard nothing. The fellow liked to talk. He was also quite paranoid. These were the only things giving Kevin hope.

"Stop looking at the cells. They're not for you. The cells are for *pussy*." The man gave the word special emphasis, like he didn't use it very often, but he wanted it to sound as if he did. Fair enough. Kevin never used it at all. "You don't interest me that way. I told you already."

"That's fine." Kevin didn't know what to say, but he was afraid to say nothing.

"Damn right it's fine. I bet you've heard of me, right? I'm famous. I've got some clippings I could show you, videos of newscasts. They call me by lots of names—I'm that prolific. But I'm too smart for them. They haven't a clue who I actually am. The Alphabet Killer. The KC Strangler, The Basher, The Peanut Butter Killer. That was because after I strangled a woman in her house I made myself a peanut butter sandwich and ate it in her kitchen. I did that a few times, numbers fifteen through twenty I believe, then I went on this paleo diet. You're not supposed to eat peanut butter on paleo, did you know that?"

"I ... I did not."

"That's because they consider peanuts a legume and legumes are a no-no. The paleo's done wonders for my A1C. I bet you've never had to diet. You were born with the perfect metabolism, right?"

"I've dieted some."

"Sure you have. You're good looking, but you're not very smart, are you? You figure if you say the right things I'll let you go. But you mean less to me than any of those women I killed. You don't mean any more to me than my morning piss. Less even, because at least I enjoy my morning piss."

He looked at the ceiling again. "Did you hear that? You know what happens when you lie to me, right?" He went over to the barred door, unlocked it, and ran up the stairs. Kevin began to struggle, wiggling his arms and legs. But the zip ties the guy used were too tight and dug into Kevin's skin.

His kidnapper didn't come back for a long time. When Kevin heard footsteps on the stairs he peed his pants. The man came into the room, stared at Kevin's wet pants in disgust, then broke into laughter, obviously enjoying his humiliation. Kevin tried to put it out of his mind, but the more he tried the more he was aware of the smell and the discomfort.

"So, what attracts you to a woman like Alicia? She's a little on the skinny side, isn't she? Not much meat to hold on to."

Back to Alicia again. Kevin wondered if talking about her increased her danger. He'd read novels about creeps like this, how they liked to torture the girlfriend in front of the helpless boyfriend. "I told you. She had a great smile. And I thought she was smarter than me. You'd hate that, wouldn't you? But I liked it. I admired her intelligence." Kevin was being stupid, saying too much. Alicia would at least know better than to trade insults with a killer. Was he putting them both in more danger?

"Had? Why, you didn't kill her, did you?"

"Has. *Has*."

"Well, that's a relief. I would have been seriously disappointed. I'm looking forward to, well, you know." His kidnapper pursed his lips and made an obnoxious kissing noise.

Kevin groaned involuntarily.

"I bet it's a sex thing for you, isn't it? I bet you don't love her at all. That's so *shallow*, Kevin. I like all kinds of women, myself. Women walking alone turn me on. So do women living alone, like your Alicia. That's a big place for a single girl. Does she like to throw big parties? She a party girl, Kevin?"

Kevin had no idea what the safe answer was here. He just shook his head.

"Or is she a shy one? Enjoys sex but won't talk about it. Won't tell you what she needs, so you have to guess. I hate guessing, don't you? When I was in high school they made you guess. In college I decided to stop guessing and, well, did what felt good. But do you know they don't like that either? They call the cops on you. A guy can't win."

Kevin nodded. He wasn't sure why. Maybe because he was too afraid to disagree. Or because challenging this guy would be too dangerous.

"You a winner, Kevin? Is that why Alicia likes you instead of me? You don't look much like a winner right now."

His kidnapper continued to believe he heard noises upstairs: a salesman, a nosy neighbor, maybe an intruder breaking in. Each time he raced upstairs to check it out he returned angrier than the time before, pacing, swinging his arms, sometimes with a knife in one hand.

"You think you're morally superior to me, don't you Kevin?"

"No, not at all. People have ... you must have your reasons."

"Are you crying, Kevin?"

Kevin shook his head, but he had no idea. Maybe he was crying. This ridiculous man talked and talked and would not shut up.

"Oh, sometimes I blow up. I can't help myself. A man has needs, and a man has limits. I get angry, in my line of work. I try not to, but Christ, those women. They bring it out of me. But that's a good thing too. I like them to be afraid of me. I like seeing them struggle. If they don't struggle I lose interest. What, they're giving up that easy? They're just going to let themselves die?"

The fellow went on for hours. Kevin began to nod, and when he nodded he waited for the blows, which sometimes came and sometimes not. Sometimes he slept. He didn't know if his kidnapper was permitting this, or if he was so busy talking he hadn't noticed.

"I gave young women rides on a regular basis, but I behaved myself. That way they began to trust me. I was a perfect gentleman, until the day I wasn't. It was stupid of them to accept those rides from a stranger. Their deaths were inevitable."

"I strangled her with a rope attached to a stick. It was like a tourniquet for her neck. I felt a thrill watching the light fade from her eyes."

"Sometimes I'd drive around with a dead woman tied to the passenger seat. No one could tell the difference. Sometimes I'd wave at pedestrians, and they'd wave back!"

"After I choose someone I write out a plan. Things have to happen step-by-step, in a specific order. How I'm going to approach them, what I'm going to say, exactly what I'm going to do to them, how I'm going to avoid getting caught. Every move is rehearsed. When I make up my mind I don't change it. I still have impulsive urges, sure, but now I try to suppress them. Those will get you caught, Kevin."

"I've been doing this *so long*, I can't believe I haven't been caught. The police, right? They're never there when you need them.

"I've come to understand that nobody out there is going to stop me. I'm unstoppable, Kevin, how about that? That's my special power. But I can't keep doing this forever. It must end sometime. Suicide is my final solution. I get to choose the time, the place, and the method. You can't do better than that. I'm one lucky man, but you, Kevin, are not."

His kidnapper was pacing again, frenetic, slurring his words. Was the man high, or angry?

"I smell kaka. Did you have an accident, kiddo? Have you been listening to me? You know, I thought you were a good listener, that I could tell you everything, but I think you've been faking it.

"The world's a better place without certain people. You can't argue with that. I don't like kids, but I don't kill them. I've got rules, Kevin. It's total chaos if you've got no rules."

He pulled a knife out of his pocket, flipped it open. "Remember how I said I loved using a knife? It's practically the only intimacy I allow myself. I'll slice them open, but I do it with loving care. I don't have sex with any of them, I swear. I wouldn't give those bitches the satisfaction. So, I can't really use a knife on you, now can I? Because you're a guy, and like I said, I don't swing that way. So, what am I supposed to do? Kick you to death maybe?

"If I untied one of your arms and gave you this knife, would you kill yourself Kevin? Because that may be your only way out of this."

The kidnapper read his mind. If Kevin had a knife he wasn't sure if he'd try to cut this guy's throat, or his own.

The guy stopped pacing, and again stared at the ceiling, legs spread, arms raised and shaking with tension, the hand clutching the knife visibly vibrating. He emitted a low growl, fumbled with the keys in the barred door, slung it open, and pounded up the stairs. Kevin could hear an incoherent shouting, and then the door at the top of the stairs slammed.

There was a series of violent vocalizations overhead, but he couldn't make out any of the words. Some sort of argument maybe? Then things were quiet for a long time. Kevin listened carefully, but heard no voices, no footsteps, nothing.

Then he heard light footsteps on the stairs.

At this point Alicia must have figured out something was wrong. They didn't go a day without a phone call or two and several emails. Besides, they'd made plans to go to the mountains, check into a romantic B&B. They'd been looking forward to it for weeks.

She would have called the police by now, but without a lead what could they do? Maybe this guy made a mistake, left some kind of evidence in the alley, but that seemed unlikely. Still, he was unhinged, and maybe ...

Maybe he'd gone back to Alicia's place. Maybe he was with Alicia now.

A small face dissolved out of the darkness at the bottom of the stairs. It was Alicia, running toward him.

"Alicia! How ..."

"We have to hurry! He's gone outside. Did he hurt you? Are you hurt? Kev, I was so scared!" She was barefoot. She had a smear of blood on her cheek. She ran over to him, started jerking on his arms, his legs. "I can't see how you're tied!"

"Zip ties. Can't you see them? They're so tight, they're cutting off circulation. You'll need a knife. Get a knife."

But Alicia kept jerking on his arms, hurting him. She was crying. Was she hysterical? Something shiny caught his eye. Her earrings. A cluster of pearls surrounding a purple stone. She wasn't crying. She was laughing.

"I've got a knife." She held up the kidnapper's knife.

A shadow loomed behind her. A blocky hand came around and grabbed her waist. She leaned back and let his kidnapper kiss her on the mouth. All the breath went out of him.

"Alicia?"

She smiled that killer smile. "Oh, Kev. I never said we were *exclusive.*"

The kidnapper stepped around her, pushing her aside. "You know, you were right about one thing, Kevin. You ask enough times, and one will eventually say yes."

L is for Love

He couldn't remember the last time he'd been outside. The neighbors probably thought he moved. The arm of the letter L by his front door had broken off, leaving a tilted and ragged-edged I. He couldn't decide whether to replace it or remove it entirely. It probably didn't matter. He couldn't remember the last time he'd gotten his mail.

Through one corner of his bedroom window, he could see the dead weeds covering his lawn, the leaves piled up on his porch steps and spilling onto the porch itself, the growing pile of newspapers, the notices from the city torn away by the wind and scattered across his property.

Luscious. Lover. Lamia.

Sometimes, when the morning light through the trees and the half-closed curtains spotted her body with flecks of shadow, she looked sleeker than normal, more dangerous, her fingers leaving almost invisible lacerations in his flesh, her nails practically glowing against his skin. And Alan thought, *leopard*.

Sometimes, after a long night of making love, when it was pitch-black in the room and it seemed Alan could never get enough of her, never get beyond the feeling that however much they made love he was still alone when he was with her, she was the *leviathan*, the consumer, the monster without edge.

"Are you asleep?" she whispered in the close, warm darkness. The question unaccountably bothered him. He would have expected her to ask *Are you awake?* and that small difference in emphasis disturbed him. "Are you asleep?" she asked again.

So he feigned sleep, keeping his breath so shallow as to be almost nonexistent. He feigned death.

"Are you dead?" she whispered, and he could detect no humor in her question. He lay still, locking himself up in his death imitation, became a lie, even though lies had always frightened him. Her mouth loomed over him in a darkness that seemed absolute. "Are you dead?" she whispered.

He waited for her to reveal herself, to say whatever she really meant to say, to do whatever she'd always wanted to do, now that she thought he was asleep, or dead. He waited for the *lycanthrope* in her to come out. He waited for her next question. She became the law. She became a legion. She became a mouth nibbling at the base of his spine, working its way around each buttock, leaching the sweat from his body, scraping its way so intently down the insides of his thighs he thought she intended to work down to subcutaneous tissue. Her mouth flensed him, cleansed him, and then was gone.

In the darkness, in the absence of her touch, of any signals from her, he felt alone. He was in limbo, neglected, his skin still tingling from her teeth and insensitive to any other touch, as if his body had suddenly floated free of the bed and he was turning in the warm dark air like meat on a spit. She had always frightened him. He had never known what was inside her, and could never know. When he first met her she was raven-haired, doe-eyed, languid in her movements, flesh cool to the touch. But the time after it seemed she caught on fire, her hair flaming, her skin reddened as if pinched repeatedly by calloused fingertips, her warm breath rolling off her swollen lips.

And the time after that she had been a blonde, almost white-haired. An ancient woman, or a wisp of a girl. Her voice was a whisper and manners so demure he felt like an old lech.

She might be thinking anything. He could never know for sure. He could marry her and still never know for sure. Sometimes he would hover over her at night hoping she might whisper her secrets from sleep.

He would always be terrified of losing her, knowing he had never really had her. At the same time, he would always be afraid she'd stolen him, and swallowed him whole. To be inside her, and she inside her own thoughts where he could not reach, it was all too frightening. He felt murdered, lynched. It enraged him. He imagined her some giant cold Lucifer full of laws and regulations. And later he was ashamed of these resentments.

His naked form shivered on the cool, damp sheets. Her hair fell over his chest, spread pleasurably across his skin, moved slowly down his belly. Listless hair. Wanton hair. Unruly hair drifted around his penis, curled over the shaft, rode up to its tip, floated away into the darkness. He regretted its absence, but its disembodiment also disturbed him.

Ask me a question, he thought. *Please.* And then, *Let me see your face.*

He imagined she could see him, even though he could not see her. He imagined she had special eyes that could see in the dark, that could see the embarrassing wart on his chest, critically measure the middle-aged sag of his breasts and belly. He reached, but his hands could not find the sheet to cover himself.

He could imagine her invisible fingers weaving arcane patterns in the night air. He tried to protect himself with his too-soft hands, moving them about his body in an aimless attempt to find the portions of skin which might be most vulnerable to an attack from her fingers.

Her voice was an absence in the air. He knew the sound of it would leave him anxious, but he needed the oxygen that curled inside each vowel.

She watched him, he knew. She saw what was behind his clothes and beneath his voice. His silence gave her permission.

His desire for her was limitless.

He waited for her voice, but it was her fingers which came instead. Or rather her fingertips, for he was aware only of small circles of contact which appeared suddenly on either side of his neck, then moved slowly down to rest on his nipples, then traveled to his hipbones, carrying out an imagined resculpting of his body, then in ever-tightening circles closing in on his groin.

"Are you dead?" the voice came, but now it was unrecognizable, heavy with desire and filling him with dread. "Well, are you?" it sang, an octave deeper.

The fingers had grown teeth. The hot breath descending upon him had edges that cut and lifted the skin. She draped herself over him, and he could feel his skin shrink, then swell.

"Who are you?" He forgot himself and asked the question aloud.

She laughed once, gently, then surrounded him like a landslide.

M is for Mother

First trimester. Purely a guesstimate. Paula's pregnancy had hardly been normal.

She was a storm of anxieties and delights, always leaking tears. But it was early spring, and she'd found the ideal house for raising a baby: a Craftsman bungalow on a quiet street, a shade tree out front perfect for a tire swing, the rent mostly affordable.

A large, wooden M was mounted by the front door, ornately painted with rabbits and eggs, orchids, and cows. "They're fertility symbols, Ma'am," her future landlord said. "The last tenant did that. A good omen."

"Why would you say a good omen?"

He blinked. "Oh God, I'm sorry. My wife says I never think before speaking. I shouldn't assume, I mean you look perfectly *healthy...*"

"It's okay, I'm not mad," she said, absolving him. "Yes, I'm pregnant." She rested her hands on her bump.

"Let me guess. Our daughter had a baby last year. Five months?"

"Something like that." But it had only been three weeks since her strange one-night stand. She could still smell his cologne: magnolias and champagne, and something underground. Last week she'd seen her doctor for stomach pains; he said she was four months pregnant. *Impossible!* He urged her to return for a follow-up, and commented on the pale diagonal scar across her belly. But she'd never seen it before.

He guided her inside. "It's all on one floor, no stairs to climb. The original oak and mahogany, rare these days. A bedroom for you, and a smaller bedroom for the child. Unless you're having twins, or triplets." She didn't answer. "Nice big kitchen and front room. If you need help with anything, just ask."

"Thank you so much." The last thing she wanted was her landlord dropping by.

He went on and on and she let him, though she was already sold. She wrote a check for the first month's rent and deposit. He was a nice man, if a little nosy. She was relieved he didn't ask about the baby's father.

Paula had gone to the hotel that night because they held a dance every Friday and women got in free. She hadn't dated in a year. She worked long shifts in a warehouse, spending little and saving money for college.

She'd had too much to drink, and it was the end of the night. He was tall, dark, and thin, and she couldn't quite see his face, not even when he bent over and said hello. Not even when he held her close, smothered in his fruity cologne. She couldn't remember him speaking, but she believed him to be devastatingly handsome. Later, upstairs, he showed his face as he was removing her clothes, but she couldn't remember it. He understood exactly what to do, but then he did *that*, and even though she couldn't remember what *that* was, she knew it was something no one in their right mind would want. She woke up alone. The room had been taken apart and stained maroon. She hurried past the housekeeping cart in the hall, embarrassed.

It took a day to move in. She had few possessions, but a wealth of baby supplies—diapers and furniture and the right foods, medical supplies, and every book she could find on pregnancy.

She remembered Mother saying, "Women have been having babies at home forever." She'd read the books and watched countless videos online. She wasn't a genius, but she was a fast learner. She'd felt from the beginning having this baby alone, where no one could see, was the right thing to do. If she got into trouble, she would call someone.

Her body ached and skin hurt. She kept getting bigger, but she couldn't feel the baby inside. Maybe she was something worse than pregnant. The littlest things—a crack in a mug, scrambled eggs looking ugly—set off a frenzy of weeping. Her breasts were tender and swollen. She had heartburn. She was often constipated but still too late getting to the bathroom.

One afternoon Paula discovered a gray rabbit in the backyard, sunning himself on a bench surrounded by beautiful trees. She decided to keep him as a companion. She knew nothing of rabbits, but figured if she fed him, he would stick around. After a day she brought him inside, because if he ran away, she'd be inconsolable.

Paula didn't know how to housebreak a rabbit and spent a lot of time cleaning up his messes but thought it good training for raising a child. Once she picked up a piece of vegetable he dropped—too chewed to determine what kind—and she ate it. She and the rabbit snarled at each other. It was the best whatever vegetable she'd ever eaten, and a healthier meal than all the mac and cheese and macaroons dipped in mayonnaise she'd been munching.

One day several lumps appeared on her belly, small as mosquito bites at first, but growing into masses the size of kittens. After a week they vanished, but eventually she realized they'd burrowed deeply inside.

She was having daily talks with the rabbit. He appeared distracted, but at least he listened. "Mister Rabbit, I'm afraid I'm going to have a miscarriage. This pregnancy is like nothing in my books. I'm no martyr, but maybe I deserve this. I know nothing about the dad, and I'm not sure I want this child." The rabbit stood up on his hind legs and stared at her. Paula found this mildly encouraging. "Thanks for being a good friend." She paused. "I always wanted my life to be my own, and now I know it never will be."

Second trimester. Strictly metaphorical, of course. Great gobs of her auburn hair littered the floor, clogging the drains. She'd read hormonal changes could cause this, but she hadn't expected so many bald patches.

Her belly was a taut balloon. She could feel all those lumps inside moving. Was she having more than one? They were naughty babies wandering where they weren't allowed to go.

"It's too soon for it, or them, to be moving, isn't it?" she asked Mister Rabbit. He lay on his back and displayed his belly in sympathy. "I'm way too big, and it's only been three months."

After another few days she began having Braxton Hicks contractions. She wasn't far enough along for those. Patches of color emerged on her skin, but not the brown ones the books talked about. Her belly blushed with the brightest Easter egg colors. She was supposed to be making joyful preparations, reading about breast feeding, but she felt no joy, only fear.

Mister Rabbit started running away when he saw her approaching. Even her best friend found her too much to bear.

―――――――

Third trimester. It had no relevance to what she was experiencing, but she marked it on the calendar anyway. The contractions were much stronger, waking her up in the middle of the night. She had dreams of the father coming back to the hotel room where she and her babies snuggled in bed. She still couldn't see his face. He gathered her and the kids in a sheet, carried them to the balcony, and threw them out. She woke up trying to snatch her babies out of the air.

She recalled the sex talk Mother gave when she was twelve, about the "ordinary miracle" of childbirth. If Paula's mother were alive, would she still be so confident, or would she, too, be terrified?

Paula believed she might deliver at any moment. A lot more movement. A great deal more pain. Everything was dangerously ahead of its time. She had such a powerful sense of *internal* gravity, a heaviness she could not get rid of. She felt mutated. It took everything she had just to crawl out of bed.

Her babies weren't ready. But they had to come out.

―――――――

Birth. So many of them.

The magnitude of her misery was beyond anything she'd imagined. It was a vivisection, a mutilation. Somehow, she'd gotten herself into the kitchen and was lying on the fake marble tile. They came out in the middle of a contraction, one so convulsive and painful she blacked out. When she awakened, she was covered in yellow and magenta goop. She thought she must be hemorrhaging. She felt one—no, two, no, *several—*

tearing at her breasts. She wanted to be nurturing, but they were going to kill her. Too many frenetic mouths. Paula recalled when she was a kid and her dog Angel had ten puppies, but Angel had ten nipples to feed them.

Mashed together, wriggling like a pile of giant maggots. She couldn't tell many details, or where one left off and the others began. But as they started to separate, each eager to seize some part of her, she could see how sickly they were, pale skin thin as paper, scrawny arms and legs and long narrow claws scratching, drawing blood. One opened its eyes. It had *her* eyes. Another opened its mouth, and she couldn't quite understand what she saw, but there were teeth continuing all the way down its throat like a lamprey eel. She suddenly remembered seeing that mouth before. It had its father's mouth.

They weren't getting the milk they needed and abandoned her breasts in search of other nourishment. At some point she would have to get up and evaluate her wounds, assuming she could manage to stand.

Of course, these weren't normal babies. Their human heads were smaller, their bodies thin and malnourished looking. Their jerky movements reminded her of baby birds. Like birds and reptiles, they only had one little hole, *cloaca*, where their genitals were supposed to be, the rest of their nether regions smooth as Barbies'. They used those holes generously, the poop and pee running constantly down their scrawny legs and all over her kitchen.

Yet she had no trouble seeing herself in them. Their enormous, human eyes were full of enough tears and longing to break her heart. They had little noses above their mysterious mouths, not beaks, and little pointy chins. Maybe no one else would ever find them endearing, but she certainly did.

She counted at least thirty, but there might have been more. They moved so quickly—running, or crawl/walking, in and out of rooms—an accurate count was difficult. She saw no way to distinguish males from females.

Mister Rabbit retreated to the top of the kitchen cabinets. He didn't look exactly afraid, bunny faces being not particularly expressive, but he was watchful. Three of her babies climbed the cabinets trying to reach him but their arms were too short. They opened and shut their mouths repeatedly, teeth clicking loudly. She decided then there would be no more attempts at breast feeding.

The next few weeks were spent walking around with babies hanging all over her. They still bit her now and then. The wounds were ugly and painful, but they healed.

How could she be a good mother to this clamorous brood? Mewling, whining, ferocious kiddies. They were hungry all the time, and they needed *her* all the time. She couldn't shower or bathe because they might drown. She was beyond sleep deprived. She struggled to corral them. She couldn't hold them all at the same time, and the ones left out raged. They ran away and she might not see them again for hours.

She tried to produce some names. She began with Frank, the largest, the calm and thoughtful-looking one, then Jane, George, and Susan, but still not knowing if they were male or female, continuing with Peter, Flopsy, Mopsy, and Cottontail, then began naming them after foods—Macaroni, Peanut Butter, and Pizza Boy—and the smallest Bitter, Sweet, and Sour, but it rapidly became futile. She was sure of only a handful.

Some, Frank, and Pizza Boy especially, were quite affectionate, climbing into her lap when she was depressed. Many of the others came when hungry, hurt, or scared.

Her birth wounds healed quickly, like that long diagonal scar which she now thought had something to do with her impregnation. But her abdomen was misshapen. Women complained their husbands didn't find their post-pregnancy bodies attractive. Well, screw those myopic men. Those bodies were where their children came from.

It would have been nice to take her children to the doctor for a wellness visit, but that wasn't an option. One look and her babies would be taken away.

A few of the kids liked to bite each other, and they bullied the weaker ones, but so far none had been hurt too badly. She pulled them apart before too much damage was done. She made giant batches of formula mixed with bits of bread and potato which they lapped from bowls like kittens. Her biggest worry was running out of money. She had no idea what she'd do then.

They grew rapidly but were still relatively small. She was scared a few of them working together could topple her. After another few weeks they developed an appetite for tougher foods, raw carrots, and meat. The change in diet settled them down. They became content just to cuddle. She could read them bedtime stories, all her kids perched on and around her like one of those Southwest Native American storyteller dolls.

Despite her concerns about the landlord, he hadn't been by since he gave her the keys. No one else knew where she lived except the delivery drivers, who left orders on the porch. The knock on the door was a huge surprise.

It was a windy day, and the kids were on edge, fighting each other and clinging to her, leery of the shadows sweeping the windows and tapping against the glass. She told them about trees, and promised if they were good, one day she would show them the beautiful trees in their back yard. She had no idea if they understood, or how much language they could grasp at this stage, but she had to try.

Initially she thought windblown branches were the reason for the persistent knocking, but then the beating became more forceful, shaking the door.

Whoever it was would have to wait. She climbed out of her chair, babies complaining, falling, landing on the floor, squealing. Some of them took it as a game and tried to climb back up. She had to waddle, as babies hung on to her ankles, gripped her knees and thighs. Whoever it was continued to bang on the door, and she shouted, "Wait!"

The door swung open and slammed into the wall. The shadowy figure beyond leaned into the doorway, having to duck to get through. She fell to the floor and couldn't get up again. From her angle he appeared unnaturally thin, dangerously sharp within his voluminous black coat, then as he turned, he broadened into something monstrous, his overcoat momentarily morphing into enormous wings above multiple, reptilian arms. Abruptly Paula could taste magnolia blossoms floating in champagne, and she knew who he was.

Her sweet and curious child Frank toddled calmly up to his dad. The creature bent over, his face an indecipherable blur of motion and disintegration. A long scythe of arm swept down and gathered Frank up, and his father swallowed him whole.

"Why did you do that?" she asked faintly, instead of screaming. It was a strange thing to say, but she was struggling to put together what had just occurred. "Why!" she shouted this time, and it shattered her to feel so helpless. Yet she continued to sit there, mesmerized, watching.

The father paid no attention, crouched now, sweeping children into his arms, stuffing them into the folds of his massive coat, where they disappeared, a few chubby hands and arms appearing outside its bounds. Some of their children laughed, thinking this a game.

He took half the children, picking them up, examining them, tossing some back her way, who she hung on to desperately in case he changed his mind. *He's taking his share,* she thought.

Then without a word (Had he ever actually spoken? She didn't know.) he rose and swung around, his coat flaring out momentarily so she could see all the children inside, hanging from their feet like rabbits ready for the hunter's knife.

"Wait! What are you going to do with them?" But she knew. She ran after him with all her clinging kids, although one or two might have fallen off, she couldn't be sure. The door slammed shut behind her as she chased him through the yard.

Paula screamed, and made a desperate dive, grabbing the back of his coat and bringing him down in giddy triumph before he could reach the street.

In retaliation he stole the children still clinging to her, adding them to the collection inside his coat.

She scrambled around searching for them, frantically tearing open his coat and beating on his hard, slick shell, but now his coat appeared empty, her kids passed on to somewhere else.

Suddenly she was on the ground again, and he was on top. She was certain he would do to her the same as he'd done before, that brute act of animal husbandry, and she'd rather die.

But he only gazed at her, as deep within the obscurity of his face the lights of his malicious intelligence gleamed. *There are many things you cannot change. This is one of them.* Those words, mysteriously conveyed, possessed a semblance of pity.

But not so merciful as he abandoned her there in the wind and the dark grass alone with her memories: a child struggling to comprehend the dead cat in her lap, or the tortured illness which took her grandparents away. "They're only sleeping," Father lied. It was left to Mother to set her straight.

But children push death away because they know it can't happen to them, and then a neighbor dies, a cousin, a boy she barely knew at school, a teacher, a best friend.

She recalled the drowning which swept her brother away, leaving her parents awash in unending grief, the unwelcome surprise of a familiar name in the obituaries, the news of loved ones dead in distant cities, followed by the swift losses of her father and then her mother, and someday it would be her gone to dirt and ash and then whatever children down through an eternity of mourning, a sacrifice of flesh and pain given up to the insatiable appetite of nature as mothers delivered both life and death into the world.

The landlord pulled up in front of the bungalow on a late summer day with a FOR RENT sign he hoped he wouldn't have to use. His tenant had missed two months' rent. He'd sent a polite reminder with no response. He knew she was a new single mother, or almost. This was a welfare check as much as anything else. His wife said he should call the police, but he wanted to do this himself. He should have checked earlier. People fell through the cracks, and it was a terrible thing.

The yard needed mowing. He should have called someone or done it himself. He never expected her to do yard work, not in her condition.

The mailbox overflowed with junk. The single personal piece was his letter asking for the rent. This spoke of someone with few or no friends. He knocked on the door, waited, knocked again. He knocked steadily for a minute or two. He didn't want to bang on the door; it might scare her.

A layer of dust and grit covered the front porch, along with broken branches, drifts of leaves. He'd had tenants abandon properties when they couldn't afford to pay. He peeked through the front window. He didn't believe this was the case here. From what he could tell the front room looked pristine.

He knocked one last time, then unlocked the door. He opened it a few inches and called. "Paula? It's your landlord. I hope everything's okay. I'm coming in."

The house was clean and tidy, but no one answered, and he couldn't find anyone in any of the rooms. The refrigerator was mostly empty, but there was milk, a covered plate full of mashed potatoes, some condiments, some pickles. A bowl at the center of the kitchen table was full of fresh fruit. Nothing looked spoiled. Someone must be living here.

He found them in the backyard. "Paula?" She didn't answer. She lay on the bench among the beautiful trees, staring at him with such sadness, such solemnity. He'd seen that look before in people after some terrible event. It was the weight of knowing.

There was a flower in her auburn hair. A rabbit sat beside her on its haunches, head up and alert. The rabbit did not flee but appeared to be watching him with vigilance.

A naked boy sat on the ground nearby, his legs folded beneath him. He had red hair like Paula's, so perhaps they were related. Maybe a cousin. He was ten or so. He was thin and gangly and a little goofy looking, as boys that age tend to be.

The landlord realized then that Paula no longer appeared pregnant. If anything, she'd lost weight. So, she'd miscarried, and that explained the way she looked, and why he had not heard from her. It was a terrible thing. He wished his wife were here. She would know what to do, and exactly what to say.

The boy had the most beautiful, wide-set eyes. He was quite friendly, smiling and nodding at all the landlord's questions, but he would not open his mouth and speak.

N is for Night

He had little understanding of human relationships. None of his had lasted long enough for him to acquire any notion of expertise. Yet he believed they were an uneasy balance of truth and pretense. Despite everything human beings managed to commit and care for each other. The pretense was not only what you said or did to make yourself appealing, but any confidence you had that you understood what someone else wanted or cared about or how they perceived the world in any way. Impossible. No one was a mind reader.

Jeffry never outgrew his fear of the dark. He'd never shared that information with anyone. He was ashamed. It was an embarrassing relic from a frightful childhood. He remembered as a boy lying in bed with the covers over his head listening to every sound. At least as an adult he kept the covers down. How did it help to make things even darker? But he still listened. He still quaked.

He imagined if he were married, he would have a companion for those long dark nights. He came to understand the fantasy promised too much. Everyone takes such journeys alone.

An aging bachelor, he bought the house on Alphabet Row after a significant drop in price. Something was probably wrong with the property, but he could not find it. He had simple needs—he wanted a comfortable place for reading during the day and sleeping safely at night.

The house was set further back than the others on the street. He had no idea why this sudden break in uniformity, except it allowed for more trees. Nine large, leafy maples in the front and side yards kept his home permanently in shade during the summer, spring, and early fall. When the leaves fell, he felt buried, and kept the blinds and curtains closed so he wouldn't have to look. The realtor bragged how the numerous windows in the front of the house let in the maximum amount of natural light. But windows which let in light let in dark after the sun went down.

The house was difficult to light at night. It had two stories, although no one looking from the street would have known because of the obscuring trees. Both levels had high ceilings with an unnecessarily steep staircase connecting them. There was no hall light, or ceiling fixtures of any kind. Jeffry had to make do with plug-in lamps whose illumination reached barely above head-height. The walls were broad and had too few outlets. No matter how he positioned the lamps there were always dead spots, broad patches of shadow, and recesses so dark they disappeared.

The night found sanctuary inside his home. After dinner the ceilings faded into non-existence. The walls were awash in gloom. The interior geometry never appeared normal. The worst were the closets. Wary of their nasty implications, he never opened them after five.

Not that he necessarily deserved light. His had never been a sunny personality, and for someone who was so unsettled by darkness he never bothered to fortify himself with more sun during the day. Since his college years he'd kept largely to himself, and now retired could see little reason to venture out. Sunshine was wasted on him. He had no desire to garden and if the grass died beneath the intense shade of all those trees at least he wouldn't have to mow.

Jeffry understood sunshine to be a kind of medicine, a balm against depression and a source of vitamin D. He made it a practice to sit in a chair in his backyard every morning within the small patch of ground which received direct sun. He closed his eyes and allowed the sun to warm his face and heat his head, almost until they burned. If he got out early enough, he imagined he saw jewels of sunlight nurturing the surrounding plants before blending in with the sky's spreading illumination, a process opposite to what he witnessed in the late afternoon. He didn't take such visions seriously—he was a hermit hiding away in his nonconforming nest, and therefore prone to exaggerated experiences.

Late afternoons the darkness spread from shadows beneath the bushes and trees and drifted down in soft gradients from the sky. If the weather was warm enough the crickets took over and sang the night into full, black bloom.

He had a working fireplace, but he was afraid to use it. What if he fell asleep and some embers tumbled from the grate? But a good fire might be a welcome comfort. The Neanderthals, didn't they require fire to survive? Perhaps not. They were shorter, stockier than modern day humans and much better suited to the European cold. Fire was useful, for cooking, for toolmaking, and for keeping the night at bay.

He familiarized himself with all the sounds his house made, the furnace coming on, the buzz of various bulbs and electrical appliances, the creaking, and the groans of old timbers as they settled and resettled their bargains with gravity, the thumps and the cries and the weeping. He thought if he catalogued these noises, he would feel less alarmed by their presence in the dark. But every stray sound seemed the beginning of a nocturne he'd deal with poorly if heard when half-asleep. His own company kept him constantly nervous.

Every evening as bedtime approached, Jeffry practiced certain rituals meant to both distract and calm him. He had his dinner early so a full stomach would not keep him awake. He listened to music on the radio, but he avoided the chat shows and their endless opinions. He read copiously but stopped the last hour before bed to prevent an excess accumulation of language. He double-checked the security of doors and windows, and he took a last look outside, even when it was too dark to see anything. The air under the trees was opaque and inky.

Once the downstairs routine was complete Jeffry turned out the lights and negotiated the steep stairs, never looking back. It occurred to him how the second story would someday become inaccessible because of his aging legs, and he would need to sleep downstairs. Even on the second level the lights failed to reach the corners so any intruders would have numerous places to hide. The upstairs hallway felt narrower at night. Some nights it seemed he could hardly squeeze through. He became less nimble every day. He ran into furniture whose locations appeared to change without warning. Shadows which had once been mere nuisance became obstacles.

Every night he hoped for dreams to sweep him away from worries over the noises and the hidden things meaning him harm. He slept naked because it seemed to make it easier to slip into dream. He kept his clock near, referring to it every time he was startled awake so he would know how many hours he had left to bear.

Every night he heard someone coming up the stairs, someone forcing their way in, someone trying to open a window, someone pounding a door, jiggling a knob, kneeling beside his bed hiding their presence. He didn't know what they wanted—he owned little—but older people often presented as victims. Thieves and murderers were drawn to the aged like flies to rotten meat.

He needed something new to happen. Even something negative might lead to positive change. He was certain she'd spoken his name. Forgetting his nakedness, he got out of bed and went to the window.

She stood beneath the trees. She looked familiar, but he couldn't remember her name. Was she a neighbor?

Things were wrong with her appearance. She resembled some sort of negative image. The next morning, he remembered getting up in the night but wasn't sure if he'd actually seen her. Perhaps he hadn't left his bed at all. His dreams were numinous, compelling, but incomplete.

In winter, after the trees lost their leaves, Jeffry was surprised by how many branches hid beneath the missing foliage. The complexity of their intermingling limbs seemed an impossibility, as if the sky had fractured.

The biggest change was now he could see the sidewalk and the street in front, and the people and cars passing by, although they looked much further away than he knew they were. His was the last house, on the corner. He'd always heard corner houses were the ones most frequently robbed. In the distance was the M house across Alphabet Row. An elementary school lay beyond. Children were always walking down the Row towards the library. He often heard them, but almost never saw them.

He had not seen the woman under the trees again, although he looked for her every night. He hadn't decided whether she'd been there, but the possibility nagged him, and the search became part of his routine. Every morning he lay in bed, staring at the ceiling, listening. The sounds he heard were not that different from the ones he heard at night—creaking and breathings and footsteps on the stairs—yet they seemed less ominous in daylight. In fact, there were far more sounds to sort through, traffic on a distant highway, children on the school playground, people on the sidewalk out front, the noise from neighboring yards. None of it particularly sinister.

When Jeffry eventually climbed out of bed, he did so gingerly, as if not to awaken whatever might be sleeping in his house. A nonsensical notion, but it persisted. His feet were numb in the morning, not quite ready for the floor. Once he put on his shoes they felt better, but his footsteps made too much noise.

He wasted an hour or two each day sitting by the large front window, watching. There wasn't much traffic. Many people preferred to walk. A number carried book bags as they made their way to and from the old library. As much as Jeffry was intrigued by the building and the books which might be found there, he hadn't yet worked up the nerve to go.

A few couples walked by, the younger ones holding hands. They didn't understand what was in store for them. The older people appeared to walk together but separately, intent on their own missions. Many of the pedestrians were women. He paid special attention to them, looking for some resemblance to the female apparition who'd lingered beneath the trees, but it was difficult to draw comparisons with these quite real women under the harsh glare of daylight.

Now and then, one would pause on the sidewalk and glance his way. It was some distance, so he wasn't afraid of being seen, but if they smiled, he felt foolishly encouraged. He assumed many locals never saw his house when the trees had their full complement of leaves, and so were curious what the place looked like. As far as he could tell his was much like the other houses, at least the few two-story ones. The houses on this street were lettered rather than numbered—he'd never seen such an arrangement before. But he didn't know what his house letter was—that character was long gone, and for some reason it wasn't on the deed. All his paperwork referred to an outdated lot number. When he called for grocery deliveries, he referred to it as "the house on the corner with all the trees out front" and they knew which one he meant.

Perhaps that explained why he never received any mail. He had a cell phone but used online grocery lists and text messages to order food, and seemed to have been spared the unwanted sales calls which plagued the modern world.

None of this seemed entirely natural. He couldn't always distinguish his days from a pointless, languorous dream. He was eager to see the woman under the trees again, no matter if she were real or not.

Despite his fears his life was best at night. Even when he woke up in the middle of the night, terrified, at least he felt something. His breath quickened and his heart beat with urgency. It also seemed his thoughts were far more interesting between nine p.m. and dawn. Ideas and perceptions came in such a flood he couldn't keep track. He'd leave notes to read the next day, but most were illegible.

One night in midwinter he peered out his bedroom window and saw the woman moving across his front yard. She had a paler look, and moved among the trees haphazardly, as if a long twist of newspaper caught in the wind. He might have thought she was no more than a bit of trash, but he heard the fretful sounds she made, distressed weeping, and moans of disappointment. Twice the twisted debris turned its face to look at him as if wanting something.

He threw on his bathrobe and raced down the stairs, risking catastrophe. The open front door made him stop. Had someone gotten inside or—as unlikely as it seemed—had she come from inside his house? He went out into the yard in his bare feet. The rough frozen ground felt like broken glass. He had trouble breathing, his chest seizing with a fierce cold pain. He stayed out as long as he dared, but he did not find her.

He turned on all the lights when he got back inside and searched the house. He found no traces of a break-in, or indications of any kind that another person had been in his home. He left the lights on, unable to sleep the rest of the night. There seemed to be several possibilities, but none appealed.

The rest of that evening and all the next day Jeffry spent looking out his windows from various angles, thinking an optical illusion involving distortions in the glass and accidental geometries might be involved. His neck was sore from straining to see what wasn't there. When he grew exhausted, he searched his problematic closets on the off chance the woman might be living in one. He discovered items he did not recognize but assumed they'd been left by the previous owner: old china, men's leather gloves, a hairbrush, an old hatchet head, a spade with a cracked blade, and a rope studded with hard, blood-stained knots. Perhaps these things had been hers. Had he overheard her mumbled prayers or was that his imagination?

During the next few weeks Jeffry suffered from extended bouts of narcolepsy, unable to stay awake for days, so numb with worry over what the night might bring he could not keep his eyes open. He would wake up in the dark not knowing where he was, having lost hours, in a chair or on the couch and more than a few times lying on the floor. The experience was humiliating. For safety he began spending most of his time in his bedroom, lying down on the bed at the first sign of somnolence or even a noticeable period of inattention.

He stopped having dreams, or perhaps his waking experiences were his dreams and those periods of dead unconsciousness his newly awakened life.

One day he woke up to numerous sharp objects littering the bedroom floor: fragmented metal and broken glass, pins and needles and knife blades and jagged bone.

Another morning his pajama sleeve was nailed to the headboard. That same morning, he could not feel his nose. When he examined his face in the mirror, he saw that his nose was there, but it had been nibbled on, altering its shape. Dried blood caked his nose, cheeks, and chin. After this event Jeffry couldn't smell anything after dark. Either his nose had been ruined, or the scents themselves had translated into something else.

His life had departed any sense of a consistent narrative. His clock had stopped running. He had no idea how long ago. Not that these human-conceived numerals had any meaningful relationship to time. If it felt like nine a.m. when he woke up, it was nine a.m. Surely somewhere on this vast world it was nine o'clock something.

After the narcolepsy passed, he noticed he could stay awake for days. He sat cross-legged on his bed and stared out the window through the trees and to the street and houses beyond and the neighborhoods beyond and even the skies and fields beyond the city. He couldn't remember having been able to see so much before. He used a small hand mirror to examine his eyes. The pupils were hard to catch the way they kept darting around, anxious to witness everything. It felt as if they were two untamed creatures over which he could no longer claim ownership.

Black ink began to drip from one pupil and then from the other. The ink streamed down—he was literally weeping ink—over his chest and over his bed, flooding the floor and pouring out the window until nature itself disappeared into the endlessly spilling ink. Night had arrived again, and with nothing left to see Jeffry fell back asleep and slept for days or maybe even longer, it was hard to say with his clock stopped.

When he awakened again, he could not open his eyes without nausea. He had reached the nadir of his season, it seemed, when he understood he could feel no worse, and could look forward to a climb back into normalcy.

He practiced opening his eyes slowly until he could keep them open without getting sick. He mustered enough determination to put his clothes and shoes on, thinking that increased his chances of having a normal day.

Outside his window a noirish quiet had settled in. It appeared to be late afternoon, the air looking heavily polluted, but he decided it was only fine bits of darkness, the first suggestions of evening. There appeared to be more black silhouettes of trees than the nine he owned, or at least more limbs, multiplying as the darkness deepened.

He crouched on the floor by the window, at first self-conscious being seen from the yard or the street. He considered turning out the bedroom light, but he heard the front door open, and saw her rushing out into the yard, arms stretched overhead in dismay, a sound like wind pushing in front of her, but he grasped immediately she was making that soft howl.

He got downstairs as quickly as his stiff legs would allow, but this time he slipped into a coat and woven cap. She was still making a mournful noise, and it was certain to draw the neighbors, and the idea of meeting them under such circumstances disturbed him more than the less than substantial female standing in his yard.

"What can I ..." He paused, the sound of his own voice unsettling. He couldn't remember the last time he'd heard it. The figure fell silent and moved deeper into the trees.

He couldn't tell what she was pointing at, so he stood beside her, and it was difficult to focus on anything but the way the minimal light from his window lit her form, reflecting an eye, a bit of her open mouth, shining through most of her torso so he saw more ground than belly, more tree trunk than leg. Then there were the bruises: dead black splotches on her face, neck, and shoulders where no light shone through. He shouldn't have stared, but he hadn't been this close to anyone, and certainly not a woman, in more than a year, so he had to force himself to look at the exposed roots of the first tree, where a fragment of discolored hip bone lay revealed, much like a piece of stone, but he had no doubts what it was. Nearby lay scattered finger and toe bones like worn pebbles—he couldn't remember their names—and above a limb penetrated a section of yellowed sternum with a few attached ribs, and an entire mandible wedged into a fork further up the tree which would have to remain because he had no way of getting it down.

Because that was what she wanted wasn't it? All this evidence brought inside, all this dirty laundry, so the neighbors wouldn't see, and ask their nosy questions, and call the police.

———

Jeffry had never seen such a snowstorm, a hard wind, and blinding white blasts lasting for days. The storm made him nearsighted. He couldn't see anything beyond their trees, beyond their yard.

The wind died down, and seeing how the white clung to almost everything, so bright it hurt the eyes, Jeffry considered how the landscape looked like a reverse night. No human beings, no creatures of any kind were in evidence. He might have been staring at an expansive still life. The neighborhood had become a necropolis. He remained inside, cozy within the nest they'd made.

He was a novice at this. He didn't know what he was doing. He followed her lead.

He did not know her name. He supposed he could call the realtor who sold him the house or do a little research at the local library, but he didn't think it mattered. She had lost her reticence. She often sat at the table with him at meals. He set a place for her with one of those cracked china plates from the closet. It was a ridiculous thing to do he supposed, but she did sit there and stare at the plate as if recalling past meals. She spent most of her time wandering the house, floating up and down those stairs. Sometimes it looked more like falling—was that how she'd met her death?

Sometimes she lay in bed with him. They did nothing untoward. He felt her tickling his nape as if seeking entrance into his skull, but he could have told her she was already there. Touching her left his fingertips numb.

Had she killed an abusive husband? That's what the few details he had would suggest. But it was an interpretation from too few facts. Human beings made up stories out of a need to know, but it did not mean they had acquired any degree of truth.

Other people looking at his story might pity him, might think his personal narrative a sorry excuse for a life. But did they know their lovers any better? Were their lovers any more real? Like everyone else he lived at the nexus of now and yesterday and only imagined what he knew.

Dust continued to accumulate. Spiderwebs filled the corners. The front steps overgrew with nettles and rabbitbrush. Neither had a knack for housework it seemed. Night and day blended into long stretches of sepia.

He wondered if she would let him know when he died. He might not recognize it otherwise.

O is for Occult

It was hard to miss the large wooden O mounted by the door of the bungalow. O as in obedient, onerous, obscene. The stain along the bottom of the letter conjured an image of ragged teeth and a tongue. Gray and black rotting leaves filled one side of the porch. The window screens were rusted and torn. An omnipresent carelessness suggested abandonment, but this was the address she'd been given. It was nothing like what she'd expected. It didn't appear sinister enough.

Before she reached the door, it opened. A thin man in a gray suit too small for him gazed up at her. "Miss Whyte?"

"Please, Darla."

"Come in Miss Whyte. Welcome to Pembroke House."

The interview took place in the front room, at a card table with two folding chairs. A sleeping bag and bathrobe lay folded in a nearby corner. The wood-paneled walls were decorated with a variety of African, Northwest tribal, and Inuit spirit masks. It was bitter cold, but as far as she could tell the furnace wasn't on and the fireplace was dark. She zipped her coat up to her throat. With growing impatience, Darla watched the man study two sheets of paper covered in dense handwriting. Finally, he looked up. "Are you married?"

"Nope."

"Boyfriend? Girlfriend? Children?"

"No to all three. Happily, purposefully unattached. If you're trying to find out if anyone might miss me enough to call the police, well, that won't be a problem. I have no one."

He scribbled a note in the margin of one of the sheets. "Do you drink or use drugs?"

"No." She'd come from an AA meeting. She'd lied to them as well.

"And you're a student at the university? Religious Studies?"

"I am. All independent study. I don't go to classes." The thought of attending class, with *classmates*, made her shudder.

"And you'll be working at the library down the street as well?"

"I'll be doing some cataloguing for them, yes."

"Eve Pembroke was the original head librarian."

"I know. It's one of the reasons I want to work there. Her book collection is here, right? In her old house? My faculty advisor promised I would get to use it."

"Professor Jay Douglas, yes. A good friend of the Institute. You will have unfettered access to her books on the premises, but you must never take them from this house, or bring in any outside materials from the library or any other source whatsoever. We cannot risk … contamination."

She was beginning to suspect he might be an officious prick. Darla did not obey rules, especially silly ones. "Of course. I promise."

"Your event occurred ten years ago, when you were twelve years of age?"

"By *event*, if you mean my *exorcism*, yes."

He frowned but kept his eyes on the papers. "Have you experienced your first period?"

"I was having my first period at the time of the exorcism. It made it quite memorable. I didn't know. I thought that's the way it was going to be *every* month. Can you imagine?" He frowned but said nothing. "Why? Does that disqualify me?"

He looked surprised. "No, not at all. That's what it says here. I just need to verify."

"Does it also say that my mother, my own mother, performed that exorcism *because* I was having my first period?"

"Yes, yes it does. And unfortunately, this resulted in your mother's demise?"

"*The demon fucking ate her!*" Darla hadn't intended to shout. But this was a big deal in her life, and it demanded acknowledgement.

He gazed at her unblinking, as if he could see right through her. "My condolences." He glanced at the papers in his hand again, then folded them into thirds and slid them into his coat pocket. "Perhaps you would like me to show you the ... well, it's in the next room."

"Is that it? Have I been hired?"

"The Institute does not want you to think of this as a job interview. It is far more important than that. You may move your things in at any time. It will be up to he-who-comes whether you shall remain. Only he can judge you as a vessel."

"So like any other man."

"He is not a man. Do not make that mistake."

"I know not all demons are male."

"Correct. Females certainly exist. *Ardat Lili, Batibat, Empusa, Lamashgtu, Lilitu,* several others."

"So, which one are we angling for?"

"I haven't been informed, I'm afraid."

"Above your pay grade, huh? No blood oath, no ironclad NDA?"

He didn't answer. He turned and walked toward the frosted French doors at the back of the room.

"Hey! Was I the only candidate?"

He looked over his shoulder, clearly annoyed. "I am not allowed to say." He flung open the doors.

It was a beautiful room, probably the original dining room, done in the Craftsman style with box-beams across the ceiling, intricate molding, an arts and crafts chandelier, and built-in bookcases around the perimeter. The curtains were open, exposing stained glass. Red and blue rays patterned the books, those gorgeous volumes in their worn leather bindings with raised cords.

The massive emblem which covered most of the oak floor was from a different design tradition entirely. A thick layer had been scraped away from the surface of the dark boards to expose their much lighter interior. At first glance this scraping appeared frantic and uneven, as if animals had been confined here. But when she looked closely, she saw the depth of excavation was consistent over the entire design, and the finer scratches radiating from the circumference created a halo effect which must have been purposeful.

Superimposed over this thoroughly worked area was a complex engraved design of interlocking oval mandalas containing interior circles and squares. Darla couldn't quite figure out how these onion-like layers had been accomplished. They appeared both raised above the scraped area and embedded deep within it, the appearance changing as she walked around the outer edge. The design was suggestive of celestial navigation. Within each mandala were countless internal connecting lines, fine as hairs. Depending on where she stood, she thought she could see various figures worked into the design: exotic creatures, landscapes, and architecture which transformed as she moved.

There were hooks embedded in the floor at various connecting points. "Those hooks are where you'll be tying me down?"

"Oh, there are no such plans. Ms. Pembroke had someone tie her to those hooks, or she tied herself. We don't know. But all we want you to do is to take notes concerning anything you see, hear, or feel while you are staying here. If some sort of possession were to occur, you would then receive the proper guidance."

"Guidance from whom? I'm surrounded by higher powers, it seems. Everyone thinks they know what's best for me, and I'm supposed to trust them."

He shrugged. "Honestly, I have no idea. As you so succinctly phrased it, above my pay grade." He gave her the keys. "If you don't mind my asking, why do you want to do this? Especially given your traumatic history. I realize that was one reason you were selected, but why put yourself through that again?"

Darla smiled. "My therapist thought it would be a good idea. She's tried everything else."

"This is a *terrible* idea," Dr. Sorros said. "Don't do this, Darla." She waited for Darla to respond, but Darla had learned her therapist couldn't bear the silence and would eventually speak. Increasingly this woman reminded her of her mother. Overdressed and too sure of herself.

While waiting for her doctor to speak again (the poor woman couldn't help herself), Darla glanced at her bookcase: *Trauma Treatment, Attachment, Diversity in Clinical Practice, Psychopharmacology, High Risk Clients,* bound volumes of *Psychological Medicine, The Lancet Psychiatry,* and *Clinical*

Psychology Review. Those were shelved either quite high or quite low.

Arranged on the easy-to-reach shelves, among scattered romance novels, were titles like *The Silva Mind Control Method*, *Crystals for Beginners*, Linda Goodman's *Sun Signs*, and *The Secret*. Not for the first time Darla wondered how she'd gotten stuck with such a crap therapist.

"I respect your beliefs, Darla, but as I've told you before this is outside my area of expertise. Demonic possession is not a valid psychiatric or medical diagnosis recognized by either the DSM-5 or the ICD-10."

Darla struggled to control her temper. "My mother was trying to get the bad stuff out of me. Open me up like an abscess to release the pus. But that allowed more infection to come in. The doctors at first thought I had epilepsy, or Tourette's. My OB-GYN thought I might be pregnant! I lost memories. Christ, I was having fits! I could use a good purging, don't you think?"

"I know it may seem as if a supernatural being took control of you when you had those attacks, but isn't an explanation other than the occult possible? You were deeply traumatized. Mental distress is a common response to such trauma."

"Nothing you've done has helped me!" She got out of her chair and went to the bookcase. "How can you read this crap? Can't you feel your brain rotting?"

"Darla, please return to your seat."

"Yes ma'am." She sat primly, hands on her knees. "My life needs purpose. I need to count for something. Maybe this new occupation, adventure, whatever you want to call it, can point me in the right direction."

"I know you love books—"

"I don't always understand what I'm thinking. I don't always recognize my thoughts as my own thoughts. Books speak to me—I find myself in *them*."

"I've suggested journaling before. Writing down your innermost feelings, your ordinary thoughts, might reconnect you, discourage your habit of obfuscating. Also, some exercise, walks in nature—"

"I need new drugs. I still have a lot of pain from my exorcism. Can you help me with that, Doc?"

"Clearly opioids are not the answer. How is AA going, by the way?"

"Wonderful! Brilliant! I can't remember the last time I had a drink."

———

Darla hoped the Queneau librarian couldn't smell the alcohol on her breath. She'd used mouth wash, coffee, peanut butter. Those usually did the trick, but some people had better olfactory abilities than others. She was convinced her brain worked better after a few drinks. Alcohol possessed her just enough to be useful.

Ms. Reynolds wore a 3D-printed plastic compression mask strapped to her head to cover her severe facial burns. No one warned Darla. The most surprising thing about the transparent mask was how much Darla envied it. It allowed enough of the underlying flesh to show through, and yet the damage, and her likeness, were nicely obscured.

"It's really quite lovely," Darla said, after Ms. Reynolds provided a brief, matter-of-fact explanation of what had happened to her. The librarian's home lay in ruins across the street, her son, the presumed fire starter, still missing.

"Thank you, but we needn't speak of my injuries again. You have a time-consuming job ahead of you. Professor Douglas says you have extensive experience with the evaluation and cataloging of fragile collections?"

"I'm well-versed, yes." Jay had exaggerated her part-time junior college library experience considerably. She was nervous about whatever repayment he expected. "And I have a lifelong passion for knowledge and learning."

"Very good." The rattle of the birdcage elevator made conversation difficult. Darla worried there might not be an escape option if it stopped working. She could feel her claustrophobia blooming.

The cage opened and they stepped out. There was a pronounced odor: sour musk, mold, and was that oysters? Ms. Reynolds flipped the light switch and various grimy bulbs struggled to burn. The Gothic architecture might have once been opulent: pointed arches and ribbed vaults, ornate iron brackets which were now badly oxidized. The walls had been drabbed down with olive-colored paint randomly applied. The books Darla could see were a mix of the common and the obscure, inconsistently arranged.

"This is the second basement. You'll start here. The level above, for all its mess, will be less of a challenge. The contents of the level below have mostly liquified, I'm afraid, due to frequent water incursions. There is at least one level below that, completely flooded and lost."

"What's the caged area in the corner?"

"Ms. Pembroke made it her office space. It hasn't been touched since her demise. The shelves contain some of our more outré items. It's where you'll be working. No one will bother you. My staff refuses to come down here. Perform light repairs if you will, but most will require expert conservation. At best you'll have chipped and bowing boards to contend with, foxing, wormholes, that sort of thing. Many are in disastrous shape. Are you familiar with Ms. Pembroke's studies?"

Darla could barely contain herself. She'd expected Pembroke's items either to be lost or off-limits. "She's part of my independent study. Early twentieth century female occult investigators."

"So, you believe in demons and evil and all that?"

"Evil is a human construct. I don't know if there is a spiritual evil or not. Perhaps it's simply a set of behaviors we do not understand. What do you believe?"

The librarian didn't answer. Darla started to turn around to make sure Reynolds was still there when she heard, "I'm not a believer in much of anything. I'll leave you to your work. If you need anything just come upstairs. And remember, none of these materials can leave this room."

Darla turned and smiled. "Of course not. They're safe with me."

She spent the next few hours searching Pembroke's cage. She found the sketches, notes, and diagrams Jay told her about, secreting them inside the lining of her coat. They smelled bad. She hoped the stench wouldn't alert any of the staff when she left the building.

———

Professor Jay Douglas stood before the blazing Pembroke House fireplace, a glass of wine in his hand. He'd stripped down to his tighty-whities. Darla thought he resembled an unattractive Oberon.

Darla was drunk, but not *that* drunk. "Put your pants back on, Jay. I'm not having sex with you or anybody else. To be blunt, I don't like things *inside*—"

"That's an unsophisticated view of sex. There are other—"

"Jay!"

He stared at her, looking disappointed, and finished his drink. While he was sitting on the ottoman getting dressed, Darla continued her study of the papers she'd stolen from the library along with some related volumes she'd pulled from the

Pembroke House shelves. "How are your classes going, all the ones I don't have to attend thanks to you?"

"None of the students are up to your standards of course, although many think they are. Charles, the one you hate, is worse than ever. He thinks he can get away with anything, the snobby little prick."

"Maybe we should use Charles for a trial run. Tie him to the floor and see what happens."

"I wish." Jay had his pants on, but his shirt was still off. He was standing next to her now, a little too close. "Some spirits *delight* in causing suicide."

She stepped away from him. "I won't traffic in that." Although a test subject was not a bad idea.

"Sweetheart, you don't know what you want. You never have. You needed someone to protect you—you never had that. But I'm here now. I'm the one who can protect you."

His words almost appealed to her. That was the frightening thing. "That thing my mother brought into me, when it left it took from me something essential. If I get it back I won't need your help or anyone else's."

"You don't know if it's the same demon, or a demon at all."

"I've read all of Pembroke's notes. She did this more than once you know. She experienced numerous visitations from the same creature. The size and the shape, what facial features she could make out, even the smell of it. I'm sure it's the same."

"Don't be obdurate. It could be a hungry ghost, or a *dybbuk*, a refugee from the other side needing a physical body it can use. Maybe it was someone who died a drunk, a parasite who wants to be able to drink through you via spiritual osmosis. You know Pembroke was an alcoholic, too."

"What? Get out of here! I don't need you to doubt my scholarship, especially not now." He didn't budge, but stepped closer, looking down on her. He'd done this before, his way to dominate.

She tried to slap him, but he grabbed both her wrists. "I *understand*. You're *torn*. She almost killed you. But you're an orphan. You miss her. You don't want to hurt me. You love me. You would never hurt me."

Darla gazed up at him, barely in control of her anger. "You really *see* me, don't you? No, I could *never* hurt you."

———

They drank some more. A lot more. Jay drank everything she put into his hand. He casually tried to undress her. She kept pushing him away.

She talked him into sitting on the floor. "If we pass out we'll have a shorter distance to fall." He laughed but kept complaining about the hooks snagging his pants and tearing his skin.

She put on one of the African masks, a brightly painted surprised look with a wide-open mouth and enormous eye holes. He stared at her dumbly, then exploded into hysterics, falling over, nearly out. She gently spread his legs, pushed his arms to ten and two. "Oh, darling," he murmured in a distorted voice. She took out the rope and stretched it through the hooks and over his body, testing various star patterns and pentagrams, studying Pembroke's drawings, trying to match them. Finally, she had a design similar to the last, most complex sketch of the series. She hoped it was similar enough. "Professor Douglas, how do you feel?"

He groaned. "Snug. It's … snug. Can't move."

"Perfect."

She positioned the candles at the prescribed points and read aloud a few passages in Latin from a volume with tattered edges and a badly water-damaged leather cover. Her Latin was a little rusty, but Jay's was not. She watched his eyes widen as he began to realize what she was doing.

"Darla, untie me." She enjoyed hearing, then felt vaguely guilty about, the shakiness in his voice.

"Of course. After we're done."

She had the books and papers stacked and marked in order according to Pembroke's notes. At first she'd been annoyed by the woman's marginalia, a nervous, jagged scrawl marring most of these rare, priceless books. But those jottings proved essential. She didn't understand half of what she was saying or if she was pronouncing the words correctly, but hoped her passion and commitment counted for something. Other than a few passages from the gospels of Matthew, Mark, and Luke, the items were rare and esoteric, including a 1702 edition *Grand Grimoire*, *The Munich Manual*, *The Book of Soyga*, *The Picatrix*, taped together photocopies from the gigantic *Codex Gigas*, and something Pembroke referred to as *The Orange Book*, handwritten in French bearing no publisher's colophon, bound in the skin of an orangutan.

"Pembroke *died* during the rite!" Jay squirmed, fruitlessly trying to loosen the rope.

"We don't know that Jay. All we know is she disappeared. I expect a bit more precision in the pronouncements of a tenured professor."

Twenty minutes into the rite he began spouting nonsense, or she simply didn't recognize the words. "Jay, honey, what language is that?" He stared at her with bloodshot eyes, then spoke more gibberish.

His face began to change. Subtly at first: a raised eyebrow, a thicker lip, the eyes morphing into different shapes and colors. When Jay began to resemble her mother, Darla didn't want to see it. She ran and took the Inuit spirit mask off the wall and placed it over his face. The mask was distorted, lopsided, consistent with the warping flesh underneath. Still, Jay wouldn't shut up. "You were always a whore, even at twelve! You lie to everyone! You've always lied!" It was her mother's voice.

The voice grew huskier and more hateful. "I ate your mother and I'll eat you too." The eyes peering from the holes in the mask had lost their whites to pools of ochre, the giant obsidian pupils bulging.

His body took on an odious aspect, his belly swelling unevenly. She was embarrassed that it made her grin, thinking about this misogynistic male suffering some of the more uncomfortable indignities of pregnancy. His skin rippled as he expelled an offensive gas. Beneath the mask he produced an orchestra of sounds which should have been impossible for any human tongue.

He went still for several minutes, the skin of his torso so pale and bloodless she thought he might be dead. She hadn't intended to murder him. This was supposed to be a test run before she performed the same ritual on herself.

She hadn't thought this through. Instead of checking for a pulse she became distracted by her errors, her lack of preparation for contingencies. She'd have to record herself reading the passages—no way could she memorize all that. She could light the candles before she lay down inside the pattern. How could she tie herself down?

But the essential thing about the rope was not its security, but the pattern it made. With enough practice she might be able to thread the pattern while propped up on one elbow, then tighten the rope when she lay down. It might take hours, even days of practice beforehand, but she thought she could manage it.

Or maybe she just needed to sucker some horny and bookish college kid into helping her. Whatever was required, she would get back what had been taken from her all those years ago.

Jay began to weep. Faintly at first. At least he was still alive. She could hardly hear him. But as the volume increased ... where had she heard that voice? That little girl's voice coming out of a grown man's mouth. That shy, awkward, polite, soft-spoken little girl.

Darla leaned over, pulled aside the ropes framing his head, and jerked the mask away to expose the smallish face.

It had been her face when she was only twelve, before the innocence and the kindness had been stolen away. She'd made a terrible mistake. The little girl she had been was now irretrievably stuck in him, and it was her own damn fault.

P is for Phantasies

Six months following his death I began having my father's dreams. I hadn't seen him in years, but to my surprise he left his house to me. It's an understatement to say we were estranged. My father was a monster.

The house was a small bungalow built sometime between the world wars on Alphabet Row, where the homes are lettered rather than numbered. Twenty-six of them. I thought it peculiar, but quaint. Some displayed a large wooden letter by the front door. Dad's place was #P. His P was a couple of feet tall and several inches thick, covered in cracked and peeling yellow paint. The fat loop on the P recalled the potbelly he had when I was young. I used to imagine he stored his considerable anger there.

When I first arrived, I heard the peeps and chirps coming from that letter, begging calls from a nest of fledglings stuffed inside the loop. No sign of the mother. The letter was an ugly, rotting thing, but I chose to leave it alone because of those innocent beings.

The first thing I did upon taking possession was to check the backyard for holes, cavities wide and deep enough to trap a little boy inside. Rotting squares of plywood were scattered across the ground, and I looked under each one. Thank God I didn't find a single pit, or a body.

I had never lived here, but for the first few weeks I experienced this discomfiting sensation of déjà vu. Maybe it was Dad's familiar old furniture, or the way he'd arranged things, or the clear evidence of violence in the damaged walls, doors, and woodwork. I could feel his presence, and his absence, his abuse, everywhere. He bought this house after I left high school and moved away. We never spoke after that.

I didn't want this place, but money was tight, and I had no home of my own. He owed me for everything he'd done to me. The house was filthy and full of trash, rotten food, ragged clothing, broken glass, disintegrating furnishings. But it was a small structure, and it didn't take long to make it more or less presentable. I threw a rug over the spot where they found his body.

The first few nights I didn't sleep well. It was still a stranger's home, and even after all that cleaning an unpleasant smell lingered. But eventually fatigue dragged me down into slumber, and then into dream. Normally, I don't remember my dreams, but to my surprise this was about to change.

―――――

I'm a young boy in the nightmare, but I don't feel much like myself. My body is naggingly different. My shoulders hurt, and there are burns on my arms and hands. That much is familiar. He used cigarettes, or sometimes just a lighter to toughen me up.

But I also have a limp. I never had a limp before. I remember my dad had a limp from a bad break which never healed. He never told me how he got it, just that it happened when he was a kid. So I'm like his twin in this dream, a notion which disgusts me.

In the dream I'm walking these dogs, two hulking, snarling brutes. They are so huge I can't control them. They drag me wherever they go. Sometimes they stop, turn their heads and snap at me. Their massive teeth get a little closer to my face each time. I'm terrified. But my father makes me walk them every night. This has become both my chore and my punishment, although I have no idea why I'm being punished. He loves these monsters more than anything, far more than he loves me.

The path is dark and there are few lights. I rely on the full moon and these beasts' sense of direction to guide me through the neighborhood.

Three mountain lions block our path. They have descended from the ridges high above us. They are even larger than my father's dogs who begin to mewl and back up against me as if I might be able to protect them. I don't know what to do, so I drop their leashes and run. Behind me, I hear their human-like screams and the sounds of rending meat.

Later that night, I sneak back into the house. I don't know what my father will do to me, but I'm afraid it will be worse than what the lions did to his dogs. I stop in the hallway and look at myself in the mirror. I've seen that face among the pictures on the mantle. It is my father as a young boy. He is alarmingly skinny and nothing like the big man I remember. His face is so pale it glows.

A large bald man staggers out of the bathroom. I am frozen and cannot move. He is looking my way, but I don't believe he sees me. This is my father, I think, even though I do not recognize him.

The next morning, I could hardly move. I felt as if I'd been beaten. I realized the large bald man in the dream had been my grandfather—I'd seen photos of him with those same ferocious-looking dogs. I couldn't make sense of it. Bad enough my father turned my childhood into a nightmare, but now his nightmares had become my dreams.

But I didn't want to read too much into it. Dreams are mysterious, their rules illogical, and they're ultimately beyond interpretation as far as I'm concerned, despite all the books purporting to explain them. I was living in my father's house. Echoes from his life were bound to appear.

That afternoon, I was up on a ladder on the front porch examining an area where the roof had leaked into the porch ceiling. I carefully peeled away some rotting beadboard, hoping it was something I could fix myself. I heard a distant rumble and then a nearby growl. I got off the ladder and looked around, keeping the prybar in front of me in case I needed to protect myself. The growling continued, and I looked out at the yard and checked the bushes on each side. The noise stopped. I waited, then climbed the ladder again.

The prybar slipped easily between the worst of the rotting boards. I exposed a discolored joist, but it appeared to be merely stained. I pulled down another section, and a large volume of dust exploded in my face. Or was it smoke? It was hot and smelled like smoke.

Wisps of vapor gathered into whiskers, then teeth, then huge milky eyes. The hound's head jerked forward, snapping, and sent me flying off the ladder. I lay on my back, the wind knocked out of me, feeling for pain. I gathered myself and stood up again. I saw the yawning cavity above my head, with nothing protruding, not even smoke. But still I knew I was done for the day.

I heard the growling, or rumbling noise several times over the next week, but I never found a source, and of course I knew there was no vicious dog hiding behind my porch ceiling. Sometimes when you're anxious you see things, and I'd understandably been anxious since moving into my father's house. But it was my house now, wasn't it? My house.

I knew I was spending too much time alone. I hadn't planned it that way. I just hadn't made any friends in the neighborhood yet. I'd gotten a new job working from home. The company required me to come in once a month for in-person meetings. Most people would envy me, but spending too much time alone, you get a little panicky. You lose confidence in your ability to hear or see things accurately.

———

The boy who is not me is in the pit again. Or I am. I can't always tell the difference. But of course, I've been here before. I know what the inside of one of my father's pits looks like. I know this setting so well: the slick muddy sides of the pit, that disgusting liquid texture impossible to climb. When it rains, even with the plywood cover my father drops over the opening, a few inches of water get in, and I shake uncontrollably, especially when he leaves me in here overnight. I don't know what we've done to deserve such a punishment—probably nothing at all. I scream and scream, but no one comes. I don't know whether they can't hear me, or if they don't care.

A flagstone covers the bottom of the pit. This is my father's version of kindness. I can crouch on the stone and avoid most of the standing water. The boy who is not me is even skinnier than me, able to fold himself into a small, inconsequential package, where he can sleep and dream his dreams within dreams.

I know something which most do not: dirt has its own distinctive voice. If you know how to listen, you can hear its laments: how we bury our secrets here, how no one knows all the mysteries dirt contains, how weary the dirt is of our cruelty and murder.

Sometimes I answer and the dirt answers back. But it offers no sympathy. The dirt doesn't care.

In the morning, the plywood is lifted, and I stare up into the face of my grandfather: his hairless head, his small dark eyes, his brutish jowls. Now I understand where my father got the idea for the pit.

———————

In the days which followed I found small, muddy footprints on the back porch and in the kitchen, and once in a staggered trail leading to my bed. Muddy handprints, or paw prints, splattered the edges of my sheets. I thought it was possible they belonged to some animal, although I could find no other signs of the creature. It seemed unlikely they belonged to a little boy. But I still re-examined the backyard anyway looking for holes. Every morning a milky mist rose from the ground and filled the backyard. The bordering trees appeared as no more than streaks of charcoal on a white canvas.

Several mornings in a row I was awakened by a distinctive, sharp barking in my left ear. I received a reprimand for consistently not signing in to work on time. I had no idea what I'd been doing all those mornings. I hadn't been sleeping. Or had I?

The growling returned sporadically. I tried to ignore it. Maybe there was some rational explanation for the sound I hadn't yet discovered: air in the pipes, some loose boards, a mechanical issue with the refrigerator's compressor. At least it gave me an excuse for continuing repairs and improvements— I figured during the course of the work I'd stumble upon an answer. Every spare moment I wasn't on the computer for work I was doing something around the house: painting walls, replacing carpet, prying up boards, installing new flooring, tearing into plaster.

At the end of the day, I'd fall into bed exhausted, but sleep was fitful and full of stories. I never felt rested the next day. The dreams were more exhausting than my labors had been.

At some point the growling morphed into a kind of loud snoring, like some giant was sleeping fitfully in the next room. The hissing and the throat sounds were extended, and troubling to hear, as if this unseen behemoth were in a desperate struggle to breathe.

I always thought of the house I grew up in as a kind of cave, a man's house, a manspace. A man cave. This place felt much the same, my father's final burrow, a hole suitable for animals to live in, where some growls were to be expected. Missing a woman's softness, a woman's touch. I never knew my mother. If she had lived a little longer maybe things would have been different. If I could have seen her at least once, maybe I'd have some memories of her now. My father would never talk about her. He didn't keep any photographs of her as far as I know. Was that why I was being punished? Because my birth had killed her?

Even on nights I couldn't sleep, I lay unprotected from his dreams. In the dark, the dreams walked and wept. They filled the house and spilled over into the yard. Yet they brought me no closer to understanding him. He had been like the weather, elemental and unreliable. The smallest things would set him off: a dirty dish, a misplaced jacket, a Sunday newspaper left out of order. I failed him in every way imaginable, at least in his eyes. More than once he'd described his punishments as his "duty as a father."

A forest has taken over the living room. A white vapor passes slowly through the trees. Deep within these woods, I hear a monster snarling, but I cannot find the creature responsible. I sweep up the pinecones and leaves and needles and the other debris the trees drop and take them out to the trash. This house will never be entirely clean, completely tame, nor will it ever be fully mine.

It begins to rain. The windows are shiny with tears. Periodically, I have to scrape the remains of suicidal birds from the floor.

I follow a path into the bedroom, intending to rest. Life in the forest takes a lot out of you. It is not the same bed my father slept in; I was wise enough to replace it. But it is in the same spot. I start to lie down when I notice blood has permeated the bedding. I search the sheets and blankets but find no signs of a corpse, and no signs of a wound.

The phone cries out.

I go to pick it up, but it has hidden itself, not wanting to be touched.

Each day I woke up more tired than the day before. I couldn't keep my eyes open. Lying down for a nap only gave my father's dreams another opportunity for access. Every time I closed my eyes, I was pulled into another dream, losing any possibility for calm.

After many of these dreams, I woke up to an overwhelming stench of booze and urine. It was a smell I knew well from my childhood living with my dad. This stink eventually faded, leaving behind a devastating sadness.

I think I have awakened, and perhaps I have. My bed is in the backyard beneath an overcast sky, surrounded by withering trees. I know they are dying, but I have no idea why. Some turn into smoke even as I am watching them.

The bed begins to sink into the ground. I try to get off, but the sheets are wrapped around my legs holding me down. I can barely move.

The bed continues to sink with increasing speed. Walls of mud rise around me, and as the bed descends into the pit it begins to shrink in size. Finally, I am able to kick the covers loose and stand at the center of the ever-diminishing bed. I try to leap for the opening above me, but it is now too far away.

The bed continues to dwindle until it is less than two feet on a side. The walls are closing in. I spin around seeking a solution and come face to face with the skinny little boy again, this early version of my father. This close I can see just how thin he is, so sickly, pale, and trembling from the cold. He is shirtless, and his torso is layered in bruises. Despite our proximity, I try not to touch him.

"Am I going to die now?" he whispers. "I think I am going to die."

I interlace my fingers in front of me, palms up. "Step into my hands. Hurry! I'll boost you up!"

He steps into my hands, and I am shocked by how light he is. He weighs no more than a dream. I jerk my arms upward and he is flying. A few seconds later, his head appears in the tiny opening above. "But how will you get out?"

I sit down on the tiny patch of bed, close my eyes, and try to wake up.

I can feel the rumbling beneath me, a steadily building pressure which makes my ears pop. Within moments I am rocketed upwards in an explosion of mud and water. When I open my eyes again, I'm lying in the muddy field, this diminutive version of my father hovering over me.

"Thanks," he says. "Are you okay?"

I don't want to speak. I struggle to my feet and look around. I am surrounded by shadows, shimmering as they breathe. Above us the sky rolls by so quickly the clouds begin to smear, creating white streaks across my eyeballs. A storm is rapidly descending, full of ragged, squawking birds.

"We should get inside the house," he says.

"Just so you know," I say. "Even with understanding, I can never forgive you."

He stares at me blankly. Of course. He has no idea what I'm talking about. He turns and starts toward the house, and I follow. We cross over numerous holes with their little boy heads protruding. Like eggs, I think, and perhaps just as fragile. I accidentally kick one or two.

"I'm so sorry," I say, but none of them answer.

In our father's house, there are many doors. We're both confused. But finally, we find the front door, the one which leads outside. I race ahead of him. When he doesn't follow, I turn around.

"I can't. I just—" he says, fading into the light. "This is where I live."

———

After many months, I felt settled in. It seemed as if I had lived in this house forever. And after weeks of seemingly dreamless sleep, I had my father's final dream.

The big man is giving me a bath, but he always forgets I can't breathe underwater. Perhaps other children can—I don't know—but I sure can't. Maybe the big man has made an honest mistake.

The big man holds me under and holds me under until the giant black bubbles arrive. The black bubbles take up more and more space until I can't see anything else. I close my eyes. They aren't doing me any good, anyway.

When I open them again, I am at the bottom of the sea. What a wonderful place!

There are caves full of eyes! Trap doors in the seabed hide creatures which peer at me with curiosity. There are fish which are all skeletons, with enormous eyes and teeth! They have the oddest appendages imaginable. If I am going to die—and surely this is what is happening—I might become one of these strange fish myself, if I am lucky.

Sometimes I am chased by bigger fish. There are creatures within shells, and I want to join them. I hide inside a large one. The big fish swim back and forth looking for me.

When the world looks a bit safer, I swim out from the shell, and I swim as far as my diminutive fins will permit. Below me lies the vast ocean floor, and the bodies of the pale little boys who came before me.

To be yourself you must remember who you are. It's not as easy as you think it's going to be.

Q is for Queneau

At seven a.m. Dodge walked to his boss's house on Alphabet Row. It was only a few houses away from his own, but it was foggy, and he hated walking in all that quaggy mist. Even in this short distance, with so many similar homes, it was possible to wind up at the wrong front door, and in this neighborhood that could mean serious consequences. Most of his neighbors didn't understand this, but Dodge knew more than most about the kinds of houses they had on this street, and what they contained.

It was a modest bungalow in decent repair. Nothing special about it other than its owner. The landscaping was a little overgrown, but that's the way the old man liked it. Keeping it at that precise degree of wildness required a great deal of Dodge's time. No power equipment was used, with each plant or branch receiving individualized attention.

The iron Q mounted by the front door was badly corroded, weathered from its original curled dragon shape into that of a dying worm. It was ancient, over a hundred years, but was that old for iron? He didn't know where his boss got the thing, but he should've asked for his money back. Of course, tracking down the original maker was questionable.

He punched in the lengthy security code. The key hung up in the lock but worked after a practiced wiggle. The door scraped slightly as Dodge pushed it in. Both were on his list to fix when and if he got around to them.

The front room was smallish and quaint=looking. Queen Anne style antiques for the most part, not used in years. Dodge dusted them now and then, but neither he nor the nurse were allowed to use them. They were just for show. To show *who*, Dodge had no idea. No one visited. No one would want to visit. According to the stories this rich, inventive man had always been bitter and alone.

The original wall between the single bedroom and the dining room had been taken out, as well as a portion of the kitchen, to accommodate all the equipment. Forty monitors provided rotating views from inside the houses and the Queneau Library, as well as panoramic glimpses of the neighborhood. The bottom row was reserved for internal and external communications. When John D. Queneau could see and hear these monitors provided him with a great deal of entertainment. The monitors were not the latest models, but the standard here was quantity over quality. Some of the houses were also equipped with infrared sensors, both EMF and EVP reader/recorders, and instruments for which there was no settled nomenclature. Everything possible was captured, including the most unlikely data.

When he was first hired Dodge asked him once (as awkward as those initial attempts at communication had been), what was the reason for all this surveillance. Queneau conveyed that since he built these houses he had the right to know what was going on inside them. In those early days on the job Dodge often wondered if the old man got some vicarious thrill from spying, but it was hard to imagine this dour individual thrilled by anything.

Some of the monitors were grayed out. The address at #A was still a burned-out husk, and both #G and #V remained under reconstruction. As part of his compensation package, Dodge's house at #U went unmonitored. This house, #Q, was monitored only for security purposes, with an additional feed going to Dodge's bedroom so that he could evaluate any alarms or emergencies. Many of the residences—like at #I, #R, #S, #W, and #Y—had active feeds, but rarely showed anything. This made up for the houses which regularly showed too much, scenes Dodge never wanted to see again. Queneau had a strict no-interference policy in place, but this did not stop Dodge from placing the occasional quick anonymous call to the police and fire departments, or more frequently, for an ambulance.

There hadn't always been remote monitoring, of course. When the houses were first built in the late twenties and early thirties Queneau employed a staff of snoops and photographers. The first tape recorders were installed in the early Fifties, and a staff of three had the job of interpreting what they heard and filing reports for Mr. Queneau's perusal. Later those reports were bound and stored in a shed at the back of the house. These records were later lost in a fire. The first video monitoring system was installed surreptitiously in the Eighties at great expense. Better technology led to their one-by-one replacement in the Nineties. Part of Dodge's job was to service and replace these cameras as necessary. He hated doing it and tried to find excuses not to. As far as he was concerned, they had no business prying into other people's affairs.

Once the video system was in place Queneau had the wall of monitors installed and let his small group of investigators go with non-disclosure agreements in hand. He much preferred to make the observations himself. This changed in 1993 when John D. Queneau, no longer the young genius/entrepreneur, technically "died" at the age of ninety-four. That was when the really expensive equipment was brought into the house at #Q.

Apparently, his doctors detected a spark, what the resurrected Queneau liked to call a "quark." Something very small, yet quite significant. Which led to all this.

Queneau had been a small man, thin, and slightly over five feet tall. The figure on the narrow bed was even smaller, shrunken, seemingly more homunculus than human. Its color was an orangish brown due to the protective covering which had been applied to the skin, a kind of breathable plastic meant to prevent infection and decay. A metal girdle covered the private parts and took the body's waste away (although the nurse confided to Dodge that very little waste was involved). The body was skinny with almost no body fat, which left the face almost unrecognizable as Queneau (his portrait hung in the front room), but rather a kind of skull mask, thankfully not grinning.

An array of wires and tubing penetrated the body from all angles. They led to a conglomeration of computers and other equipment covering the back wall. These provided nutrition, breathing aid, blood purification, stimulation, communication, data input, and a variety of other functions Dodge had never been privy to. These were the province of the nurse and whatever medical and legal consultants were currently involved. Dodge had very little contact with these people. He suspected they were a collection of quacks, hacks, and opportunists. The nurse, Elaine, had slightly more interaction, although sometimes, she'd confessed, she was afraid maybe they'd been abandoned. But paychecks continued to arrive, bills were paid, and outside services occasionally engaged. Dodge had only the fuzziest of notions as to the administrative structure involved with Queneau's continued maintenance, which was clearly Queneau's original intent.

Dodge determined long ago not to question any of this. His role was *technical assistance*, but he was actually not much more than a glorified janitor and private duty orderly. Elaine's role was far more important, and he treated her as his superior.

Elaine didn't come in today. Dodge advised her not to.

It unsettled Dodge how quiet everything was, far quieter than any ICU. Despite all this equipment the room remained largely silent. No hum of machinery, no pump sounds, no beeps or clicks or alarms. Audio from the monitors was fed directly into whatever complex of processes and materials which currently constituted Queneau's "brain." Signs of life in Queneau's body were subtle. The chest's expansions and contractions were barely detectable. Occasionally an eyelid twitched. Sometimes Dodge thought he'd seen other movements, but Elaine explained those were illusory. "I once did morgue duty. You stare at a dead body long enough, at some point you would swear it moved." Queneau was not dead, yet Dodge found it impossible to think of him as alive.

Dodge had no interest in voyeurism, but he periodically checked the monitors for events he needed to handle, whether with Queneau's permission or not. He would not stand idly by and watch someone become injured or die. His call brought the fire engines to the house at #A across from the library, an act for which he was reprimanded and docked a week's pay.

Queneau knew what Dodge had done. Queneau seemed to know everything, and Dodge wasn't always sure how. His boss rarely took action, but when he did he made sure Dodge was aware that Queneau's personal hand had been in it.

A screen in the bottom row of monitors flashed red and words appeared.

GOOD MORNING DODGE. QUERY: STATUS REPORT?

"Good morning, Mister Queneau. It's been relatively quiet. Some new graffiti on the north exterior wall of the library. I'll take care of it this afternoon."

WHAT DID IT SAY? WAS IT DISRESPECTFUL, OR WAS IT ART?

"I don't know, Sir. What's art? The kids, they code their messages. I have no idea what it says."

WE NEED A CAMERA ON THAT SIDE OF THE BUILDING. I'VE ASKED FOR ONE BEFORE. SEND ME A DIGITAL PHOTOGRAPH.

"Yessir."

I WON'T HAVE MY LIBRARY DEFACED. WE MAY NEED TO TAKE ACTION.

"Yessir." Queneau's suggestions for unspecified *actions* were occurring more frequently of late. This trend made Dodge nervous and reinforced his decision as to what needed to be done.

QUERY: WHAT OF THE BASEMENTS? HAVE YOU STARTED INSTALLING CAMERAS YET?

This again. "It's difficult to gain access. I know how important secrecy is to you. I could fake a break-in, but not in every house. That would draw suspicion."

JUST GET IT DONE. I NEED TO KNOW WHAT IS GOING ON IN PEOPLE'S BASEMENTS. IMAGINE WHAT THEY MUST BE HIDING. I SHOULD HAVE HAD CAMERAS INSTALLED A LONG TIME AGO. THIS SHOULD BE YOUR HIGHEST PRIORITY. DO NOT LET ME DOWN DODGE.

"Yessir." This wasn't going to happen.

The monitor went dead. Queneau was done with him for now. Dodge could feel the man's dissatisfaction. Likely he'd be fired soon. It was a puzzle Queneau had kept him on this long, but his boss had been occupied with other concerns. And once he was fired, what could Dodge expect then? Certainly not safety.

The other screens on that bottom row suddenly brightened and began filling with letters and numbers. Dodge had seen this kind of display with increasing frequency over the last several years: a mixture of alpha and numeric characters, at times appearing to be entirely random, but eventually resolving into formulae as names and places from the news were assigned numbers and those numbers added, subtracted, and multiplied with the results translated back into other names, connections, and historical dates. These seemed to be Queneau's primary focus at this stage of his life, if *life* were even the proper word for it: an obsessive stream of numerology and gematria, a madman's exegesis, QAnon nonsense which determined that John F. Kennedy, General George Patton, and Donald Trump were related, all direct descendants of Jesus Christ, blessed by God and soon to return to Earth as prophets and rulers of the world albeit in a multitude of disguises.

Elaine first alerted him to what was happening on these monitors. Dodge had noticed the increase in verbiage, sometimes taking over the feeds from the individual houses and occupying every single screen. But he'd written it off simply as verbal static, an attempt by the equipment to make sense of Queneau's somnolent thoughts. Elaine had been the one who noticed the patterns, and how they related to various conspiracy theories currently making the news. Dodge himself hadn't watched the news in years. He didn't even own a television.

"In nursing we sometimes see the development of hospital psychosis in patients. People confined to an intensive care unit or a similar setting experience a cluster of serious psychiatric symptoms due to the isolation, sleep disturbance, and sensory deprivation. Imagine what life must be like for him. It would drive anyone crazy."

WHEN HE RETURNS HE WILL SMITE THE ENEMIES OF THE GOOD, THE CHILD MOLESTERS AND THE KIDNAPPERS AND THE PERVERTS WHO FEED UPON OUR CHILDREN. HE IS 89 AND HE IS 42. HE IS 131 IN THE DAYLIGHT AND 382 AFTER THE SUN GOES DOWN. HE IS THE LAMB WHO BECOMES THE LION AND THEY WILL ALL BE DESTROYED ONCE CONFRONTED BY HIS SAVAGE TEETH AND CLAWS. HE HAS AN ARMY WAITING. YOU WILL KNOW EVERYTHING WHEN THAT GREAT DAY ARRIVES.

Dodge began monitoring Queneau's internet traffic. Queneau's interest in the internet seemed harmless at first, and a way to ameliorate his isolation. Dodge hadn't given it much thought beyond that. But when he began tracking the sites and the pages Queneau visited, the multitude of accounts Queneau was using and the thousands of aliases involved, and the posts—those godawful garbage posts his employer was spewing throughout the digital space to hundreds of thousands of followers—Dodge became genuinely frightened.

Suddenly all the monitors went blank. Then in the far upper right quadrant of the monitor array, a single line displayed.

QUERY: DODGE? WHAT ARE YOU UP TO?

The screens refreshed, and a collage of rapidly changing imagery displayed on every monitor. News footage for the most part: riots and demonstrations, war in the Ukraine, violent attacks on police, white power marches filling the streets, congressional testimony, paid political announcements, panels of experts, podcasts and livestreams, rioters in painted faces wearing buffalo horns, televised trials.

All completely silent at first, but then Queneau turned on the exterior audio as the images changed more rapidly, the volume increasing until Dodge could no longer stand being in the room. He escaped through the kitchen—now reduced to a lunch nook for the staff—out the empty sunroom and into the back yard.

He turned around. The electric panel was mounted there by the back door. It had been added to over the years as the house's power requirements increased, but the main breaker, controlling all the power to the house, was still a double-width switch located at the top of the service panel. Several days before Dodge disconnected the backup power from the system. Queneau had placed him in charge of his security, but fortunately Dodge never had the desire or the necessary qualifications to do an adequate job.

He flipped the main breaker. There was nothing audible, and it might have been his imagination, but he felt a shift in the atmosphere as the lights inside the house went out.

He walked around the back yard. It needed a good weeding. Maybe he'd do that if he had the opportunity. The landscaping had actually been his favorite part of the job.

He pulled out his cell phone and called Elaine. She picked up on the first ring. "It's done," he said. "I don't know what you plan to do—"

"I'm going to go live with my daughter in Baltimore. I've already packed. Are you going to be okay?"

He was touched that she cared. "Probably. Take care, Elaine."

"Bless you—" He ended the call.

Dodge took the back gate out to the alley, then walked a couple of lots down to a pathway between some bushes which took him back out to Alphabet Row. It was only a short distance to his front door from there.

A crowd had gathered in front of the house at #Q. Dodge hadn't expected this. How could they possibly know? And so quickly? Cars and pickups jammed the street. Drivers were abandoning their vehicles and streaming onto Queneau's front lawn. Dodge couldn't be sure, but he didn't recognize any of these people as locals. They looked angry, determined. Some of them carried sticks, and some were waving guns. Several appeared to be fighting each other. But the strangest thing was no one said a word. This was all performed as silent pantomime, as if he had gone deaf.

R is for Remains

The naked man stood in the doorway, eyes unblinking. A portion of the left side of his skull was gone, but there was no blood, no gore. Gene tried to outstare him, afraid to look away, and was about to give up from the pain of the attempt when the naked man began to disappear, first his chest, then his legs and dangling bits, his pale lips and whatever lay in the cavity beyond those lips, and finally those eyes, still rigidly, defiantly staring.

They'd been told it was a double suicide but knew few of the details. Gene heard the shriek of distant sirens, and close by the soft bubbling of writhing maggots. The bittersweet stench had been overpowering at the front door, but here, outside the clean zone, they wore respirators. The two bodies had been here undiscovered for weeks, long enough to liquify in a massive meltdown, and although they'd been removed, fat deposits still pooled along one of the baseboards. There were rat droppings. Perhaps the rats had eaten off the bodies. He didn't know.

Fluid had wicked up into the drywall. The floor had an eastward slant. Decomp had traveled into at least four rooms. The event began in this room, but the couple had moved around, panicked, or determined, coughing and bleeding.

180 / Steve Rasnic Tem

Alcohol, poison, knives, and a gun were involved. Bio contaminated much of the house.

"Did you see something?" It was the new employee, Ed something-or-other.

"What do you mean?" Even though Gene knew exactly what he meant.

"The others, they say you can see them sometimes. Ghosts, whatever."

"They're just hazing you. Ignore them."

"Ha! That's what I thought."

He hadn't yet decided if Ed was reliable or not. More than once, Gene had seen a new employee run out of a job. The work had a rapid burnout rate. Besides, Ed didn't radiate competence.

He could see Ed's red-rimmed eyes through the googles. Maybe the fellow was taking drugs. Gene could have told him that only helps for so long.

Gene rarely got enough sleep, but he didn't use drugs, not sure what he might see as a result. What he saw on just a regular day was bad enough.

They both wore blood suits, boots, two pairs of gloves, goggles, respirators, but Gene could still tell the fellow was new on the job. A little too eager to prove he wasn't disgusted by the cleanup scene, moving nervously, clumsily, spreading biomaterial further than necessary. More than once, Gene had stopped him from tracking remains into clean areas. "Focus, Ed. That's the key. Just follow my lead."

Ed sprayed water over the floor, re-hydrating the blood to make it easier to clean. "At least they were together, right? This couple? At least they weren't alone."

Most of their cleanups were single bodies, the unattended dead, left alone to die. "I try not to think about what happened here. Our goal is to make the location look normal again, as much as possible. Sanitized and ready for repair. I want to know as little as possible about the families or the circumstances, Ed. I suggest you do the same. I know the others like to gossip, but I don't recommend it."

"So, it's just a job to you?"

"I didn't say that. It's a sad situation. But we can't feel their pain. All we can do is clean up after them. Somebody has to do it and that's what we've chosen to do. It's what we're paid for." Gene was talking too much. Sometimes he did that on a job.

The naked woman appeared behind Ed and to the left. She was probably beautiful once. She appeared to be running, screaming a silent alarm. Most of her hair was still by the couch, stuck to the floor. Her body was riddled with ragged holes. Gene could see through some of them to the shredded wallpaper behind her. The two of them, they must have clawed at the wallpaper in this room. He found a piece of fingernail embedded in the drywall. Much of the wallboard in this room was contaminated and would have to be removed.

"Are you married, Gene?" Ed used a long-handled scraper on the field of rust-colored human debris layering the floor. The decomp had pooled in places, traveled in rivulets down the hall, created additional pools in other rooms, spread under carpeting. There was contaminated tile and porous grout in the kitchen, and the floor in this room was soft pine not well sealed. The demo crew would have to remove a great deal. The couple's landlord was in for an enormous financial hit. "You got kids? Family? What do they say about what you do? I haven't figured out how much to tell mine. I just tell them the pay's good."

"I live alone now," Gene said. "No girlfriend. No prospects." Ed didn't reply. Gene picked up broken liquor bottles, a shattered lamp, a sticky hairbrush, and dropped them into red hazardous waste bags inside cardboard hazardous waste boxes. He sprayed and scooped dead maggots into a separate bag.

Gene didn't want to be found like this, people in hazmat suits cleaning up after him. But for now, he couldn't see how to avoid it. "We clean up life's unfortune mishaps," was the way the company's owner put it, a man who no longer went out on jobs. He'd named the company "Bio Genies." Their logo was three identical genies with tornado bodies leaving sparkling stars in their wake. It was embarrassing.

"Why do you think they did it?" Ed asked, rolling in the extractor, a powerful biohazard vacuum.

"Ed, please. I don't—" But Ed had already started up the machine, apparently not interested in the answer. *Suicide* was a small word for everything this couple had done. They had committed *rage* here.

Flies were everywhere. At one point he turned around and was confronted by a cloud of flies in the vague outline of a man. He turned around and walked the other way. He checked all the corners where debris tends to gather. In one he found small chunks of jellied flesh like rotting fruit.

They found where a few footprints tracked through the blood. The cops said someone robbed the place afterwards, even with all this carnage spread through the house.

At the end of day one, they cleaned up their equipment in the clean zone and slipped out of their gear. Before leaving Gene switched on the ozone machine to purify the air overnight. He posted a warning on the door.

After a day like this Gene was reluctant to spend a long evening alone in his apartment. He couldn't talk about what he did for a living. It repulsed most people.

He retreated into the library at the end of the street. Gene knew the neighborhood well. This was their fourth case on Alphabet Row in two years, a large number for such a limited area. With small brick bungalows built in the late Twenties and early Thirties, it was meant to be a cute, fairytale-like neighborhood with large letters on the houses to help teach the local children the alphabet. Maybe at one time it had been exactly that charming, but many of the homes were now in poor repair, and many of the letters which had given the neighborhood its name were missing or replaced with lettering of more modest size. But the current client's house still had its enormous R mounted on the outside by the door, painted a bright candy red.

Gene imagined these old bungalows were cheap enough, and small enough, they might seem the perfect places to house elderly relatives in their final years. But bad things can happen when you're left alone, when there's no one around to find you. But Gene wasn't the one to point out other folks' isolation.

The library appeared full. Gene found it calming to be around a large group of people. Of course, seeing several people wasn't the same as being *with* them. He didn't like to think of himself as a recluse, but he supposed he was. He'd lost the knack for talking to people.

Numerous chairs were placed in and around the checkout area and the stacks. They were famous here for never turning vagrants away. Like most libraries Gene patronized this one contained large numbers of the dead: lounging, sleeping, reading, and re-reading the same page. It always made him curious, what that single page might be, but he kept his distance out of respect, or maybe fear.

A few ranted silently to themselves. Several mimed dramatic scenes, a reprise of their final moments, played again and again.

Many of the dead were obvious about what they were. They wore their torn cheeks, empty eye sockets, and missing ears almost proudly, as if they were carefully selected ornamentations. Gene thought of these as the honest dead. Others were more challenging to distinguish, their scars and stains easily mistaken for the evidence of careless, difficult lives.

An elderly man whose multitude of facial wrinkles made him appear fractured had a newspaper over his lap. Gene wondered if he were hiding something there. He appeared unable to keep his tongue in his mouth.

A woman in an ill-fitting green sweater sat hunched forward, staring at her shoes, an unmatched pair. As Gene walked past her, he noticed the chunk missing from the back of her neck.

One fellow's ballcap was crushed and splitting at the seams. He turned around and stared at Gene with huge, bloodshot eyes. This one, apparently, was alive.

A few nudes were present as well, wandering the aisles. Sometimes they reached out and touched the ones who were seated. There were also people lying in the middle of the floor spreadeagle. Gene assumed all these folks were dead. Some were bodies he had helped remove or cleaned up after at various crime scenes. Some he recognized from bedside photographs at the sites of suicides.

He found his wife and his beautiful little girl in the children's section, reading together. He tried to ignore their obvious wounds, where the car he'd been driving had crushed, or tore their bodies. At one point his daughter looked up at him, but with no signs on her face she recognized him, or even that she registered his presence. Instead of being traumatized, he was grateful for the reminders: how his wife tilted her head when reading, how his daughter folded her hands into her lap while listening.

He walked out to his van and drove to his apartment. He knew if he didn't do something soon, he'd one day become one of the unattended, lying undiscovered for days, for weeks, for months.

———

On the morning of day two Gene felt restless, anxious to begin. Their boss called a couple of times, wanting to know when one or both of them would be free. They had other jobs to go to, other human messes to clean up. But seeing the house with fresh eyes, Gene found hundreds of examples of further contamination, hundreds of spots requiring a thorough cleaning.

Gene wouldn't go on jobs in which dead children were involved. He was a good employee, so his boss made allowances for him, although not always happily. A two-person demolition crew arrived to remove flooring and chip away at the tile. His boss was trying to rush him, but there was much more cleaning required in those rooms before any demo could take place. Many spots were stubbornly resistant and might require hours, but Gene refused to walk away prematurely. His task, wherever possible, was to turn back the clock.

What he did here would not redeem him, but it was responsible work, and it filled the time. For him personally, he knew there would be no fix, no matter how much effort was applied. Remorse was too small a word for what he felt.

Ed worked with the radio tuned to a country station, the volume turned loud enough to grate on Gene's nerves. But he didn't complain.

He scrubbed one wall in stages, spending hours on it. He sprayed on industrial strength disinfectant, wiped off switch plates, door frames, any place they might have touched or coughed on while running through the house, dying. He

186 / Steve Rasnic Tem

climbed a ladder and cleaned the ceiling fan blades, top and bottom. He examined anywhere flies and other insects, or rats might have carried the biological material. He sprayed blood indicator onto surfaces and followed the results throughout the house. He rubbed and scrubbed until no traces were left.

There were few pieces of furniture in the room they called location zero. A couple of old chairs, a small table, a floor lamp. They were contaminated by the decomp drawn up from underneath them and would have to be thrown away. There was also a sideboard sitting directly on the floor. That, and everything inside it, would also be thrown away.

The demo team cut the wall about halfway up and removed the bottom portion of drywall. They removed all the baseboards in the room. They began removing floorboards and subflooring. In spots the floor joists were exposed. The room appeared frozen in deconstruction, but at least it would be clean.

Ed continued to ramble on about sports, news, weather, arguments with his wife, how his kids misbehaved. Gene found those latter complaints particularly hard to take. But at least Ed kept working. Gene could tell he had a talent for the job. They both tried to be thorough. They took turns making rounds looking for things the other might have missed.

So, Gene was startled to discover a large spread of decomp in the middle of the bare bedroom floor. They'd been through this room dozens of times, sprayed and scraped and sprayed, but somehow this enormous stain had reappeared. He could see how the dying couple ran through the room, both trailing blood. Maybe one stumbled and fell and this was what he or she left behind.

But Gene cut the blood stain out of the carpet yesterday, as well as the portion where it leaked into the pad. He put those pieces into a biohazard bag and the rest of the carpet was disposed of as solid waste. The blood had not reached the floorboards underneath it. There had been no stain left on the floor.

Yet here it was, rusty red and crusted with human grit.

A hand rose out of the stain. This was not the first time Gene had witnessed such a thing. He struggled not to react. He had worked hard to regain some limited composure. Now he felt on the verge of relapse.

The hand did not go away. The fingers separated as it tilted in his direction. Unable to resist, Gene walked over and grasped the hand and pulled. He continued to pull until he'd pulled the woman out of her own remains.

She swept past him, and even though he wore a respirator he could still smell her.

Gene waited in his van parked on the street until the others left. Ed was the last to leave, waving to him and shouting that he would see him in the morning. Tomorrow would be a full day. There was both a murder and a suicide on the schedule. Gene didn't expect they would have time for both. Gene and the boss would argue, and Gene would win.

He stepped out of his van and walked across the street. He could see the dead lying on the sidewalk in a variety of distressed poses. Bodies lay up and down the lane in differing degrees of brokenness, their fluids leaking into the gutters.

He didn't leave the house until the flames were well established and unlikely to stop by themselves. He'd stashed cleaning fluids in several closets, and when the flames reached them, they went up with a gasp.

This wasn't the first time he'd done such a thing. But he always made sure the homeowner had insurance. They needed insurance to pay the company what it charged for these extensive cleanings.

But sometimes despite everything they did, they couldn't get a house clean enough. He knew he'd get caught someday. He didn't care.

Gene waited to make sure the fire remained contained and until he heard the sirens. He watched the dead walking the streets as the house burned, a sloppily organized parade of regrets. A pale figure paused and stared at him through the windshield. It was like gazing into a mirror.

S is for Subsidence

Eventually he realized his only power was letting go. Kurt bought the small house a year into Jane's illness. Not long ago she'd been fine, but nature was unpredictable, and sometimes a vicious saboteur. They needed a single-story home because she couldn't manage stairs. They had to get rid of three-fourths of their possessions to fit into the new place. Jane was past caring, and he made himself not care as he sold, gave away, or donated things he had loved for decades. But he kept her dolls and animal ceramics, artificial flower arrangements and woven wall hangings. He couldn't imagine living in a house without them.

He kept asking what she wanted. But she said she wasn't making any more decisions. It frightened him to hear that. For a while there'd been a wandering problem. The space in a smaller home would be easier to control. On good days she looked fine, but terrible things were happening beneath the surface.

At least it was a lovely house. It had a glow about it. Its roots went deep. People had lived here for a century. They were next in a long line of lives spent in this singular location. He tried to find out about former occupants, but no records were available.

Kurt held onto enough antiques to furnish their new home. They fit right in with the Mission-style built-ins and trim. Out of their once vast library he saved two hundred volumes. At the end of the street was a fine old branch library. He hoped they could walk down there together. She no longer read but enjoyed it when he read to her.

But Kurt had always been too optimistic about her illness. Following the strain of the move Jane deteriorated rapidly, sinking both physically and mentally. Most days he was lucky to get a simple *Hello* out of her. The visiting nurse said she was stable, but honestly, she wasn't likely to live the year. Kurt spent hours at her bedside, searching for vague recollections of who she used to be. He knew there was nothing to be done, and the coldness of the knowledge infuriated him.

He didn't go out. He never left the house. He had all their groceries delivered, including fresh cut flowers he put in a vase on her dresser. He didn't know if she ever noticed them.

———

Six months into their residency Kurt first noticed the cracks. He thought they were cobwebs at first. He couldn't afford a housekeeper, and even with a long-handled duster he found it difficult to reach distant crevices. But climbing a ladder—something his doctor had forbidden him to do—he could see them clearly: dozens of tiny cracks in the corners where walls and ceilings met, around lintels, around heating vents. Defects, fractures, worrying signs.

There were other issues, phenomena he couldn't explain. Rising and falling water in the toilets, faucets coming on for no reason, doors swinging open, curtains fluttering even when the windows were shut. Jane hadn't noticed as far as he knew, and he wasn't about to tell her.

He'd been initially concerned because this house sat lower than the others in the neighborhood, although the drop did make it feel nicely secluded. His yard was at least a foot lower than the public sidewalk, necessitating a few concrete steps down to his front walk.

Kurt hadn't yet investigated the basement. The stairs were dimly lit and appeared to descend forever. He stood at the top and attempted to smell for dampness. He smelled something else, but he didn't think it was damp.

A little settling was to be expected. He didn't have time for this. Kurt's focus had been, and continued to be, his wife, watching her responses or lack thereof, reading to her, playing music, even singing to her in his off-key, cracked voice. Sometimes she spoke, and sometimes her words made sense, but not always. He imagined she was already far along on her own personal journey, her mind in two different worlds.

When Kurt needed a break, he went out on the front porch and sat watching the people passing by. A lot of students headed to and from the library. A few older couples strolling by holding hands. They sometimes smiled and waved. Each time he was inordinately touched.

He lowered his eyes to his front walk and thought it looked off. The edges weren't straight. It had what? Folded? He got out of his chair and walked toward the street. There was a definite slant. A crack a good half-inch wide crossed the width of the concrete. The halves of the walk dipped as if it were a ship broken in two and sinking.

"It looks like subsidence." His name was Tom, a friend of a friend, someone who worked in construction, and a man who'd offered to examine Kurt's house for free, because Kurt's wife was dying.

"What's that?" Kurt asked. He was embarrassed. He was well-read, but he didn't know the word.

"The ground sinks because materials are moving underneath where you can't see them. It can take a while to notice something is wrong. Day to day, everything looks normal, but there's shifting, gaps developing, breakage, in the dark places unknown to you. Then one day your world collapses."

He roamed the house with Kurt in tow, examining diagonal cracks in the walls, ceilings, and brickwork. In the spare bedroom which Kurt used when Jane's tossing didn't allow him to sleep, Tom found rippling in the wallpaper. He checked all the doors and windows and pointed out where the sticking—which Kurt had noticed but ignored—might be indicative of a bigger problem.

"Your door and window frames are out of true. This house has shifted significantly."

They descended into the basement. Kurt was still hesitant, but Tom persuaded him he needed to see any problems with his own eyes. Even with the light on they required a flashlight. The steps took them all the way to the far wall of the basement. Kurt counted twenty-five.

"I've never seen such a deep basement under a house this age," Tom said. "At least you have a solid staircase." He pointed his flashlight at the stairs. "That's not going anywhere." The treads were thick, solid wood, supported by a substantial mass of concrete.

"I'm not seeing any cracks or separations down here, no signs of damp, no salt deposits on the walls." He jumped up and down. "But there shouldn't be this much give in the floor. It's as if it's unattached, floating. I don't get it."

They investigated every corner, swinging the flashlight at bare walls, the floor, the spider-like furnace hiding in the shadows. The basement was empty and surprisingly dust and cobweb free. Tom started back up the stairs. Kurt had to scramble to keep up.

Back in the kitchen Tom gave him a card. "This guy is a good soils test engineer." He gave him another. "This woman is a foundation expert. They'll tell you what you need to do."

Kurt stuck the cards in his wallet and thanked him, even though he had no intention of calling anyone. Experts charged money he didn't have and prescribed solutions he wouldn't be able to afford. What were the odds of the house falling down before both he and Jane died?

––––––––––––

The hardest part of taking care of her was knowing he was powerless to change anything. What was going to happen was going to happen. Human beings were too fragile and died too easily. They suffered from a failure of design.

The house made more sounds at night than their former home. Perhaps because it was older. Everyone knew old houses made noise. But Kurt now knew it was also not geometrically sound. This house moaned and groaned, its movements impersonating knocks, rapping, and footsteps. His eyes weren't what they used to be, but the walls appeared to move at night. They breathed. At times they shuddered.

Kurt never knew at the start of any day how aware Jane would be, or how willing to communicate. This had negligible effect on the activities he did for her: changing her clothes, combing her hair, clipping her nails, brushing her teeth, cleaning up her accidents.

Swallowing water tended to sicken her, but her lips were cracked, her mouth almost empty of saliva. He gave her chipped ice, experimenting until he found a size which wouldn't make her choke.

He gave her small bits of food he knew she could manage, delivering them slowly as if they were a sacrament. Every time she coughed, he was afraid she was choking.

He gave her pills four times a day, tracked and checked off a list. There were other pills for pain to be delivered as needed. These frightened him because he didn't want to give her too much—he might kill her—and yet he couldn't sit there while she was in agony.

One night she cried in his arms, incoherent, delirious, but he had given her the maximum. Was now the time to give her more? The moment passed, but Kurt knew it would come around again, her distorted mouth, her slurred calls for relief. There was no escaping it. If she asked him to help her die, what would he say?

Some days she slept for hours and woke up frightened and confused, not knowing where she was or the day. One night she sat up and stared at him. "I don't think we'll ever make love again." She began to cry. He held her in his arms and stroked her head.

Most nights he stayed in bed with her no matter how restless her sleep. He knew he couldn't go on like this. He would have to move into the other room. Already he had trouble staying awake during the day.

The nurse explained in grim detail what he should expect as Jane's death approached. She described how her breathing would change as mucous and saliva built up in her throat, how awful it would sound, as if she were in terrible pain, but he needed to understand she was not. This would likely last for only a few hours before her heart and lungs stopped.

He didn't believe he could listen or sit there watching. He couldn't lie in bed with her while that terrible transformation occurred. He was ashamed of himself. All she'd ever asked of him was to be with her at the end.

He lay down in the bed and pulled her against him. She woke him sometime later, coughing, pleading for water. He went to the sink and ran the cold faucet. But a fine sediment covered the bottom of the glass.

———

Not long after, Jane fell headlong into delirium.

She kept insisting she heard sounds coming from the basement and would Kurt please check it out. He could have told her he checked and found nothing wrong. She had no way of verifying. He didn't want to tell her he was afraid to go down there.

She claimed there were people in the room when he left her alone, so if he didn't want any uninvited visitors in their home he should always be where she could see him. She was more alert than he'd seen her in weeks, but it seemed cruel her alertness was tied to her delusions. She babbled on about what these invisible presences were doing, and ordered him to listen, because they were sending them a warning.

Kurt didn't know if the illness was causing her delirium, or if it was the result of being in bed for weeks on end with the same lighting and the same environment. The sameness can do terrible things to a mind. Sometimes he'd open the window, and she would turn her head in that direction, like a plant turning toward the light.

He asked her simple questions to ground her, random facts about their life together, names of parents and schools. She forgot more than she remembered, and what she did remember was often colored in deep paranoia. *These creatures*, as she called them, meant them serious harm. "Don't you understand? They're so far above us, to them we're a small, forgettable meal."

Her stomach became swollen. Kurt didn't like to think about what might be inside. She was burning up. Sweat saturated the sheets.

She was charged with an ineffable emotional electricity. Just being around her infected him. If he sat with Jane too long, he began to see a complication of shadows parading across the walls, but he couldn't match up those shadows with anything physically present.

At one point she reached over and grabbed the glass off the bedside table, shattered it on the edge, and held a shard to her throat. Kurt snatched it out of her hand, giving himself a deep cut. He wrapped his hand in a towel from the bed. She'd collapsed back into her pillow, comatose. He saw no signs of breathing. Her dolls watched him from across the room urging him to do something. But he didn't know what to do. In desperation he slapped Jane across the face, the first time he'd even thought of hitting his wife. She opened her mouth and made this shrill, inhuman sound. He crawled on top of the blood-stained sheets and held her, chanting "I'm sorry I'm sorry I'm sorry." The dolls across the room chanted with him.

The day was extraordinarily long. He picked up the phone to call 911, but got no dial tone, instead hearing waves of electrical static. There was no longer a clock in the bedroom — Jane said it whispered unpleasant things — so he had no idea how long they'd lain there. A myriad of sounds slipped into the room, but he did not look around to see what they were. Eventually she fell asleep, and he climbed off the bed and went into the bathroom to clean himself up. Thankfully, the cut wasn't as deep as he'd thought. He poured peroxide over it and tied a crude bandage on. He pulled some fresh sheets from the laundry cabinet but didn't know how to change the bed without waking her, and the last thing Kurt wanted to do was awaken Jane.

When he walked back into the bedroom he saw those spirits, those creatures, leaping from the bed and into the fractured walls of the room. He did not believe in ghosts. He never had. And it strangely reassured him these were not ghosts. These forms—rippling, multiple-appendaged, with too many orifices to count—had obviously never been human at all.

The room itself had changed. What had been solid had become soft and ill-defined. Much of what had been invisible, the very air, appeared intermittently opaque and crystallized.

Kurt experienced severe vertigo. He sat down on the floor. From this angle the ceiling appeared to have retreated. There was a fluttering and a grinding of translucency along its edges. He became aware of a terrible stench, both salty and sulfurous. He'd never smelled anything like it. The floor began to slant.

From her high perch on the bed, Jane leered down at him. "This isn't even *our* home; did you know that? The realtor had no right to sell it to us. This is *their* home. They've lived underneath this house forever."

Her shadow, cast on the wall behind the bed, began to change.

———

Kurt didn't recall falling asleep, but when he woke up, he was lying on the floor in front of the bed, using the clean folded sheets as a pillow. There was light in the room. He assumed he must have slept through until the next day.

He got to his feet and checked on Jane. She was deep in sleep, her breathing relaxed. She was covered in dried blood, his, he presumed. He got a wet sponge from the bathroom and tried to clean her. She began to sputter and choke so he stopped. She opened her eyes and gazed at him.

"They've become so bold," she said. "So obnoxious."

"Who?"

"Why the souls, silly." She smiled at him as if he were a child. "They slip out of the cracks in our house, showing themselves even while I'm looking right at them. As if my opinion doesn't matter. Don't you think that's a bit cheeky?"

Of course, he'd seen them as well. Maybe her dying body had contaminated him. He wondered how long these presences had been here. There were so many limits on what humans could know. Most of his so-called knowledge was simply an interpretation of the facts.

Kurt felt a shift in gravity, a difference in the air. Everything had changed somehow, yet he knew his wife was still dying. Everything else about this strange day was extraneous.

She heaved an enormous sigh which reverberated throughout the room. The walls shook with it. He was terrified. He wasn't ready yet.

A painful light issued from the cracks in the walls, revealing new openings he hadn't noticed before. He looked at the window. It was still dark outside. What he had mistaken for a new day was the light leaking from somewhere below.

The wallpaper began to sag as more brilliance shone through. The light manifested as a fabric unravelling into strings as it traveled through the air. Its salient aspects were its intensity, and the insignificance it made him feel.

The light crossed his arm, searing the skin. The pain made him howl, even though he tried to contain it. Jane's eyes moved as if she were searching for him. But he was standing right in front of her. He watched as the radiating fabric dropped onto the furniture, over the vase full of flowers, her small collections of ceramic animals and dolls. Everything the fabric touched developed its own glow, as if they were on fire. If their house were to burn down now, he couldn't think of anything he'd care to salvage.

The light scraped her skin. There was a scent of copper. She began to bleed. The pillow wrapped around her neck like a bloated scarf. Had they decided to kill her?

The folds of light twisted into non-humanoid suggestions, shapeless, or at least in forms difficult to comprehend, segmented bags of translucent alien viscera, gigantic cilia, liquid flowing carapace. These things traveled across the room, appearing to sample every location in curiosity or some mysterious quest for satiation. Periodically they emitted dazzling waves of light which scoured the walls. Where the light hit the floor it turned to steam, leaving behind an ashen stain.

The house shook itself as if sentient, struggling for protection, attempting to sever itself from whatever occupied it. The flowers on her dresser expanded, sending out long, ornate stalks and curling tendrils, the blossoms opening and closing like mouths. The dolls began to gossip amongst themselves, grabbing the whimpering ceramic animals and chewing them to bits.

Jane began that terrible choking rasp, the tortured rattle the nurse warned him about. Her body shook under the power of it. Kurt had feared this moment, and now he was terrified of her. He'd promised her he would stay and was mortified he could not. He turned to leave, and she jumped out of bed and snarled at him. He ran.

She scrambled after him, her face wrapped in a glowing sheen. They scuffled. He felt a sharp pain. She was biting into his side.

He extricated himself from her hands. It felt like she had more than two. He ran through the doorway and slammed the door shut behind him, pressing his shoulder against it to keep it closed. She began beating on it.

The door felt silky just before it came apart. He ran down the hall. She was close behind him, running on all fours. The silkiness spread to the walls around him, then a silvery damp spilling across the floor. Then they were out into the shambles of the living room, where the furniture had become piles of glistening sludge.

The lines between walls and ceiling began to smear. Kurt glanced back. Her face had become smooth and featureless.

The house was twisting, angles altering, tiles popping off the kitchen floor, every plane transforming as if to reveal the secret architecture underneath. Distortion popped the basement door open. Kurt went through it, not considering the basement's dead end.

He was almost to the bottom of the basement staircase, and he couldn't hear her anymore. He grabbed the railing and twisted around. He could see her head at the top of the stairs, watching him. He wondered if she was going to follow, or seal him inside the basement.

———

Kurt descended the staircase, but instead of finding the floor, he was at the top of yet another staircase. He couldn't go back up the stairs because of Jane, or whoever it was who waited, so he continued. A force, a kind of suction, drew him down the stairs.

He found himself on another landing, a deeper darkness beyond that landing, and more steps leading down. The light above, shining from the basement door, appeared to be shrinking. He himself was shrinking it seemed. He was a tiny presence on these enormous stairs.

Outside the walls of the basement, he could feel the ground and everything in it moving, taking the house somewhere new. He continued walking down. He tried to control his breathing, hoping to take in no more than a small sample of air at a time. He had his doubts about the safety of the atmosphere.

There was some variation in the basement walls the further he descended, differentiations in strata and composition. Any variety of stability seemed forever out of reach.

Several more flights of stairs and he could no longer see any light above. He had no idea how he could see at all. He concluded the basement walls contained some inherent illumination, too subtle for him to perceive its source.

The staircase lost its proper scale, either too large for the space or too small. Now and again, he thought the stairs were tilting. He seized the railing and held on tight. But he was old and not strong. The staircase began to spiral.

There was a sudden, explosive shock as the stairs ended. He was standing on the basement floor. The concrete was sandy beneath his feet, as if it were beginning to disintegrate. The floor began to smolder.

He looked down. He saw them there through the not so solid floor, their incomprehensible silhouettes, swimming or flying through that unfamiliar medium. There was nothing sane about it. His final hours had become a time of great discovery and a loss of innocence.

The police were called for a welfare check when a large grocery delivery remained on the porch for weeks without being taken inside. Squirrels had ravaged the contents, and the officer who responded to the call had to chase off a family of racoons before he could get to the door. He knocked and pounded for some time. He then announced his presence and broke in.

It was a small, well-furnished home. Somewhat secluded because the ground was lower than the street. Mission style or Craftsman. He didn't know the difference, but it felt

202 / Steve Rasnic Tem

comfortable and welcoming. The beds in both bedrooms were unmade, but the rooms were otherwise clean and orderly. The second bedroom included a bookcase full of antique books with strange titles. The light coming through the windows was warm and pleasant. It made the polished wooden floors glow. The main bedroom displayed several collections: dolls and ceramics, dusted and well-cared-for. There was a vase on the dresser for flowers. He assumed a woman lived here.

There was no food in the house, and no sign of the occupants. A door in the kitchen led to the basement. He stood at the top of the stairs and looked down into the darkness. He pulled out his flashlight, then reconsidered. The steps appeared to go on forever. He decided that taking those steps wasn't his job.

T is for Tutti i Morti

All dead. All gone.

It was late, darkness a smear outside his bedroom window, yet he decided to go out for a walk. His son would not have approved, but his son was asleep, and Lorenzo was a grown man, an old man capable of making his own decisions, despite what anyone else believed. He had nothing to do, no responsibilities, no tasks he needed to perform. At this stage in his life, he preferred the night. His mind was clearer after the sun went down, and he'd become self-conscious around other people. They were always eager to tell him he'd made some mistake.

He didn't know how far he needed or wanted to go. He had no plan. He would have called a taxi, but he no longer had credit cards or cash of his own. His son bought him a cell phone, but he never learned how to use it.

His son controlled everything. Yet his son couldn't keep his house clean. As Lorenzo moved through the house, he was alarmed by the layers of dust over floors and furniture, the cobwebs, the widespread disarray. Something trickled down his cheeks. He wiped it with his finger and looked. Was that perspiration or blood or tears? He honestly didn't know.

As he left the house, he was surprised to discover the front door had been tagged with black spray paint—an X or a lopsided T. The homes across the street bore similar signs of vandalism. The lack of civility troubled him—yet another indication he'd lived past his expiration date.

The remains of shattered pumpkins littered the front yard. Lorenzo remembered his childhood in Italy, how they carried pumpkins carved with the shape of a cross with lit candles inside as lanterns. They called them *cocce de morte*, dead people's heads.

She joined him out on the sidewalk. He wasn't sure exactly who she was, and he wouldn't look at her, but it seemed quite right she should be the one to accompany him. They strolled past the small houses at the end of this row , each one dark as a blinded eye, around the library, and beyond.

Many more people were out at this hour than he'd expected. Teens and twenty somethings. Maybe thirty-somethings, but his ability to estimate age had deteriorated over time. People were now either very young or very old.

A tall man stood in front of them, his bare face tattooed into a hideous mask. The man's coat fell open, chest exploded, heart visible inside the rib cage. Then Lorenzo realized it was simply a T-shirt design. The man wouldn't yield so they had to push around him. Lorenzo never would have tolerated such rudeness when he was younger.

Many in the crowd were elaborately costumed. Bright scarves and hats, voluminous suits and dresses, faces painted or masked or both. Some carried lumpy bags. A few were in high spirits, but overall there appeared to be a solemnity to the occasion, whatever it was.

"Perhaps it's a festival. A big one, from the looks of things." It was the first time Lorenzo had spoken to her since they started walking.

"It's Halloween, dear. Don't you remember?" He'd always loved the sound of her voice.

"Is it, already? It's that late in the year?"

She laughed so softly he barely heard her. "Look at the trees. The leaves are almost gone. It's too late for the little goblins, but the older ones are out. I imagine they still have parties—don't you think? You used to love parties."

"I *hate* parties. I never know what to say. Especially when they ask me how I'm doing. They're just being friendly, I suppose, but how do you answer such a question? Do you tell the truth?"

She didn't answer. He wasn't surprised. No one wanted to talk to a complainer. He'd always been a moaner, but in his advanced years he was worse.

Trick or treat. That's what they called it, what they did on Halloween. Extortion was what it was. *Cosa Nostra* business. When he was a boy in Italy, they did not trick or treat. What Italian parents would allow their children to wander into strangers' homes? There it had been a religious holiday, *Ogni Santi e il Giorno dei Morti*—All Saints and All Souls. *Novembre 1 e 2*. He remembered all the lit candles and the crosses. They left out a lamp, a bucket of water and a little bread, so the dead might find their way home, then eat and drink. In some houses the fireplace was kept going for the whole night and the table was set with plentiful food for the dead so they might feast.

Was the food gone in the morning? He could not remember. Perhaps his parents hid this from him. He thought of huge meals left on tables for days, rotting and swimming in sour liquid, all because the families could not let go.

It seemed they had left the crowd behind. They passed through a neighborhood which was completely dark, the houses seeming more like tombs than dwellings, except for an abundance of lit candles on the porches, the sidewalks,

206 / Steve Rasnic Tem

collected into large groupings on the lawns. Some of the candles were tapers as thin as flaming fingers. Others were long and thick and waxy like severed limbs set on fire. The largest tabby he'd ever seen erupted from the bushes in front of them and scattered dozens of the candles as it raced through a sequence of lawns. At one point it may or may not have caught fire, and Lorenzo screeched in dismay. The cat vanished before he could ascertain its fate. Lorenzo tasted ash and tried to spit it out. But once you have acquired such a taste it never completely goes away.

Across the street an angry couple herded their two children along. *Where were you? We've been searching everywhere!* The boy was throwing a tantrum, making it quite clear he didn't want to go home. Lorenzo would have gotten a beating for behaving that way.

Lorenzo looked around and could not find her anywhere. She'd abandoned him again, all because of his sour attitude. He would try to change. He would try to do better. How many times had he promised her that?

He felt a flutter of panic deep inside his throat. Was he going to cry? Old men tended to weep. They could not help themselves. He didn't know if he could find his way home without her.

He turned the corner and was confronted by the crowd again. The size of it alarmed him. He couldn't guess the total number, but it had to be in the thousands. The territory the revelers occupied had expanded. All he could see were costumed figures filling the streets, the yards, the public parkways. A giant street celebration, he supposed, for the holiday. It was all so—what was the word—theatrical? Some costumes appeared commercially made, perhaps based on popular cultural icons, but since he didn't go to the movies or watch television, he had no idea which ones.

Someone had covered themself with a white sheet and cut two eyeholes to fashion a makeshift ghost. The sheet appeared to be spotted with bloodstains.

A large number had rough brown sacks over their heads. Lorenzo thought of them as sack heads, and under any other circumstance he might consider them comical or ludicrous, but not tonight.

Deeper into the crowd the costumes became more frightening—cloth ripped and painted to suggest decay, masks and prostheses bubbling with disfiguration, mutation, and extensive injury. A few of the characters featured missing limbs and other random amputations. The mob was thick with drunkards. Every few minutes some merrymaker would fall over, intoxicated, or dead—it was difficult to tell.

He reached out for her hand and found it. She'd come back. But had she forgiven him? Her fingers were stiff at first, then gradually relaxed and intertwined with his.

"It seems in poor taste," Lorenzo said, but stopped. He didn't want her to perceive him as someone with no sense of humor. He had no idea if any of this was in poor taste or not. Fashions change, and he had lost the ability to tell. But he had never liked being reminded of people's misfortunes. Everywhere people were suffering, their fates inescapable. This was nothing to celebrate.

The density of costume made him uncomfortable. This was no minimalist masquerade. Faces and arms, hands, were painted, and on top of these, masks and layer upon layer of personalities were applied.

Risqué outfits were much in evidence: exposed bellies and butt cheeks, bare breasts, an abundance of naked skin for such a cold night. These costumes would have been taboo when he was a young man. He hadn't realized they were considered acceptable now. He tried not to stare, but these forbidden delights were everywhere he looked.

Someone started a fire near one edge of the crowd. Certainly, it was a chilly evening, but this seemed unwise. He should have brought a coat. His shirt and pants were much too thin. Or perhaps he was still in his pajamas. Lorenzo wasn't sure.

Setting a fire close to so many people was a reckless thing to do. He couldn't see them well, but a circle of costumed figures danced around the fire, at times practically touching the flames. One towering figure appeared to be toasting its long fingers.

For a moment, they stopped moving, and that portion of the crowd became a frightening tableau of fire and burnt silhouettes. The mob began to shift direction, perhaps as people realized the danger, or maybe as part of some drunken, communal sway. Lorenzo pushed against the prevailing traffic. He didn't want to be trampled, but he was also desperate not to be trapped. Finally, he had to give into the tide and allowed himself to be swept away.

She'd let go of his hand. There was nothing he could do. He'd promised he would take good care of her, and yet he'd let her down repeatedly. His tender feelings for her had never gone away, even after all these years without her.

The flood of carousers appeared to turn in a circle, then split into several disparate arms. His group was forced down a narrow street, bodies pressed tightly against each other. His body began to tilt. He struggled to remain upright. The pressure of the other bodies kept him from falling, but he couldn't stand either. He traveled this way for some distance, carried along without his feet touching the ground. A murmuring arose deep within the horde, its tone darkening, becoming more animal-like.

When the street ended, Lorenzo was vomited out into an open space. He didn't recognize the area but thought it might be a park or athletic field. Fallen leaves were everywhere, wet and sticking to his shoes. A thick layer of filth accumulated over the lower part of his body, giving his legs a ruined appearance.

Broken masks and bits of costume lay scattered across the ground, stained, tainted. Yet he was still tempted to pick them up and examine them to make sure they were pieces of costume and not flesh and body parts. Each time, he managed to stop himself from acting on this bizarre impulse, realizing he might become infected with some terrible disease.

Someone was walking next to him. He was hopeful it might be her. He heard the tap tap tap as the bearded man passed, as if the fellow had a cane. But when Lorenzo looked down at the man's legs, he could see the fleshless, skeletal feet. He looked back at the man's head and now his beard consisted of narrow threads of skin hanging from his chin.

A hand grabbed Lorenzo's. "I'm so glad you came back," he said. But glancing her way he realized he was holding a hand severed above the wrist. He shook his arm repeatedly until the hand let go.

A man approached, waving his handless arm. Lorenzo tried to tell him he didn't have it anymore. The man shouted and his tongue detached, flying over Lorenzo's head.

The field, ankle-deep in the debris from assorted carnage, resembled a massively messy meal, the plates and silverware buried beneath the leavings. The path through the wreckage was long and torturous. Lorenzo avoided touching the bits as much as possible, but the wet, gooey texture of the ground was inescapable.

Straggling survivors from the crowd drifted out of the mouths of the surrounding streets, dazed and wounded, but apparently still seeking comfort in the company of others. Some huddled standing and weeping. Others collapsed into piles, using one another's bodies for protection from whatever threats remained.

A trumpeting sound filled the air. Panic gripped the survivors, some fleeing, others clinging to each other for reassurance or resigned to share the same fate, their limbs and bodies twisted together.

Out of the tall trees bordering the field a series of narrow legs emerged—four or six or eight—so tall and narrow they disappeared into the darkness above. Lorenzo could not see whatever they were attached to, mammoth insect or beast or something even less imaginable. Sharp, blade-like appendages. The number of legs changed as the seconds passed and the legs came down on people and destroyed them, severed them, or mashed them into the ground. Then the arms came down out of the darkness, equally long and narrow and deadly, ending in claws which snatched and grabbed and tore bodies apart. Lorenzo kept looking up, still unable to see a body or a head or a physical source.

It harvested what remained of the crowd. No explanation. No trial. No reprieve. No interest in their desperate pleadings.

Lorenzo trembled as the thrashing legs and arms grew closer. He felt too old, too sad to run. Then her hand closed on his and she was there again, urging him on, practically dragging him out of the field. When and how had she gotten so strong? He remembered her always as a fragile, delicate creature.

They didn't talk for some time, but she maintained a firm grip on his hand, guiding him through the dark streets. He still couldn't bring himself to look directly at her. He didn't know why. Perhaps he was afraid of what he might see.

Lorenzo had no idea what time it was. He wondered if his son missed him yet. Trash covered the trees, the bushes, the houses.

His grandmother in Italy always had tales about this time of year. He never knew if any of them were true, but it felt disrespectful to doubt her. He remembered her saying if he were good and prayed for their souls, the dead would bring him gifts. But everything had been taken from the dead. What did they have left to give?

Lorenzo didn't understand how it could still be dark out. He'd left quite late, and he'd been gone for many hours. He could see a dim glow just above the distant horizon, but the sun appeared stuck there, unable to rise.

Lorenzo watched as scattered shapes still in their Halloween costumes returned home. Some reentered their houses without bothering to open doors. Of course, he no longer owned any doors. But what would happen when he reached his son's house?

Somewhere along the way he lost the comfort of her touch again, but she was there waiting for him in the open doorway.

"I don't know about you, but I'm famished," she said.

He gazed at her for some time. His wife appeared much as he remembered her—her wide smile, her large green eyes. But there was a fatigue in her face he had never seen before.

They sat at the massive spread laid out for them, enough food for a dozen people for a dozen meals. He tried to eat a little bit of everything, although sometimes he found the skin tough and difficult to chew.

U is for Underground

D odge wasn't sure if any of the crowd were following him. They were preoccupied with whatever outrage they believed had just occurred. They filled that end of the street and were trespassing on people's lawns. Should he alert the police? He should at least alert somebody. He kept looking back over his shoulder and caught the eye of one or two of them, which was a huge error. He should have just walked home as if nothing had happened. He started to run, which was probably yet another mistake.

He opened his front gate and trotted up the front steps. His yard, raw and unkempt, needed work. The grass was tall enough to hide someone crouching and the bushes were so overgrown he couldn't see the edges of the house or the property line. Why hadn't he seen that before? He'd been so busy with Queneau's property he'd neglected his own. No wonder his neighbors were no longer speaking to him.

Was this still his house? He wasn't sure. The house had been one of the perks of the job. Queneau kept telling him the property was all his, and yet Dodge never saw any deed. He wouldn't be surprised if a lawyer dropped by with an order to

vacate the premises. He wondered how much time he had left—
would they kick him out before or after the funeral?

Unlike most of the houses on Alphabet Row, #U had no
letter by the front door. Dodge took it down when he moved in.
He didn't want to participate in this, whatever it was. Taking
the letter down made him feel slightly safer.

Yet he couldn't evade responsibility. While in Queneau's
employ he'd seen things, terrible things, all manner of human
degradation and the end of lives played out on video screens.
Sometimes he'd called for help on their behalf, but more often
he had not. Why? Was it simply because he saw that as outside
the scope of his duties? Or because he felt anonymous, a mere
viewer of flitting images across a video screen. An innocent
bystander.

Was having a home of his own worth the moral
compromise? Everyone deserved a place to live. It was an
unassuming house: weathered brick walls, aging plaster, two
small bedrooms, a tiny bathroom and kitchen, a cramped living
room with a fireplace. But it was what Dodge had always
dreamed of. The back yard was full of junk from previous
occupants—old cars and miscellaneous rusting equipment,
stacks of rotting building materials—the paths between them
clogged with weeds, trash trees, and vines. He'd never gotten
around to having it all removed. He wasn't even sure he had
the authority. He needed to run it by Queneau first.

Dodge collapsed into the stuffed armchair by the front
window. From here he could see anyone walking down the
street or coming up the walk. But if the threat came through the
bushes from the neighboring yards he might never detect them.

His cat Winston jumped into his lap. His twenty-third cat,
and the only one still with him. He'd always had bad luck with
pets. He'd named them alphabetically, but few lasted long
enough for him to get to know them well. At least they didn't

die while they were with him, as far as he knew. They simply vanished after a relatively short stay. He always wondered if something had eaten them. But perhaps they simply found him boring. He didn't know why he still tried to have a pet in his life. Still hoping for some sort of sustained companionship perhaps.

"Winston, have I fed you today?" The cat stared at him, withholding an answer. He picked the cat up gingerly, carried him to his food bowl, and sat him down. Winston's interest picked up immediately. He raised up and rested his front paws on Dodge's lower leg.

Dodge opened a can of cat food and bent down to scrape it into the bowl. Winston kept trying to eat from the can and that wouldn't do. It annoyed Dodge to have to push the cat away. But if he hadn't fed him in a while this behavior was explainable. If Dodge lived with someone they would have reminded him about such things. Perhaps they would have talked him out of taking this unhappy job in the first place.

"Eat hearty. And I'm sorry if I forgot."

Dodge thought he saw shadows cross the dining room window overlooking the side yard. He walked slowly over and pulled back the curtain. The window was filthy, and he could see very little. Anything could be hiding out there. He listened for whispered conversation, but in his experience you always heard whispers if you listened hard enough.

He made his way to the back porch and peered into the yard. Again, almost anyone could be hiding there amongst the junk. But these people didn't seem all that subtle. He doubted they would engage in any sort of surreptitious attack. From them it would more likely be a frontal assault on the premises, brandishing weapons and trying to burn the house down, screaming for his traitorous blood.

He saw two women stand up in his back yard. Dodge couldn't tell where they came from. Had they crawled under his fence? Then he realized they were the two women from next door, the ones remodeling that wreck of a house. Maybe they were lost, or idly snooping. Or maybe they were in on it, part of Queneau's vast internet following. They didn't look the type, but in this new world appearances could not be relied upon.

He watched them wander through the vegetation and around the piles of trash for a bit, then they reversed themselves and suddenly were gone. He had no idea how.

Dodge thought he heard noises out front, but when he returned to the living room window he saw no one in the street or in his front yard. He thought about going out on the porch and looking from there, but that felt unwise, and might aggravate whoever might be spying on him. He sat down again and was about to fall asleep when he heard the noises again, bumps and scratching, footsteps on the porch maybe. He got up and retrieved his hammer and a box of large nails from his hall closet, a cordless electric drill, and a coffee can full of long screws. He went around to his windows and nailed or screwed them shut. Then glancing at his front door he did the same there, securing the door to the doorframe, then sliding his couch in front to further barricade it.

He went into his bedroom and threw the mattress and box springs off the bed, took the support boards out of the frame and used them to partially board up the windows.

He kept himself calm by focusing on his labors and ignoring the clamor of voices outside.

It wasn't enough of course. There were still a thousand different ways to get in. And people like that, worked into a frenzy by their illogical attraction to a charismatic leader, would stop at nothing to get to someone they perceived as a turncoat.

216 / Steve Rasnic Tem

Of course, these people, they weren't entirely unjustified, were they? After all, Dodge had committed actual murder, preceded by multiple instances of moral cowardice. He was no innocent. It was necessary, but don't many murderers believe so? It had been a kind of mercy killing. Would anyone understand that? If he were charged at least he'd be able to plead his case. Dodge needed some penance, some punishment to make things right, yet no punishment felt sufficient.

As much as he resisted, Dodge kept looking at his basement door. He hated the basement. He'd always hated basements: the earthy gloom, the dank smell, an atmosphere seemingly conducive to corruption. He'd barely gone down there since he moved in. And certainly, his limited knowledge of the underground life of this street had not improved his attitude toward below-ground living spaces.

He supposed a lot of people moved into their houses without looking into the basement, but eventually they used it didn't they, at least for storage? Basements, especially old ones, were drab and dirty for the most part. It was the place where you stuck things you had no immediate use for. Where you hid things.

Dodge could hear them gathering on the porch, crowding outside his windows. Soon they'd be breaking the glass, reaching through, and yanking at the boards. They wouldn't care if they cut their arms in the process. There were so many of them they could lose several of their members from blood loss and it wouldn't even slow them down.

He grabbed a flashlight and scooped Winston up on his way to the basement. To leave the poor creature to the mercy of the crowd would have been unfeeling.

The basement was deeper than he remembered. He flipped on the light, but the resulting illumination was less than adequate. He still couldn't see the bottom of the stairs. Winston began to struggle as they descended, but Dodge held on tight. He hoped he wouldn't lose an eye for his trouble.

After ten steps he stumbled, his instincts telling him he should have already reached the floor. Three more steps and his right shoe landed on something solid and slightly slippery. He moved the light and found concrete with a thin covering of loose soil. Further probing revealed a few broken-down crates, an old chair, the ancient furnace crowding one corner. Dodge never used it, preferring the small fireplace in the bedroom.

It was an ugly, irredeemable space: calcium deposits in the corners and huge clumps of dust making disturbing shapes. Various wounds in the walls appeared ulcerous. The stench was ubiquitous, a perfume of sour decay and cloistered air.

In several regions the concrete and stone floor was missing, showing exposed dirt. Much of this bare ground had been churned. Similar exposed ground could be seen in various patches in the walls, stone and brick removed and piled onto the floor below.

Dodge knew the basements along this street varied greatly in both size and content. Most had furnaces but some did not. Some residents expanded their basement space once they moved in, whereas some had those dark spaces filled. Why? To soothe some nameless anxiety?

These basements did not belong to Queneau. They did not belong to anyone. They held their own secrets, and did not reveal them easily. Although in the course of his work Dodge had gone into many of these homes when the owners weren't there, he never went into the basements. He might open a basement door from time to time, but he never ventured down those stairs.

Winston began making a mewling sound which rapidly warped into that hideous, high-pitched howl cats make when they perceive some presence which disturbs them. Dodge searched with the light and found the cat rigid, hackles raised, head pointed to a dirt spot on the basement wall. Soil drifted from the spot, then something, some large pale body, turned within it, exposing a naked white flank, then legs then long feet ending in clawed toes before it disappeared. Dodge imagined something unholy within that wall.

Winston turned and bolted, striking the opposite wall head-first, claws raking with a spray of clay and malleable rock. Much of the wall collapsed, revealing a wide tunnel, perhaps an abandoned sewer or a passage into another chamber, into which the cat vanished.

Dodge was not unaffected by Winston's disappearance, but he was not about to go in after him, until he heard the thundering overhead, a human stampede pouring into his house, tearing through his things, looking for him, opening every door. He plunged into the tunnel as if diving into his own grave.

It appeared to be a network, an uncanny labyrinth of passages. He couldn't imagine the instability this brought to the houses above. His flashlight, shaking back and forth as he hurried, revealed a number of choices, branches upon branches. He had no guide for which passages to take, but he heard Winston continue to howl, and caught the occasional glimpse of his bendable orange form, and so Dodge followed him.

Most of these routes were empty, but here and there he encountered the remnants of old utility lines, pipes, and cables, and a few scattered support timbers indicating that humans had once used at least part of this system underneath the neighborhood. But he didn't understand how they managed to hold back the mass of dirt. A collapse appeared imminent.

In one side chamber he discovered a scatter of rotting clothing: shirts, pants, flowery dresses (or they might have been tablecloths or curtains), copious amounts of underwear which he didn't care to examine closely.

There were also rats, of course, more than he wanted to acknowledge, a variety of worms and insects, some species of which he was completely unfamiliar. Some were quite long with multiple prehensile appendages, moving oddly across the floor of the tunnels, their various parts seemingly in conflict.

He occasionally stepped onto soft and crumbly places where he struggled to remain upright and not fall through into whatever levels lay below.

Twice he encountered the remnants of rotted and useless staircases and wondered if these once lead to other basements, other homes, in the neighborhood. He remembered reading about an ancient underground city in Turkey which once housed 20,000 people with eighteen levels of tunnels stretching for hundreds of miles. Could this be anything like that? It seemed unlikely but not exactly impossible.

Finally Dodge caught up to Winston. The cat was lying in the middle of the pathway, apparently unconscious. Had he tired, or was it something worse? Dodge sniffed the air for traces of gas or anything similarly suspicious. Maybe he shouldn't have followed the cat, but that was a mistake he could not undo.

Ahead of them the tunnel appeared to slant upward and disappear into the shadows overhead.

Dodge wanted to pray but he didn't believe in anything. So, who or what should he pray to? What could he possibly wish for?

Winston got up and purred, curling and uncurling his tail. Then he turned and scrambled up the incline. Dodge followed, struggling on the loose dirt and debris, bits of rotted wood, brick, mortar, rusted bolts and nails and the other miscellanea of a house disintegrating from underneath.

The cat scratched frantically on the stretch of wood above their heads when someone on the other side lifted it away. A crowd of curious faces peered down from the exposed square hole.

Dodge put his palm under Winston's rear and gently pushed him into the waiting hands. He let them grab his arms and pull him up into the house.

He was numb to the uproar at first, a mixture of excitement and was that in fact anger? Then he saw that small, discolored mummy which had once been Queneau propped up in a Queen Anne wingback chair, face frozen in a rictus smile, his holes still leaking from where he'd been unplugged, surrounded by all these worshipful strangers.

V is for Vermin

She vividly recalled what it was like as a young child before the accident: wandering through the woods behind their house, prying up rotting logs to see the teeming insects, the sad remains, the vermin feasting on both the living and the dead, a harsher version of the vivarium her class managed at school. Her parents worried over her apparent need to look under everything.

Then after, weeks lying in her hospital bed, feeling vulnerable and afraid of all those parasitic creatures waiting in the dark for her and everyone she loved.

Delia was on her belly wriggling through the crawlspace when she heard the commotion on the front porch. A chorus of vacuous laughter echoed through the dark cavity and the drubbings, vaguely suggestive of vandalism, sent drifts of dust raining across her head and back.

She saw no point in rushing upstairs to investigate because she had no means of rushing. She was too far into this debris-filled space, her bad leg throbbing from its awkward positioning, and the lack of traction against loose dirt, broken brick, and rat gnawed fragments of wood made it difficult to turn around.

She could see little with her headlamp, but what she could view of the architecture exposed above the rubble—masonry arches and keystones, stone columns with antique candle sconces—looked well out of place beneath a Thirties-era American bungalow. This hadn't always been a crawlspace.

The dust mask slipped off her nose and the headlamp kept blinking on and off. Every time she turned her head some hard-to-fathom shape revealed itself, and then her surroundings turned pitch-black again. Worse, she could hear the rats scratching about their fetid nests beyond the reach of the beam. Their acrid stench overpowering, a sour perfume of musky ammonia, not just down here, but throughout the house.

All this would be cleared, the upstairs stripped of damage, and she would experience the fullness of her impulsive purchase, but for now it appeared to be a half million dollars' worth of ruin.

By the time Delia got upstairs the vandals were gone. They'd graffitied a large white V across her beautiful antique door. She didn't understand the hate. Was it about her Jewishness, or the fact she was a lesbian? But how could anyone in her new neighborhood know these things? She shouted, "Vicious little freaks!" to any culprits near enough to hear. It was pitiful vengeance.

She hobbled down the steps, her leg almost making her fall, and limped to the street. She saw some teenagers with backpacks headed toward the library, talking, and laughing. One glanced back and smiled. She was suspicious but couldn't prove anything.

"Did they tag you? They got my abuela's house yesterday. Kids like that, they have no respect." Delia turned. A short, dark-skinned woman with a dazzling smile shook her hand. "I'm Martina. You posted a flyer at the grocers. Do you still need a worker?"

"It's dusty, hard labor."

"I'm fine with that. Show me."

Twenty minutes later they climbed out of that vile tomb she'd paid so much money for and peeled off their masks. Martina was strong and friendly, and she had some clever ideas to make the work go faster, including hiring a couple of her cousins who wouldn't charge much. Delia knew they would work well together. She made them some robust black tea.

"Did you know the Orloks?" Martina asked. "They were the family who lived here before. A woman and a really old man, her grandfather maybe. I sold them Girl Scout cookies when I was a kid. My grandmother took me to every house in the neighborhood. She said it wasn't safe to go by myself."

"No. I bought the house through their agent. It was a bargain in this neighborhood, but you can see why. I figured I could restore it with some help. I've hired a company to exterminate the rats and the roaches and whatever else is living here. But they won't step inside until I've cleared the debris and made the structure safer. The agent said the house has been vacant a few years. Was it nice before?"

"I remember it being dark inside. The one time I was here, I remember this moldy odor when the woman opened the door. She invited us inside, but my abuela, she said no, we had to hurry. I was glad. The woman kept shouting things to someone in the back of the house. Grandmother said the language was Romanian. It sounded an awful lot like Italian to me.

"I could see the old man back there, moving in and out of the shadows. He had this bald, swollen head. He glanced at me once—I was an imaginative child, so you'll have to forgive me—but it looked like the face of a giant rat. Those deep-set eyes, and two long teeth in front."

"Your grandmother didn't talk about them?"

"Those weren't good times for people who are different. I guess no times are. My grandmother was sympathetic to immigrants. She knew what it was like. Other people in the neighborhood weren't so kind. They thought foreigners carried diseases from their native countries. People said that about Mexicans, too."

"And Jews. The Nazis said we were like lice and caused typhus."

"And gays. Parents won't let their kids play with you. They think it's catching." They exchanged shy smiles.

Delia put down her tea. "I have plenty of breathing masks. And gloves." She glanced down at the gloved hand holding the cup. She wore gloves so often in this house she forgot she had it on. "You're sure you want to do this? Maybe I should have hired a crew with hazmat suits. But I don't have much money left—"

"It's okay. My cousins and I will be careful. You can stay up here and clean and organize. Your leg—I don't mean to insult you—is that permanent? You shouldn't be messing around in that basement."

Delia bristled. There was an awkward silence. "A car ran over me when I was young. They fixed it the best they could. It was okay for a long time, but now, not so much. You're right, I shouldn't be down there. But now that I know you a little, I don't think I need to be. But be careful, I'd feel terrible—"

"Our Lady will protect me." Martina pulled an Our Lady of Guadalupe medal out of her neckline and showed it. "I'm not a good Catholic, but you know, just in case."

———

Delia moved into an apartment a couple of blocks away until the end of construction. Every night after dark she left her new house and walked back to the apartment. She remembered before her accident riding her bike around the old neighborhood at night. Neighbors would have their porch and yard lights on, their kids playing outside. They called out friendly greetings from the shadows—everyone knew her name and who her parents were.

Here people retreated indoors when the sun went down. No one knew her or appeared to want to. Many of the houses were so dark she could barely distinguish their outlines. Narrow bottom floors with low roofs, wide overhangs. From a distance they resembled upright coffins.

The cousins arrived the next morning in a rusty panel van, Martina squeezed between them in the front seat. They might have been twins, short and powerfully built. They nodded and smiled when Martina introduced them, then unloaded metal buckets, pickaxes, and shovels. They shook their heads when Delia offered them masks, pulling up their bright bandanas. The three went to work, forming a bucket brigade to transfer debris from the basement to a side yard. Delia sifted through the rubble looking for treasures, but at this stage found only a few coins and corroded metal, fragments of furniture, and unidentifiable adornments including a long brass handle engraved *ORLOK*.

Martina brought out a trash bag sagging with lumpy contents. She held it far away from her body. It smelled awful.

"Your rats are eating each other. Every one of these bodies has been chewed on. I guess they don't have enough grub."

"I'm embarrassed you had to deal with that."

Martina shrugged. "*¡No hay problema!* Be careful sticking your hands into anything. The rabies vaccine is no vacation."

The work created clouds of dust throughout the house. Every evening Delia vacuumed. She wondered if it was even possible to eliminate all the dust, or if it would hide until the remodeling was complete, then creep out of the walls to ruin her things.

———

Three weeks into the cleanup Delia was working on the re-roofed second floor. She had no power in this part of the house and carried a small lantern bright enough to keep her from tripping. The windows had been screwed shut and painted over with multiple layers of black paint. Replacing them was going to be expensive.

She was removing water-damaged wall plaster and floorboards too far gone to salvage and checking for structural damage requiring professional intervention. Because of her leg she had to sit in a folding chair, but she had long pry bars and a block of wood to use as a fulcrum. The work was a struggle, but she would figure it out.

She encountered extensive rodent damage as well, chewed boards and posts, baseboards deeply clawed. She felt pity for the creatures, so hungry and desperate with only wood to snack on. Some of the damage could be painted over, but most would have to be replaced.

With all the gaps in the floor, the missing sections of wall, naked lathing and fallen plaster, wallpaper peeled in curls and landing in recumbent stiff folds, the lantern light created a confusion of expressionistic shadows across the room. The doors had been removed for refinishing, many of the closets partially deconstructed, so every time Delia moved the lantern some new mysterious realm of geometry was variously revealed.

The constant intrusion of unidentifiable sounds had been a distraction at first. Now she ignored them and focused on what needed to be done. She'd accepted that she'd be working around rats and spiders, cockroaches and other bugs, the occasional ferret or fox or squirrel which had found its way inside. So much disease, so much contagion. Martina gave her a can of animal repellent in case any of those creatures ventured too near, but she couldn't imagine having the sense to use it.

She was checking the floor joists inside a huge hole in the floor near one of the closets, moving the lantern around to find evidence of damp, when she heard a hiss. She scooted back thinking there was a snake. A chalk-white face appeared beneath one edge of the floor, its deep-set coal-like eyes burning. It hissed again, moist flecks spraying her arm. Its breath was appalling. She dropped the lantern just as the creature appeared to bend around itself, long body clothed in fur so dry and patchy it resembled a rotting coat. Delia turned and tripped over the lantern, shattering it. She landed hard on her side.

"Sounds like a possum," Martina said later as Delia was trying to calm herself. "They're rare here, but they do exist."

"No. No. It was too *big*. It was gigantic! I don't know how it even fit inside the floor."

Martina was quiet for a few moments. "Maybe the exterminators—"

"I've tried. They won't come until the basics are done. I didn't like the way he talked to me, like I was some silly teenager who doesn't understand how things work."

"You haven't been down in the cellar in a while. There's much to talk about, decisions to be made. You and I will work down there. We'll let the cousins work up here. They can put in the new windows. That will help with…visibility."

———

Delia was stunned.

"I hope you like castle chic." Martina laughed.

"I was thinking more dungeon, or mausoleum." The excavation had exposed walls, floors, and ceilings made from large stones fitted together, medieval-styled archways and columns. Martina and her cousins had placed floor lights to heighten the drama.

"I hope you're on good terms with your neighbors, specifically the ones left and right and behind you."

"I've never met any of them. Why?"

"Look at the size of this thing. It's been dug out part way under all their properties, and about halfway beneath the street out front. I'm surprised there's been no collapse."

Delia walked from one end to the other, looking up nervously. Roots had broken through from the ground above. "What am I going to do? They're going to sue me!"

"Maybe we can put some of it back. More immediately, something's been nesting down here. Maybe it's your possum, maybe something else." Martina showed her where shredded bits of cloth and wood and other scraps spilled from a large hole in the wall. She dragged out a tangle of polished wooden splinters and silky bits. Another of those metal handles with the engraving *ORLOK* appeared. "I don't want to alarm you, but do these look like pieces from a coffin to you?"

"It's an historic neighborhood. There are probably some abandoned grave plots. Not that I accept the notion I have pieces from a grave in my cellar."

Martina walked over to a patch of vines hanging down one corner of the cellar. She lifted the loose vegetation—it formed a flap covering another large hole. The stone and the rubble had been worn smooth here, suggesting frequent passage. "This is where it's been getting in and out."

"It was a big animal, but that seems a large hole for a possum."

"I wonder." Before Delia could stop her Martina was climbing through the hole. Not sure what she should do, Delia followed.

They were outside, halfway into her neighbor's back yard. She's seen him on his front porch, an older gentleman. The lot was badly neglected, a jungle of trees and thick vines, a sea of tall weeds containing islands of rusted machinery.

Martina pointed to a worn path. "There's a trail." She began to follow it. Delia glanced at the man's back porch, then hurried to join her.

The vague trail became vegetation worn down to bare earth leading to a trash mound by the back fence. From there multiple paths ventured out in a spoke pattern, one leading back toward the man's house, several going under fences into other yards.

"Skeletons." Delia limped over to where Martina stood by the trash pile. Among the cans and rinds there were some definite remains, leg bones, animal skulls, fragments of rib cage. There were also small vertebrae protruding from the dirt.

"Tell me none of those are human, Martina."

Martina prodded the garbage with her foot. "Not unless they're babies."

"Martina!"

"They're animals, sweetheart. No reason to get the police involved."

Delia smiled. She didn't want to wiggle back through that hole into the cellar, but Martina suggested it was simpler than trying to explain to her neighbor why they were in his backyard.

Once inside Martina took several large stones and cemented them into place, sealing the passage. Delia wondered if they should have made sure the creature was out of her house first.

The black hearse which pulled up in front was unlike any vehicle Delia had seen before. An apparent antique, it had large chrome tubes coming out of the engine compartment. Roaring-Twenties-style grill and running boards. Shiny script identified the car as an *Excalibur*. The side windows were blacked out similarly to her windows upstairs. Two tall men stepped out of the front. One opened a passenger door and an even taller woman dressed in black lace emerged.

Delia and Martina watched from the front window. Delia could see the cousins preparing frames in the yard. They stopped what they were doing and stared.

"That's her, the Lady Orlok," Martina said breathlessly. "After all these years she's barely changed." Delia had never heard her friend sound less than calm before.

"She's … *elegant*." It was an understatement. The woman was so tall, so pale, moving like an exotic bird toward Delia's front porch. The two men remained by the hearse.

Delia opened the door before the knock. Lady Orlok stared, looking miffed. "Our door, pardon me, *your* door, has been *defiled*."

"I know. Vandals." The woman raised an eyebrow. "I'm having it redone. It'll look better than new. Please come in."

Delia hastily prepared tea while Martina sat with the woman. She felt compelled to treat this strange woman like royalty. "Martina, here, she knows you," Delia blurted. "I mean she's met you."

"I was selling Girl Scout cookies. I was just a child, of course."

Lady Orlok nodded, unsmiling. "Of course. How are you?" She did sound musical, like Italian, but different.

"I'm fine, thank you." Martina said. "Busy helping my friend here restore this wreck of a home. Can we help you with something?"

Delia gasped, but her admiration for Martina increased even more.

"I respect ... directness," Lady Orlok replied. "When I left here, many years ago, I left something especially important behind. I was unhappy, and angry, and this made me do something irresponsible."

"Oh, I'm sorry." Delia sat down. "What was it?"

The woman closed her eyes. "You would know what I am talking about, if you were to have an encounter."

"Encounter?"

"Yes, encounter. Could you show me the house? Such a tour might precipitate...some activity."

Martina clearly wasn't happy, but Delia gave the lady a tour, starting with the basement. The woman had to duck to avoid hitting her head at the bottom of the stairs. Once inside, she stared at the walls in silence.

"Is it the way you remembered it?" Delia asked.

"Less clean. The furniture, many grand pieces, are missing. I left them behind. Were they less than suitable? Or did you sell them? Quite valuable as antiques, I would think."

"All we found were fragments. Splinters really. A lot of rat-chewed, worthless wood."

The woman nodded. "There were many candles, then. The light from the candles did not bother him. He built all this himself. He dug out the common brick and he continued to dig. He brought in the stones. He was extraordinarily strong, even at such an age. He fit everything together from memory. He said it reminded him of the old country."

Martina interrupted. "This *he*? Was that your grandfather?"

Lady Orlok stared at her. "An approximation. An *honorific* if you will."

"He must have passed some time ago."

Again, the lady stared, as if considering her words. "We became estranged. I have not seen him in a long time. I regret this. I should not have left so quickly."

"It took forever to clean the wreckage out of here you know. The way you left this house."

"Martina." Delia didn't know if she was embarrassed or afraid.

Lady Orlok looked from one to the other. "I do not understand. The house is vintage, but it was pristine when I departed, I assure you. I am sorry if there has been trouble. If there has been damage. I was not here to...control the environment."

The lady left a card, A. ORLOK, with a phone number written in elegant script. She instructed Delia to call "in case circumstances change." Delia had no idea what she meant.

The cousins left a week later. "Thank them for all their hard work."

Martina and the cousins exchanged a few words. "They say they do roofing all summer and fall. For them, this was a pleasant change." One grabbed Martina's arm and whispered. Martina smiled. "They say you should be careful in this house. They say even after all this work it hangs onto its secrets."

———

In Delia's dream she was a child again, lying in bed, her leg shattered, taped, and glued back together. She dared not move or it would fall apart. But instead of the hospital bed, she was in a bedroom in her new home, now all fixed and beautiful, the walls hung with flowery wallpapers and luxurious fabrics, paintings of peaceful country scenes, the rooms furnished in fine antiques Delia was surprised to have been able to afford.

But insects were creeping from between the paper seams and flowing down the wall. Despite their terrible injuries half-eaten rats were crawling out from under those beautiful antiques. But worse were the unintelligible whispers, and the sour breath of the thing lying beside her, now slipping out from beneath the sheets.

Delia slept late, and by the time she arrived at the house Martina wasn't there. Had she gotten impatient and left? Delia looked everywhere. She reached for her cell, but it wasn't in her pocket. She walked back to the apartment. It wasn't there either. She realized she hadn't seen it since she fell upstairs at the new house. She walked back, her leg throbbing from the exertion, and searched. Nothing. She tried not to panic. Maybe Martina was tired of working for her. Maybe she'd been offended by the Orlok visit. Delia didn't have Martina's number memorized, nor did she know where Martina or her grandmother lived.

She knew there were ways to retrieve contact information, but she didn't know how to do that. She barely knew how to use the cell phone at all.

But she knew her phone was here somewhere. She sat and had a cup of tea, centering herself. She had developed a taste for tea. She had work to do. Eventually Martina or the phone, hopefully both, would turn up.

Something thumped in the area behind the kitchen. They'd barely made a start there. It was the old pantry, the back porch, a kind of mud room, the back staircase to upstairs.

She hadn't replaced the lantern yet, but she had a big old flashlight. She heard some scraping. She got up slowly, the flashlight in front of her like a gun. It was heavy. She could hit someone with it.

She heard a rhythmic creaking on the back stairs. Something going up, or something coming down. She swung herself around the corner, aiming the beam upwards.

A furry flood of rats scurried across the landing at the top of the stairs, their eyes gleaming red in the light. Something tall and stick-thin loomed over them. She raised the beam higher. Something moved into the shadows to the right of the landing, escaping the light.

Because of her leg, Delia had never much liked stairs, but these last few weeks had made her stronger. She braced herself, then ascended, one hand firmly on the railing, the other gripping the flashlight like a club, ready to use it that way if necessary.

She kept glancing at her feet, afraid of stepping onto a rat or into a hole. She reached the landing and turned, and still looking down, almost missed it, the shape moving through a broken closet space ahead of her. She jerked her head up.

The silhouette of his great, domed head came around the wall first, then she had full view of his chalk-white face, more rat than human, the pointed ears, bushy eyebrows, sunken eyes, beaky nose, a long V-shaped chin, and those gigantic rat's incisors. His coat was rotted and falling off. He was taller than the doorway and had to stoop. His talons clicked across the naked wood frame.

They both stopped and gazed at each other. He had his hands up—those incredibly long fingers curling and uncurling like eyelashes—to shield his reddening eyes against the light, then gradually lowered them. He stared at her a moment, then raised a finger to smooth down his gangly eyebrows, then to lightly dust off his shabby dark coat—fruitlessly, because that decaying garment demanded much more than a cursory tidying. As ancient as the thing was, as hideously ugly, he was still pathetically vain. Nothing seemed either wise or venerable about the creature.

His pale skin was stretched tight against his skull. It appeared heavily veined, but the veins were even lighter than his skin, as if these vessels were empty.

He shuddered, lifting his lips away from his velvety pink gums. A narrow pale tongue peeked out as if to wet them, but she saw no saliva, and the tongue made a slight scraping noise as it crossed the lips.

Delia wasn't completely surprised to encounter this being. If anything, it was a validation of everything she'd felt since taking physical possession of the property.

"You need to leave," she said. "You don't belong here. This house is mine now." He made what appeared to be a vulgar gesture with those incredibly long fingers. "I'm serious. I paid good money—"

He lurched in her direction. She moved to the side, easily avoiding him. She wasn't sure how much he could see. The way he stumbled around seemed indicative of a serious vision impairment. She supposed his body remembered the location of things, but now with some of the walls removed he was confused.

His mouth gaped open like a snake's, and he hissed in her direction. His mouth was so dry, and smelled vile. She could see the terrible splits in his lips.

He'd lost his power of speech it seemed. His mouth silently conveyed his rage. She supposed he was still a villain, but she couldn't help but pity him.

He'd gone to all fours, and he found the stairs again. She could hear him hurtling down the steps, groaning and making hideous whistling noises. She no longer felt afraid, and followed.

She heard him crashing through the kitchen, then into the ruined space she hoped would one day be her lovely dining room. She heard him weeping, or at least his version of weeping, and it saddened her, thinking how trapped he must feel.

She followed him into the cellar, where bugs congregated into a moving carpet flowing across the floor. He crushed and smashed his way across them to the large debris-filled void in the wall, and clawing through the contents, tossing dirt and garbage and dry vegetation everywhere, he dug himself back into his nest.

Delia stopped, wondering if she should pursue. She didn't want to. She looked at the trash spread around her feet, dead rats, bones, the desiccated viscera of some small animal, a shiny bit of metal. She picked it up. It was Martina's Our Lady of Guadalupe medal. The chain had been broken. Then she heard the muffled, distant ringing of her phone deep inside the nest.

She dived into the hole, pushing debris away from her, swimming in it. She was unsuccessful at keeping it out of her mouth, which left her sucking for air, on the verge of vomiting, when she touched him.

He swung his arms at her in vicious swipes. No, too soft and weak for that. No strength at all behind them. These blows weren't any sort of defense. They were the sad gestures of a desperate, failing thing.

That didn't mean he wasn't dangerous. He might yet be able to hurt her, she thought, when she felt the hands around her feet dragging her out.

Delia and Martina sat on the front steps watching as the two men loaded the deep red mahogany coffin into the back of the hearse. Lady Orlok stood nearby, murmuring cautions.

"I should have come sooner when you didn't answer your cell. I'm sorry," Martina said, brushing the filth out of Delia's hair. Delia hadn't yet had time to shower. She didn't understand how Martina could stand being next to her, much less groom her.

"You couldn't know. Your grandmother being sick, that's where you needed to be." Lady Orlok had arrived right away. As it turned out, she'd been staying in a hotel downtown, waiting for Delia's call, knowing it would come.

Martina sighed. "She is beautiful, and a strong woman. You don't suppose …"

"His condition runs in the family? The sunlight doesn't appear to bother her."

"Should we have called the police instead? This doesn't feel right."

"We didn't find any human bones, at least as far as we know. He appears to have sustained himself on the rats. I'm sorry about your medal."

"It just needs a new chain. I lost it weeks ago. I didn't want to tell you."

"Do you think you can get your cousins to come back?"

"Perhaps. Why?"

"I'm ordering several tons of gravel. I don't need a cellar, all that empty space, space I don't even own. We're going to fill it in."

W is for Whispers

In the quiet, you will hear us, our voices rising above the hush.

How do you tell the difference between thinking and hearing? It used to come so naturally. Clarence had lived alone for some time. It should have been easy.

One weekend he tried counting all the people on his picture wall he knew were dead. Some deaths he knew because he'd seen a notice or received a phone call, others because they'd already been old when he was young. His children and grandchildren were alive, although he rarely saw them. They spent their time with his ex-wife, who he assumed was alive. No one had informed him otherwise. Few photos of her adorned his wall. Just the family portraits, where he and Paula bracketed their handsome brood. He believed the divorce had been his fault, although he was fuzzy on the details.

Sometimes a photograph exposes our true nature. Paula looked lovely and kind in hers. He yearned to find such kindness again.

His face in photographs was always difficult to read.

Did you hear what we said? Do you even care?

Some whispers might have been hers. Things she said while he wasn't listening, come back now as memory. She'd had such a soft voice, although he hadn't heard it in years. He couldn't remember it exactly, so maybe one of these voices could be hers. He'd read that whispers don't require vocal cords. But didn't they require breath?

Sometimes the moments captured in these pictures—an angry look, a raised hand—he'd prefer to forget. Occasionally he spotted other faces within the frames, reflections in the glass. Someone behind him? Their images were too dim to identify. Perhaps that was where they lived.

If Clarence had it all to do over, he might have decorated like a minimalist, uncluttered spaces with clean lines and useful, functional furniture. He would have followed the advice to use small rugs instead of carpeting, gotten rid of the flower-patterned upholstery, and paid attention when the magazines said more than two pictures in a room screamed *Grandmother's House*.

Well, he was a grandfather, and he wasn't embarrassed by it. He didn't always remember how old his grandchildren were, but he still loved them. Perhaps he was even a great-grandfather by now. He couldn't quite remember.

He did not own a nice house. He couldn't afford one. When Paula divorced him decades ago, they sold the big home where they raised their kids. She took her share and moved to California. He took a few furniture pieces no one else wanted, and these photographs. This one-bedroom bungalow had been constructed in the late Twenties, one of several such houses built at the same time on Alphabet Row. His was the smallest on the street which made him wonder if they ran out of bricks. A large wooden W once decorated the red front door. All that remained was its dead gray silhouette.

The house wasn't big enough for a couple with a child, so families might have been started here, but they never stayed long. The turnover in occupants must have been high. He imagined there had been other single people like himself, widows and unattached men, old folks holed up for their final days.

Perhaps these were the voices he heard. They'd left something of themselves behind. Were they talking about him? Sometimes he assumed his brain wasn't working properly, or this house wasn't working properly, maybe both and the same.

The dining and living rooms shared a continuous wall which he'd turned into a gallery. The pictures started just above the wainscoting and continued until four or five inches below the ceiling. Photos of his children at various ages, family group photos, friends both distant and close, memorialized milestones and accomplishments, dead relatives, including several he never knew or could not identify. His memory wasn't what it used to be.

Your grandfather's cousin Emma. You never met her.

The voice hadn't been his. Clarence's hearing had become unreliable the last few years, but sometimes he heard things he couldn't know.

———

Choosing which pictures to hang on a wall is a serious concern. You're advocating that these people and events are worth remembering. It seemed a kind of idolatry. It shouldn't have surprised him, having elevated them this way, that some would feel compelled to talk back.

A warm summer day. I was in love then. I hadn't yet lost the ability.

Clarence spent hours studying these pictures. He'd lost so many names, and confused others. He hoped looking at these faces day after day might bring those names back to him.

What troubled him most were the things he couldn't see, hiding in the unfocused shadows of the backgrounds. He wondered if there were similar things to be worried about in the shadows of his own house. It was a small house, but there were many shadows.

Either your son or your grandson. They both looked the same at that age, as did you.

During the day, the picture frames were like windows into other times and other lives. Some—his children, grandchildren—he knew very well. Others were only vaguely recalled strangers. The number who were strangers increased with each passing month.

He dusted as often as he could, but he couldn't keep up. Cobwebs and spiderwebs formed, flies were caught, and flies devoured.

It's filthy on top of these frames. Don't you ever clean?

Some months he waged all-out war on the dust. He always lost. It didn't matter whether clarity or confusion reigned, the dust accumulated. Dust always wins.

Such disrespect. You say you care, but where is the evidence?

At night he kept the lights dim to save on electricity. He couldn't see the frames and the picture wall bubbled with shadow. Yet the photos never slept. He heard subtle movements within the frames, shifts and tilts as imbalances were created. He'd never felt secure in how they hung. He'd never bought expensive frames. In the dark the whispers were indecipherable. They sounded more like the inarticulate complaints of the dying. He had never been a religious man, but he resorted to mumbling prayers in the dark. He didn't know what else to do.

The whispering continued in the mornings, and occurred throughout the afternoons, a low volume sibilance with occasional breathy vowels, floating through all the rooms. The best reception, if he could call it that, was when he was standing by the picture wall, but the voices were evident in other rooms as well.

One afternoon he noticed a photograph on the wall he hadn't seen before. It was him, or someone who looked like him, waltzing with a young woman, but he didn't recognize her. She might have been a younger version of Paula, but if that was him in the picture the ages didn't match. The young woman might have been their daughter, but he couldn't remember ever dancing with his daughter, which was a shame.

Perhaps the arrangement of the photos was too random. If he reordered them chronologically, they might make more sense. But Clarence's memory wasn't up to the task. He couldn't reliably remember what day it was today. In his life every day was the same.

There he was in a shiny green jacket and a gray newsboy cap. A misguided attempt to look dapper. Yet he couldn't remember ever having such items in his wardrobe.

You've never looked worse than now.

In a more familiar photo, he sported a full black beard with long, ragged hair. He looked like a werewolf. Beside it, a more welcoming photo of one of the children blowing bubbles. He couldn't tell which of their children it was. They all looked the same at that age. Or maybe it was someone else's child altogether. Perhaps a neighbor's.

If you don't remember who will?

———

Weeks went by when the only human beings he encountered were the ones in these pictures. His other frequent companions were spiders and flies and the occasional roach. Once a wren landed on his windowsill. Clarence wept when it flew away.

He could hear them talking even when he was in the cellar. Their voices seeped through the walls. Perhaps some were buried nearby, and he was the only one available to listen.

What did you forget now?

His cell phone for one. It was for the best. No one ever called with pleasant news. Usually they were salespeople, or thieves eager to take his money. He hated the sound of their tiny, distant voices, like buzzing wasps, begging.

Now and then he heard his lost phone breathing, but that sound could have come from anywhere.

Clarence had met few of his neighbors. He never intended to be a hermit, but he supposed that had become a reasonable interpretation of his behavior. A terrible man lived next door. Clarence could hear him screaming at night. He wondered if that man's walls whispered as well.

Gazing at his grandfather's photo one afternoon he was surprised to discover the old man had shaved. A few weeks later he'd grown it back again. As Clarence recalled, his grandfather only married once, but there were different women with him in the photo every time he looked.

One morning Clarence woke up with a headache affecting his vision. The glare off the pictures was painful to look at. Then he realized the frames were all missing their photos. The wall appeared riddled with rectangular holes.

When he next looked, only the photographs of him had returned. In each one his face was grim and waxen, his eyes closed. They looked like those Victorian post-mortem photographs taken as a memento for the family.

The body decays, but an image lasts forever.

———

Clarence's driver's license was taken away a year ago. It was for the best. He'd become problematic as a driver. Distraction was his normal state. He didn't miss it. There was nowhere he needed to be. Sometimes he forgot his phone number, but he never called himself anyway. He did have a problem choosing clothing. He left his house so seldomly he was never quite sure what to wear. One weekend he went out to shovel the snow from his sidewalk and found it unbearably cold. Then he realized he was only wearing shorts, a T-shirt, and slippers.

It is cold outside, but colder in here.

On sunny afternoons, the glass in the picture frames bloomed into a complex pattern of reflections. Often images moved from one frame to another. He couldn't be sure—he didn't have time to take an inventory of every photo—but things had gone missing, items, people, or both, reappearing somewhere else.

He started drinking alcohol at meals and between meals. He'd never been a big drinker, but now drinking seemed a useful way to fill the time. He saw nothing wrong with this, but he'd be humiliated if any of his children or grandchildren found him in such a state. More than once he was eating at the table when he discovered none of the pictures on the wall were familiar to him.

He often woke up in the middle of the night, climbed out of bed, and went to the picture wall to see if anything had changed. A beach scene with children—he believed they were his cousins. He was supposed to be in the photo, but he couldn't pick himself out. The water in the photo moved. Had one of the children drowned?

He found a portrait of himself he'd never seen before. He was lying on the floor, embracing a bottle of whiskey as if it were a small child. It was the worst likeness of himself he'd ever seen. He removed it from the wall, tore the photo out of its frame, wadded it up, and threw it in the trash.

We're always here if you need to talk.

It was a tiny house, but now and then he became completely lost in it. More than once he was convinced he was in some wayward room of their old, much larger home. Paula was calling for him, growing increasing impatient, but he couldn't find a—something—which would lead him to her. He'd lost the right word, but it didn't matter. If he only tried the right *bottle*, he would find her. Yes, *bottle* was the word he wanted.

A bottle was what you always wanted.

The seasons changed in these photos from one day to the next. He'd see the same outdoor snapshot in summer, winter, and fall. Trees died and had to be cut down. Houses were bulldozed and the wreckage scraped down to bare earth.

You cannot argue with progress. Or stop it.

Photos rearranged themselves. Photos went completely missing, but then reappeared again weeks later. None of the people in his pictures ever offered an explanation, even after he'd questioned them for hours.

He watched as one pale, thin woman traveled from frame to frame across the wall. He believed it was his great-grandmother. Legend had it she'd gone walking across the fields one day and never returned. The vegetation in these photos withered, followed by the people themselves.

Despite his best attempts to save them, the people in these pictures kept dying. Wisps of dust gathered on their shoulders and in their hair.

How can you see us through all this dust?

The man in the photo in front of him moved closer to the glass. Now he looked walleyed and distorted. The surface of the glass was wet. Clarence realized the photo was an underwater scene, and the man inside was drowning.

Do something!

Clarence did something. He took a nap. While he was sleeping the wind blew through the house knocking pictures off the walls. One frame sprouted wings and flew out the window. At the end of the storm the house was a wreck.

Whenever. Whatever. Life is chaos.

He woke up, went into the dining room, and stared at the picture wall. Everything looked fine. Everything seemed as it should be. The house itself smelled of polish and freshly cut flowers. A pie was baking in the oven. But he had a challenging time finding any photos in which he was included. They were all of Paula and the kids, Paula with the kids and Paula solo, along with the usual assortment of relatives, friends, and strangers.

When Clarence finally found himself, he was disappointed by the quality of the photograph. A tiny candid snapshot near one end of the wall, one of the last to be hung. He is turning away from the camera. He doesn't want his picture taken. His features are a blur.

When he turns back he is looking out of the frame into the dim space beyond. It is difficult to see through the dusty glass. But there is Paula with a worried expression looking in.

Clarence?

X is for Xenophobe

E dna heard the shuffling and the giggling on her front porch with dismay. She suspected it was those young hoodlums again, the neighborhood terrorists. Her Shih Tzu Tingling began barking. She hugged him to comfort them both.

They'd harassed her before, simply because she was an old woman living alone, who refused to put up with their foolishness. More than once they'd roughhoused on her lawn, trampling her carefully curated flowerbeds. Of course, she called the police, and of course, the police did nothing.

She waited until they left—a confrontation might be dangerous. Then she opened her door. She almost had a heart attack. They'd spray-painted an enormous yellow X across her beautiful, polished front door. Were they cancelling her? She'd heard about cancelling people—was this what they meant?

She felt a pain in her stomach. The young hoodlums had given her an ulcer. She supposed it was a small pain, a discomfort, but it had persisted for weeks.

It was the worst timing. Her new renter would be arriving soon, an injured man requiring a quiet place to recuperate. What would he think of the neighborhood? What would he think of her?

She surveyed the street looking for the perpetrators. The schools had let out and there were students in the street and on the sidewalk, headed for the old library. Many of them carried backpacks of sufficient size to hold numerous cans of spray paint. Many were laughing and chasing each other. She didn't see anything funny about destroying property.

"I can clean that for you." The voice was low and muffled. "Expunge it completely. I have the necessary skills."

Edna glanced around. At first she didn't see him, then spied him standing in the shadows just beyond the left edge of the porch. He wore a long charcoal-colored coat and matching scarf, a floppy hat pulled low in front. What little of his face she could see was wrapped in bandages, leaving only small holes for the mouth and one eye. "Mr. Caliban? Is that you?" When he'd told her over the phone he was damaged, she'd imagined nothing like this.

Before she knew it, he was up on her porch inches away. He was short—an inch or two shorter than her—and he stood with a pronounced twist, one shoulder lower than the other. He smelled vaguely of spicy fish. She reached out to touch him but stopped herself in time. What was she thinking?

"At your service," he said. "I saw the ones responsible running away. Perhaps next time I can catch them for you, brain them, batter their skulls."

Caliban did not have a short person's voice, but that was a silly thought. Edna admonished herself, saying a silent prayer asking for forgiveness. He did have an accent, but she couldn't place it. Italian maybe. One of those hot countries. But as much as she liked the sentiment of *brain them and batter their skulls*, it frightened her to hear him say it aloud.

Tingling came rushing out, stopped, and stared at the man, then began barking furiously.

"I'm so sorry. He barks at—" She stopped herself, about to say *trouble*. "Hush, Tingling! Your luggage," she said, "is it coming later?"

He stepped aside to show her the wheeled suitcase with an attached book tote he'd been dragging behind him. "I travel light. A change of clothes and some medical supplies, and of course my books. Do you enjoy reading, Missus Gerber?"

"It's Miss, and of course I read." She'd just lied to him. She'd never had the patience for reading, but he didn't need to know that.

Tingling sniffed the suitcase, the edge of Mr. Caliban's coat, his shoes. He reached down and petted her. The dog allowed it. It would be nice having a man in the house, especially one who spoke so politely. It had been years.

Edna noticed the crazy lady across the street staring at them from her front door. She'd drawn a red oval around her mouth as if she'd forgotten where her lips were. Edna stared back defiantly. Edna wasn't sure where the woman was from, but she certainly wasn't American.

———

The rental included one meal per day, dinner with her at the kitchen table. Edna could hear Caliban moving about—upstairs, on the steps, in her living room, outside—while she cooked. It made her nervous. He was everywhere at once. When dinner was ready, she went looking for him. She found him on the porch, gazing at her now-pristine door.

"How did you do that?" She could find no traces of paint, and if anything, the door looked nicer than before the vandalism.

"I have a knack," he said. He raised a gloved hand. It occurred to her then he'd been wearing gloves this entire time. "I believe I've inherited it from my mother." He'd removed his outer garb and now wore a loose-fitting shirt and sweatpants. His head was completely wrapped in bandages, like that old movie; what was it? *The Invisible Man*, yes. Claude Rains.

He continued to wear the gloves at dinner, which seemed outlandish to her. Was this the way they behaved where he was from? She'd made a nice stew, but she never anticipated she'd be so repulsed watching him eat. He stained his bandages getting the food through that little hole. It looked as if he'd been eating blood, or mud, or worse. A dull gray eye peered at her through the other, smaller hole, like that of a dead fish.

"Can you tell me what your ailment is? Will it get better?" It embarrassed her to ask, but she had a right to know. What if he carried one of those Asian viruses?

"It's a disfigurement. A birthmark of sorts. It hasn't gotten much better, but it's unlikely to get much worse."

"But I thought you wanted your room for recuperation."

"I do. I expect my recovery to take the remainder of my days."

She was angry. He'd tried to fool her. What else hadn't he told her? "Pardon me for asking, but exactly what nationality are you?"

He tilted his head, as if to pour something out of it. "I am between nationalities now I'm afraid. I once owned an island, but a powerful man took advantage of me and caused me much suffering. Then rich developers moved in. I'm sure you can imagine what followed."

"The rich have their own rules. They're not like the rest of us."

"Quite true."

"You were royalty then?"

He laughed a laugh so hideous she wondered if he might be faking. Then he began to choke, and more reddish-brown spots spread through the lower quarter of his bandages. It was a terrible thing to see, and Edna got up immediately and pounded his back. But what she felt beneath his shirt was far from normal: a mass of ridges, bubbles, and bones where no bones should be. She jerked her hand away in disgust.

He jumped up. "Terribly sorry. I must change." He moved hurriedly but awkwardly toward the stairs. Tingling tried to follow, but Edna pulled her back. Edna couldn't imagine allowing this man to live in her house for long. She didn't know what to think about someone whose face she could not see.

A pain ran through Edna's torso, extending from her private area to right beneath her heart. It was an agonizing moment, but so quick the pain was gone the moment it registered. Tingling barked at her. She hoped it wasn't cancer. So many she knew had died of cancer. She should have her new doctor check it out, she supposed, but she didn't really trust him. She wasn't a racist or anything, but she figured he got his diploma from some Caribbean medical school.

She sat down. Tingling crouched before her, growling and snapping at...what? Edna's female bits?

Later that evening she brought up some towels. The door to Caliban's room was open a couple of inches. He was lying on the bed, reading. Several books were stacked on the bedside table. *Robinson Crusoe, Treasure Island*—at least she'd heard of those, but *Nightmare Alley? The Geek?* They sounded horrid. He did have fresh bandages on, thank God.

"I have fresh towels," she said through the narrow opening. She supposed she could open it farther. She had the right; it was her house. But it was a man's bedroom. This was safer.

"Oh, thank you. You can bring them in."

"No, these go in the bathroom. What...what are you reading?" She could see that gray eye again, the dull gleam of it. Wouldn't it give you a terrible headache to read with one eye? Did he have another?

He didn't say anything for a moment. Then he held up the book. "This? It's *Grendel* by John Gardner. It's based on the creature from *Beowulf*, that ancient poem? He's a monster, 'a creature of darkness, exiled from happiness and accursed of God, the destroyer and devourer of our humankind.'"

Was he playing with her? "I don't like...monsters," she said. Something stirred in her belly. She was afraid she was going to be sick.

"You and the rest of world," he mumbled, but she was obviously meant to hear. She hated when people did that. He sat up and put the book down. Within that narrow two-inch gap, she felt targeted. "I came to reading late in life. As a youth I didn't really talk. I gabbled. The first words I learned to say were curses. They called me *moon-calf*, as you would name a pet or livestock. They were my gods. I was a slave; there are still slaves, did you know? People like you, you cultivate ignorance of certain facts. But I learned how to read. Then when I was left alone I kept reading. When I was forced from my island and spent all that time on ships, I didn't do anything but read. Whenever I finished a book, I tossed it into the ocean, thinking I'd teach my cousins, the fish, to read."

He was joking. Why was he joking? "And you like to read about monsters?"

"I like reading about myself!" He laughed. Why was he laughing? Edna could feel the pain begin in her abdomen again. "We're all monstrous to somebody, haven't you heard? But I've never found myself in any of these books, just a few poor souls no one cares about with similar tales of woe, of toads, beetles, and bats, and suffering from being pinched more stinging than bees. But I have learned many new words besides the ones for the bigger light and the less—words like *exile*, and *expulsion*, *monster* and *beast*, and *xenophobe*. I love the Xs, both letter and symbol in one."

"Well...well." Mr. Caliban was crazy. She had no idea what to say. "You have yourself a good night." She pulled on the doorknob until that terrible wrapped face disappeared.

———

Edna had made a terrible mistake letting this stranger into her home. Clearly he was dangerous. No one safe ever talked that way.

She thought about calling the police, but she had no idea what to tell them. They never took her seriously. She couldn't lie. She'd tried it before with an annoying neighbor, reporting what awful things he was doing, when she was just describing what she imagined he wanted. She didn't see much difference, but they did.

She dreaded her meals with Caliban, afraid he'd do something disgusting with his mouth inside that hole, afraid of that dull eye, afraid of his jokes, which she never understood, but most of all afraid the bandages might slip. They were old, and he'd been reusing them, and once or twice she'd seen some bit of twisted skin or blistered callus. Every dinner felt like a catastrophe in the making.

"I intend to become a citizen of your great country," he announced one evening. "You have such a great library system. America for Americans, as you people say."

"What people?"

"Why people like you, Edna, of course. Wasn't that what you told your Japanese families during World War Two?"

"I never—"

"Oh, I suppose you're too young. But wouldn't it have been grand to live during those times?"

Edna's stomach roiled. She had to run from the table.

She was in pain again, doubtless from the aggravation of Caliban's foolish, insufferable behavior. She could not stand the way her clothing scraped against her skin, like a rabble of hungry insects with their barbs and claws. She wanted to wear as little clothing as possible, but she couldn't risk it with such a male living in her home.

She went out onto the porch in search of a cool, soothing breeze. But he was already there, sitting on the edge of the porch, reading. She felt betrayed. He rarely went outside. The outside, at least, had been hers.

"I thought you were in your room."

He looked up from his book. "Noises, sounds and sweet airs that gave delight and hurt not, a thousand twangling instruments, and sometimes voices so terrible they brought tears to my eyes."

"I beg your pardon?"

"I've been dreaming about home, the island. But so often those dreams turn into nightmares. I came out here for a momentary escape. I've been studying up on your biology."

"*My* biology?"

"That of human beings, a sorely self-inflicted race, best avoided."

"But *you're* human." It felt like a lie in her mouth.

He gazed at her, or his bandaged head was pointed in her direction. It was disconcerting, staring at that expressionless bust. "Of course. We are all the same here. Did you know there are microscopic creatures which live on your face? Skin mites. Demodex. They eat your oils. But they do not have an anus. Imagine that! They eat until they explode and die."

She needed to get away from this vile creature, whatever he was. But a sharp pain was playing with her lower belly, teasing her with intimations of how terrible it might become. Then she felt a slight itchiness within her panties which was almost pleasurable, then a scratchiness on her leg, tracing down inside her pants, then spilling out onto her porch.

It was a kind of insect, or not. A rusty red thing with claws and many segments, a hard shell, eyes on stalks moving this way and that, but one of the stalks was broken, so she wondered if it was half-blind. More like a baby crab, and yet not a crab. And she could feel another on its way.

"Oh my. Is that yours?" Caliban asked.

It hurt when she exhaled, as if something were broken in her lungs. She was terrified of vomiting, of what might come out she would be forced to see. She stripped naked; they'd already reduced her clothing to rags. Those creatures emerged from her all afternoon, until they were a red tide covering her kitchen floor. Sometimes they pinched and clawed and bit her in their hurry to get out, making her an island amidst a rusty sea of carapace and claw and clickety clackety taps, a tempest of sound, motion, and color. Tingling barked and snarled and hid beneath whatever shelter was available.

Caliban had retreated upstairs some time ago. The sight of her must have disgusted him. But he was the one who brought all this into her home. He was the one who had infected her life. She'd had enough. She stomped her way out of the kitchen. She could feel them snapping and struggling under her bare feet. She kicked several out of the way as she ascended the staircase. There were none on the steps themselves, or on the landing above.

Caliban was on his way out of the shower, naked and dripping wet. They met in the hall outside his room.

She stared at his hideous form, worse than she imagined. Not merely non-human, it resembled something extraterrestrial. One eye had been closed by rigid folds of flesh, the other, the one Edna was familiar with, gray and in constant motion. The lips appeared misplaced, as did the teeth. The neck was several stacks of muscle, and those muscles continued down like roots or stalks ending in a bubbled field of blisters across the belly, and what hung between his legs…some sort of giant, twisted root?

She realized then she was holding a knife, and she quickly used the knife to cover her sex. She could feel more of those vermin dropping out of her, seeking fresh territory on the upstairs floor.

He laughed. "Don't worry, madam. There are no females of the Caliban species. Even if there were, I lack the desire."

"You, you brought these!" she cried, running forward. Before the horrid jokester could reply she slashed an X deep across his belly, making four triangular flaps. He sank to his knees as his insides began to spill. He smelled of fish, but held no secrets inside, no parasites, no vermin of any kind.

He coughed a laugh up again, burbling off his lips. "All…*yours. Your* legacy…madam," was the last thing he said, as he fell across her teeming red offspring.

Y is for Yesterday

For he would be thinking of love
Till the stars had run away,
And the shadows eaten the moon.
                    — W.B. Yeats, "The Young Man's Song"

The house is a small 1930s bungalow in a neighborhood in decline. The yard with its flower bed and a few tidy bushes is well-tended by the landscape company your firm has hired, and a caretaker comes regularly to make exterior repairs. No one has been inside since Mikołaj Dworkowicz left in 1945, except in 1991, when a storm-damaged roof resulted in a leak into the kitchen. Permission was granted for some quick interior repairs, and nothing else could be touched.

A dog yaps nearby. You adjust your skirt and blouse. You've made it a practice to be presentable even for casual assignments. You always wear a skirt, a feminine blouse, matching earrings, and great shoes. Your makeup is pristine.

You wear latex gloves to protect your nails. You smile and try to look friendly. Someone in these neighborhoods is always watching from behind the curtains.

You walk up to the house carrying a shopping bag containing a note pad, cell phone, hand sanitizer, keys, makeup, and new shop rags. The brick is clean and repointed, the wooden porch recently painted.

A large wooden Y lies in broken pieces stacked by the front door. Some of the other houses display similar wooden letters originally intended to please the local children, although many letters are missing. This saddens you.

The curtains in the front window are closed, but there is a gap. You walk over to the window, the glass streaked and yellowed on the inside, and you lean in for a peek.

The furniture is draped in gloom. You move closer to the glass. A young man in a beige shirt and baggy brown pants sits in a chair, staring at you, motionless. You put your hand over your mouth afraid to make a sound. You don't move, and the man fades away. This has happened before, your brain filling the gaps between light and shadow to create an image.

You walk over to the door and unlock the deadbolt, then use a different key in the knob. You turn the knob and push, but nothing happens. You try again, using your shoe to press against the brass kickplate. Good thing you wore your black pumps. But you can't afford to ruin them. Your size is expensive and only available online.

The bottom of the door gives a little, but the top remains jammed. You turn the knob again, but this time you ram your shoulder into the door. You feel it give and pop open. For once you're thankful you still have broad shoulders.

As you enter the home you feel the cobwebs dropping over you. *Damn.* You furiously brush the soft debris from your blouse and out of your hair. You flip the switch and the dirty chandelier glows. At least they got the power back on.

You take out your cellphone and start taking pictures. You scribble some impressions into the notepad. The room is layered in dust, fine gray bits like ash. Even when a house is shut the dust always finds its way in. Insects die and decay, mice leave droppings, wallpaper flakes and glue backing breaks down. Dust leaks from the ceiling cornices and attic spaces, and the tiniest gaps around windows and doors allow the dust to blow inside.

Webs decorate the corners. A wasp floats by. This stresses you. As long as you can remember you've been afraid of being stung. You doubt the house's interior has ever been sprayed. You make a note to call the exterminators.

You take dozens of pictures. You're not about to be blamed for taking too few. The living room wallpaper has vertical green stripes with clusters of cherries. They had busy tastes back then. The space has an excess of furniture: a coffee table in front of a long floral couch, a matching chair, side tables with lamps, a white hutch full of dusty plates. The carpet is so dirty it's impossible to know the original hue.

You open a door expecting a closet, but it leads into the damp smelling basement. You don't do basements. You'll leave that for the inspection and cleanup crew. Whoever buys this house will doubtless strip it down to the studs and rebuild from there.

A bookcase holds two prayer books, the Tanach, the Mishnah, a commentary on the Talmud. Your mother had similar volumes in her house. You barely glanced at them, much to her dismay. You pull out a small volume of Sholem Aleichem in Yiddish. Perhaps you can arrange to buy the Aleichem and give it to her as a peace offering, a last-ditch effort.

You're surprised Dworkowicz left books this important behind, but he walked away with little more than the clothes on his back and some savings in the bank for a new life in Chicago.

For all its dust and disintegration, the room is remarkably orderly and uncluttered, the furniture aligned and nothing unnecessary intruding. The one exception is a dirty rectangle lying on the floor beside the coffee table. You nudge it with your shoe. It's a magazine, too soiled for you to pick up.

Closed French doors lead into the dark dining room. Still, you can see the edge of a dining table and chairs placed around it, and in one of those chairs that same young man you'd seen earlier sits bent over the table as if in prayer.

He wears a skullcap and a dark shirt with rips in it. He nods ever-so-slightly back and forth, mumbling, and tugging on these torn pieces of shirt. His fingers snag small bits of paper from a pile on the table before him. He folds and unfolds them, dropping them back onto the pile.

In its muted stillness the scene resembles a painting by Edward Hopper: the quiet, the isolation, a barely contained misery. You wait, but this time the image does not fade. You walk slowly to the left side of the living room where a narrow hall leads to the back of the house.

The first room off the hall is a bedroom, the bed still made. You're struck by the floral-patterned wallpaper, the matching bedspread, and the flowery upholstered chair. This was a man who decorated for a woman, you think, but you don't believe a woman ever arrived.

Above the chest of drawers hangs a diploma from a Polish yeshiva dated 1936. Nearby is a bare nail. You can still see the vague outline of a snapshot-sized frame. So far you've found no photographs or art on any walls. Searching the drawers might yield further information, but you're afraid of whatever might be living there.

You turn around and you're startled to see that same young man dressed in brown and beige sitting on the edge of the bed, elbows on knees, hands over his face, leaning forward. He is all too solid, except when his shoulders heave as he weeps into his fingers. With every minute shudder he becomes slightly less substantial, as if a spirit striving to escape its body.

You quietly move around him, not knowing what might happen if you touch this less than substantial form, and not wanting to find out. You still have a job you must complete.

The next room is smaller, and contains a baby crib, the faded twelve-dollar price tag still attached.

You like the bathroom's look. Green tile on the walls and a green wall-mounted sink with two chrome legs, a matching tub. The medicine cabinet still contains a variety of glass medicine bottles and pasteboard boxes.

The bathroom mirror has grown cloudy with age, but it is all you have to work with. You brush the remaining dust out of your hair and off your shoulders until you reach a reasonable semblance of professionalism. You apply a bit of foundation around your mouth and smooth it out. You add a little extra concealer under your eyes.

Your cell phone is buzzing and you glance at the message. HAVE YOU FINISHED LOOKING AT THE ESTATE? WE NEED YOU BACK IN THE OFFICE NICOLE. This is from the same person who sometimes still calls you Nick, but each time insists it is an honest mistake. So far HR has done nothing.

If you had the funds, you'd get the surgery to soften these square facial edges and reduce the width of your nose. You've already gotten your hairline lowered and it's made a dramatic difference. You have a friend who's had a tracheal shave, so people won't notice their Adam's apple. You were supportive of course, but you can't even imagine. A scalpel touching your throat.

When Mikołaj Dworkowicz resettled in Chicago he insisted everyone call him Nick. So, another Nick. At some point he changed his last name to Divari. It's all in the deceased client's file back in the office, an entire life history, but with a few pieces missing.

People thought Nick Divari was Greek and as far as you can tell he never corrected them. It was even in the Chicago obituaries. Did the name change give Dworkowicz a completely new life? It appeared to. But it couldn't change his past.

The kitchen could use a good sweeping and a mop, but otherwise appears ready for meal preparation. You're grateful not to smell anything foul. The icebox is empty, as is the pantry. Dworkowicz knew he wouldn't be coming back, but he still cared about what he left behind.

The color scheme is red and white: red-and-white-checkerboard linoleum floor, apple-red-and-crisp-white enamel metal dining set, quarter circle shelves at the end of the white wall cabinets, wallpaper with a rooster pattern. An enameled bread box and cannisters, a wood-burning cast iron stove, a leaning farmhouse cupboard on the verge of collapse.

Like all the rooms in this house, despite the dirt and the grime, there is an order here. The house was left ready for its next resident, but Mikołaj Dworkowicz decided there would be no next resident and paid a considerable amount for over half a century to make sure people left the house alone, until his death, with no descendants, the beneficiaries several Jewish charities.

The door to the dining room is open. You peek in, and you're relieved to see no phantoms inside. The dining room set is of better quality than the rest of the furniture. The wallpaper is more subtle, cream-colored with an embossed pattern, but again heavily soiled. A sideboard matching the table is centered against the wall. You ignore the temptation of its many drawers. You turn on the light, and the chandelier fills the room with fragmented brilliance.

A stack of letters lies on the table's dull surface, alongside a small pile of letter fragments, correspondence which has been torn apart. Another letter lies stretched out like a body on an operating table, covered by yellowed, disintegrating tape, an apparent attempt to reconstruct those fragments into a whole. You can only imagine the labor and focus required. Nearby is an antique circular metal tin of "Scotch" cellulose tape.

Intrigued, you dust off a chair and test it with your weight. It creaks but holds. You take a rag and wipe around the letters and the pile to create a cleaner surface.

You take off your gloves and pick up the taped letter for examination. The tape begins to separate, and you lay the letter back down. It's in Polish, which you can't read. That's fine; you're not looking for secrets to share. But there's a year, 1940, and his name, Mikołaj, at the beginning, and at the end a signature, Stasia. And you see a word you recognize, *Ahava*, the Hebrew word for love, repeated throughout, and again at the end.

The handwriting is small and lovely, and you imagine this letter must have been written by a delicate hand. Your own hands embarrass you, so large and clumsy, your thick wrists and long index fingers and that bent, ringless ring finger. There's nothing you can do to change any of that. Yet you have your nails painted a vivid purple. Painting your nails has been important to you as long as you can remember. This was the first bit of yourself you chose not to hide anymore.

You tore up the letter from your mother asking if you still observed Yom Kippur and recommending a matchmaker. She doesn't get it and never will. Maybe you should have taped it back together. It might be the last letter you ever receive from her.

You go through the stack of letters, carefully removing each from its envelope, looking it over, then putting it back. Every one of them are signed Stasia, every one of them postmarked Warsaw. Apparently the taped letter is the final of the bunch, or else her final message is lost among all those little pieces.

You have found only two examples of disorder amid the orderly remains of a house closed since June of 1945. You put the gloves back on and go back into the living room and pick the magazine up off the floor. The dust slides off, revealing an issue of *Life Magazine* with three men on the cover. The one in the middle has a bandaged hand. The words at the bottom are "The German People." The date is May 7, 1945. The price is ten cents.

You don't sit on the couch because you don't know what might be living there. You choose to glance through the magazine standing up. You remember that mourning sometimes involved a lot of standing. Memories are stirring. You've held this magazine before.

Your mother kept several boxes of papers at the back of her closet among old shoes and stacks of books, her private property forbidden for you to see. Of course, you felt compelled to go through these things. That's how you discovered what your father looked like and the things he had done in his life, although you found no answers as to why he left your mother. You have always assumed it had something to do with you.

In one of those boxes, you found this magazine, hidden away as if it were some forbidden piece of pornography, and pornography is exactly the way you treated it. You thumbed through its pages with a growing sense of shame.

"Speaking of Pictures" is the opening spread, a layout of light-hearted black and gray panel cartoons meant to elicit a giggle. Then an ad for The Prudential, a man putting a wedding ring on a woman's delicate finger, her nails darkly painted, you think probably red but it's a black and white photograph so you can't know for sure.

Then "War In Europe Draws To Its End," the Nazis are decimated, and everyone is smiling, Russian and American soldiers shaking hands. But what follows is a feature on the "Atrocities." This is what you remember, the first images out of the camps, the photos by George Rodger and Margaret Bourke-White. The skeletal survivors peering from their bunks, the scatter of clothing and bodies. German guards knee-deep in bones and decaying flesh, forced by the British Tommies to dig a mass grave at Belsen to bury the corpses of the victims.

You don't know if your mother knew you'd found this box and rummaged through it, but several months later when you went back for another glimpse it was gone.

You can only imagine what Mikołaj Dworkowicz felt going through these pages. You don't know if he saw anything familiar, if a bit of clothing or a pale, wraith-like face might have recalled someone dear, and what all this has to do with the torn and untorn letters on the dining room table, and why he left this house forever a few weeks after the magazine came out.

All you know is he dropped this magazine on the floor, and he tore up those letters, and tried to repair at least one, and then he left it all behind sealed up like a tomb.

You yawn. You rarely yawn when you're tired. You yawn when your nerves get the best of you.

Your phone buzzes you again. NICOLE WHERE ARE YOU? ARE YOU AT LEAST ON YOUR WAY?

You don't remember closing the French doors, but they're closed again, and through the yellowed glass you see the beige man poised as if in a painting, bent over a scattered pile of paper remains.

You gather your things to make an escape back into your everyday life, where people you've never met wish you murder, where people you've never met would reduce you to ash.

Z is for Zombie

Lee was ill for a long time. Then he felt good again. Then he felt sick again. This cycle went on for at least ten years. After a while he couldn't always tell the difference, with all the time he spent in bed, and living alone.

Eventually the casting people stopped hiring him. He'd gotten too old, too crippled up with arthritis. He'd never been more than an extra, a background actor in zombie pictures and TV shows—more than a hundred films and episodes. But he'd taken it seriously; he was good at that one thing. He was expert at playing dead. He'd had loads of practice.

He tried to convince casting directors his arthritis was an advantage—he argued it made his living dead stumble more convincing. But he would fall at unexpected times and ruin scenes. He was too unreliable, they said, an insurance risk.

The decayed face in his bedroom mirror wasn't perfect. Some of the edges weren't glued down and the paint job was splotchy, and Lee didn't know how to give his eyes that dead fish look, although the shadows he'd applied did a pretty good job of making them recede. He'd had no training in special effects or makeup, but he'd always watched the professionals while they did their work. Filming always meant much waiting around, and he'd had nothing better to do.

The scar above his left eyebrow rose worm-like off his forehead and fell onto the surface of the dresser. He scooped it up and put it in a tray. Later he would return it to one of the display cases with his other treasures.

He practiced zombie looks, alternating fierce, hungry grimaces with loose-lipped and sometimes zany expressions of brainlessness. He spoke a few lines, if a string of phlegmish gargles could be considered language. They had always been the extent of his permitted on-screen vocabulary.

Lee still rehearsed every day in case he ever got the call again. Lacking his old stamina he quit after an hour or so. His little bungalow had always been shadowy and dim, even when his mother was still alive. As his eyes weakened with age he found he could see very little after a certain hour and mirrors were especially challenging. They possessed depths of gloom he could make no sense of.

He gently transferred his bits of putty, silicone, and rubber to one of the glass cases in the living room. This particular case held makeup items from his early zombie pictures: "The Dead Are Alive," "The Dead Aren't Dead," and "The Dead! The Dead! The Dead!" All low-budget, all primitive in both their effects and working conditions. In each he'd been part of a group of zombie actors who wandered from scene to scene, occasionally changing a ragged shirt or a facial appliance in order to make it seem as if they had a cast of hundreds of undead instead of the twenty or so they could afford. The makeup had been hot and smelly under the summer sun. He'd been denied water and almost passed out more than once. On "The Dead! The Dead! The Dead!" he'd broken his middle finger when his cadre of zombies fell into a ditch. He'd suffered through all three films, but he'd loved the work. He kept the splint from the incident in the case along with whatever makeup bits he was able to squirrel away in his pockets at the end of filming.

That was wrong of course. Lee was fully aware it was wrong. But it didn't feel unfair. Those pieces of zombie makeup—scars and wounds and simulated rotting flesh, decayed organs—were everywhere. Not infrequently they dropped off and you stepped on them during the midst of some rambling zombie advance. He wasn't paid much, and this was physical evidence of the most important work he'd ever done. His dream job. Still, his mother would have been so ashamed of him if she had known.

He caught a glimpse of something in the tall glass case against the wall. In the glass door or leaning against the bits of rotting wardrobe hanging inside. A skeletal hand maybe, some bony fingers trying to reach in and take what was his.

Lee went over to the case and peered inside. Everything looked to be there, but sloppily arranged, as if it had been gone through. Of course, he might have done it himself. He was always taking things out and wearing them, stumbling around the house as he choreographed his moves. He always resolved to put them back the way they had been, but he didn't always recall the original order. He'd never catalogued his collection, which was a mistake, but he'd never been much good at organizing things. His mother usually did that for him, but she wouldn't touch his zombie bits—they disgusted her.

Lee did the best he could, but more than once he'd wake up in bed with fragments of makeup stuck to the sheets or his pillow. And it wasn't unusual to step on a makeup piece lying on the floor. He went barefoot around the house, not wanting to damage the delicate pieces with his shoes.

A dead face loomed in the cabinet by the front door. Lee smiled at it, too far away to tell if it smiled back.

He'd always worked hard on these roles and would ask some of the featured actors now and then for tips. Often they brushed him off, but some were nice. "What's your name again?" they would say, or "What do you want? An autograph?"

Once he'd asked a second unit director about his motivation for a scene. "You're a freakin' zombie," had been the reply. "You have no motivation."

Although the official line was the zombies were no longer people, their souls and personalities gone, leaving only these strangely animated shells behind, Lee never played them that way. Maybe it made no difference in the end, but he never thought of them as dead. He thought of them as just really old people with some rare disease. And, after all these years of playing them, he'd reached that advanced age himself. Minus the disease, although he hadn't seen a doctor in a very long time. Doctors never delivered good news. His mother would have vouched for that. He'd prefer his death be a surprise, a twist ending.

Even the teenagers and little kid zombies were just old people in his eyes. A bit empty, sadly alone, just walking out of habit because that's all they knew. Nothing ahead of them and everything behind. Their bodies did rot, the flesh fell off their bones, but that was just a symptom of their malady.

He heard something toward the back of the house. A scratching, or a rubbing. Maybe some shifting weight, poking and prodding, touching his things. Lee was always worried about rats. If a rat got into one of the cases it could do tremendous damage. Most of the makeup appliances were soft and chewy, just the sort of thing to appeal to rodents.

But it could also be someone trying to break in. He started in that direction, thinking he should at least double-check the locks. He moved carefully. He knew how clumsy he could be and the space between cases was quite narrow with not even enough room to turn around. There wasn't a chair to sit in or a single piece of furniture unrelated to his career. Most of his house was like this, a museum devoted to his collection.

Lee kept hearing those noises, but his passing reflections in the glass doors and display tops continued to distract him. Sometimes he forgot some of the things he had. All these shredded zombie face masks, rotting cheeks and protruding tongues and broken teeth, staring out at him as he passed, breathing hard through their torn lips, glancing at him with nervous eyes, needing to scream when all they could do was growl.

He stopped in front of a framed article on the wall. The newsprint had yellowed, the edges frayed, but the print was still readable if he got close enough. Lee had always thought of himself as anonymous—zombies were intended to be anonymous for the most part, unless it was a featured player who recently turned, because he or she wanted out of their contract or because they had become difficult to work with. But years ago he had been interviewed for the local paper, and he'd been proud of his small moment of recognition.

But it had come with a cost. Fame always came with a cost— he'd learned that from watching the better-known cast members in his various projects. It didn't matter whether it was the movies or the TV shows; once you became famous you became another sort of creature entirely.

After the article appeared people would show up at his door wanting to ask him questions and see the collection. Younger people mostly—teenagers and college kids. And him with no security in place whatsoever. He'd never put locks on the cases. He'd never thought he needed to. These young people with all their energy and their barely-controlled enthusiasm, they frightened him. What if they took something? He was too old and weak to stop them. He had no idea how to protect himself and his things.

More than a few times he had the urge to bite one of them. Crazy, of course, but biting was something he knew a lot about. A bite could turn an enemy into an ally.

In his observation the world had changed. Alphabet Row was not the same neighborhood he'd first moved into. There had been break-ins and robberies. There had been murders. People went missing. Strangers gathered in the street and eyed you with suspicion. Even the beloved Queneau Library had fallen into disrepair. He no longer felt safe going there for research, even though the library was right across the street. Sooner or later, he knew, the city would bulldoze everything and erect a high-rise in its place.

When Lee had the opportunity, and no one was watching, he went out front and took his address, that big letter Z, off the wall by the door. He figured the postal carrier must know his house by habit and wouldn't need it, not that he ever received any mail. Anyone else would be looking for a house address that no longer existed.

He didn't go out anymore. He didn't need to. He could always have his groceries delivered if he remembered to do so. But Lee hadn't had much appetite in a very long time. He supposed it was an age thing. Food just didn't taste the same.

He was headed toward the back door, but he couldn't remember why. That happened sometimes. He was a man with a lot of things on his mind. He had this huge collection to take care of, and all these memories to protect and organize. All the zombie reflections surrounding him snarled their agreement. This made him smile, and he snarled back his encouragement, or was he the one who had snarled first?

He could hear those young fans at the back of his house trying to get in. Or maybe they were already inside. He wondered how they had gotten in—he had triple locks on the door, or at least he had intended to. And where were they all hiding now? His house was too small for anyone to hide anywhere.

But there were always mysteries in this world. Like what had started the zombie plague in the first place? They almost never explained that bit in the movies, and when they even bothered it was usually the silliest, most unbelievable sort of explanation. Zombies were simply inevitable—that was Lee's basic theory. Just like solitude. Just like dying.

His best display case was near the back door. He'd planned it that way as a grand reveal, his collection becoming progressively more interesting as you moved toward its end. In this case he had a variety of large latex prosthetic appliances simulating dead skin, deceased skin, burnt flesh, corrupted hands and fingers and chest pieces, all of it finely detailed so as to be suitable for extreme close-ups. These were major pieces the makeup artists guarded closely as each represented an enormous amount of labor. All of these, he was ashamed to remember, he had stolen off the set when his role was done.

The last piece was a full set of fake abdominal viscera, magnificent in its realism, although the colors had been brightened some so they would show up better on film. Lee had heard that a butcher, one of the investors in the original *Night of the Living Dead*, provided actual animal entrails for the effects in that film. Lee was grateful he'd only had to wear foam or rubber for his roles, and the occasional acrid smelling paint, although sometimes the effects were so realistic he still became nauseated.

A ravaged face leered at him, making him stagger, and his left arm came down so hard it shattered the glass top and his hand became tangled in the nest of latex and silicone organs, tearing several and scattering the rest. He snarled inarticulately, thinking all those young people had come back to steal his treasures, and he did a crazy little zombie ballet, a kind of Zydeco dance, thinking it might scare them away.

But he appeared to have almost no control over his movements. Arthritis had spread through his arms, hands, legs, feet, stiffening some joints and making others swing in the wrong direction. All the shambling and drunken stumbling he'd done through barren, dismal fields and post-apocalyptic wreckage over years and years—how many and how long ago?—must have done considerable damage.

He raised his arm and looked at it. The flesh was torn and ripped all the way to the bone, several inches of which gleamed nakedly through gaps in the meat and the rotted threads of fat and sinew. But oddly—he couldn't say luckily—there was no blood at all except for some rust-colored powdery debris, as if the pump attached to his special effects arm had run dry.

He turned his head to the glass wall cabinet beside him and stared at his reflection. When he grinned the zombie in the cabinet door grinned back, exposing its receding gums and enormous teeth, its missing lips and ears. The nose had rotted away to a pair of bone cavities. The eyes lay deep in the shadows of its skull, but clearly panicked.

Someone was beating on his front door. Lee dragged his feet through the broken glass, making his way past his precious display cases. He thought maybe he'd damaged his shoulders because one hung lower than the other, putting a labored twist into his ungainly stride. His hands appeared broken, the way they kept slipping off the doorknob, but he felt no pain at all, and was able to wedge them around the stem of the knob, twist, and pull open the door.

Two police officers waited on the porch. He saw the looks on their faces and wasn't at all surprised when they raised their weapons.

"Jubst ..." Lee knew he had to enunciate as best he could, even though he had no idea how the words would come out. He struggled to contain his excitement for at last he had a speaking role. "Just aim for the head."

Alphabet Row still exists, at least in some form, but urban renewal has stolen much of its charm. Companies specializing in overnight rentals now control several of the properties. Disturbed and disappointed renters have kept ratings low, and demand has rapidly deteriorated. Even those seeking a bargain have stayed away from the many empty homes.

Forever ago this street was full of families living their lives. Gone now are the voices of children learning their alphabet, the aging grandparents calling from their porches, and the quiet conversations taking place around dinner tables.

Sickness still permeates the house at #Q. Junk dealers have stripped it of all that was either salvageable or sellable. Killings are often made in real estate, but not here, not on Alphabet Row. Leveling the place to the ground seems like the best thing the city could do.

Many letters exchanged and countless proposals later and still no concrete plans for what to do with either the houses or the land. No one wants to live here. No one wants to think about Alphabet Row.

Ongoing police investigations continue, but with no apparent progress made. Paranormal investigators continue to beg for access, but permissions in all cases have been denied.

Queneau Library lies abandoned, decommissioned by the city's library system. Renovation plans lie unread in several city offices. Supervisory personnel of the closed branch have been unavailable for comment.

The whereabouts of numerous former and current residents remains unknown. Underwriters for many of the homes have so far denied all claims. Various lawsuits continue to make their way through the courts.

Websites focused on the street's mysteries have become quite popular. Ex-residents, the few to step forward, have been interviewed in depth concerning their odd or frightening experiences living on this block. Yellow police tape has become a semi-permanent adornment on many of these old houses.

Have you met the old/young man wearing a wool cap and heavy coat? His name is Carl, and he has an interesting story to tell.

Acknowledgments

Some of these stories have been revised since their original publication.

"A is for Alphabet" originally appeared in *The Dark*, November 2023

"B is for Baby" is original to this volume.

"C is for Clown" is original to this volume.

"D is for Dog" is original to this volume.

"E is for Eye" originally appeared in *Oculus Sinister*, ed. CM Muller, 2020.

"F is for the Farm" originally appeared in *Fiends in the Furrows III: Final Harvest*, eds. David Neal & Christine Scott, 2023.

"G is for Ghost" originally appeared in the collection *Here with the Shadows* by Steve Rasnic Tem, Swan River Press, 2014.

"H is for the Hunt" originally appeared in *Horror Library Vol. 8*, ed. Eric Guignard, 2023.

"I is for Infestation" originally appeared in *Shadowplays*, eds. Peter Coleborn and Mike Chinn, 2024.

"J is for Jolly" originally appeared in *Nightmare Abbey 7*, 2024, as "Jolly."

"K is for Killer" is original to this volume.

"L is for Love" originally appeared in *Footsteps 8*, Nov 1987.

"M is for Mother" originally appeared in *Mother: Tales of Love & Terror*, eds. Willow Becker & Christi Nogle, 2022, as "The Sire."

"N is for Night" originally appeared in *Nightscript 8*, ed. CM Muller, Sept. 2022.

"O is for Occult" originally appeared in *Wilted Pages*, eds. Christi Nogle & Ai Jiang, 2023, as "Higher Powers."

"P is for Phantasies" originally appeared in *Never Wake*, ed. Kenneth M. Cain & Tim Meyer, 2023.

"Q is for Queneau" is original to this volume.

Meet the Author

Steve Rasnic Tem was born in Lee County Virginia in the heart of Appalachia. He is the author of over 500 published short stories and is a past winner of the Bram Stoker, International Horror Guild, British Fantasy, and World Fantasy Awards. His story collections include *City Fishing*, *The Far Side of the Lake*, *In Concert* (with wife Melanie Tem), *Ugly Behavior* (crime), *Celestial Inventories* (contemporary fantasy), and *Figures Unseen*, his Selected Stories. His novels include *Excavation*, *The Book of Days*, *Daughters*, *The Man in the Ceiling* (with Melanie Tem), *Deadfall Hotel*, *Blood Kin*, and the recent *Ubo*.

Steve Rasnic Tem's short fiction has been compared to the work of Franz Kafka, Dino Buzzati, Ray Bradbury, and Raymond Carver, but to quote Joe R. Lansdale: "Steve Rasnic Tem is a school of writing unto himself." In 2024 he received the Lifetime Achievement Award from the Horror Writers Association.

NOVELS

Blood Kin
Deadfall Hotel
Excavation
The Book of Days
The Mask Shop of Doctor Black
Ubo

WITH MELANIE TEM

Beautiful Stranger
Daughters
In Concert

The Man on the Ceiling
Yours to Tell: Dialogues on the Art & Practice of Writing

COLLECTIONS

Absences: Charlie Goode's Ghosts
Celestial Inventories
City Fishing
Decoded Mirrors: Three Tales After Lovecraft
Everyday Horrors
Everything Is Fine Now
Fairytales
Figures Unseen
Here with the Shadows
Out of The Dark
Rough Justice
Scarecrows: Appalachian Tales
Thanatrauma
The Far Side of the Lake
The Harvest Child and Other Fantasies
The Hydrocephalic Ward (poems)
The Night Doctor and Other Tales
Twember
Ugly Behavior

Curious about other Crossroad Press books? Stop by our
website: http://crossroadpress.com
We offer quality writing
in digital, audio, and print formats.

Subscribe to our newsletter on the website homepage and
receive a free eBook.